To Kill A Diver

Mike Hughes

C2C Publications

To Kill A Diver
By
Mike Hughes

Copyright 1998
ISBN: 0-9664130-4-0

Other Books By Mike Hughes:

The Northwest Dive Guide
Harbour Publishing. Copyright 2009

The North American Dive Guide
Amazon-Createspace. Copyright 2012

This is a fictional story I first completed in 1998. None of the characters are real, nor were they based on actual living persons except for the mention of Ron Akeson who is a good friend and owner of Adventures Down Under in Bellingham, Wa. Underwater Sports is the actual name of a dive shop in Edmonds where I spent a short period as a park volunteer and several years as a Divemaster all the way up to Master Instructor. Underwater Sports has six locations in the Seattle area. The dive park setting was based on Edmonds Underwater Park in downtown Edmonds, Washington. The park has been renamed as *Bruce Higgins Underwater Trails* in honor of Bruce and all the divers that were encouraged by him to make the Edmond dive park the biggest and most well known underwater parks on the west coast. Many artifacts, sculptures, ropes, boats, and trails have been placed beneath the sea by countless volunteers and made home by millions of sea creatures of every sort and size. The park is still one of my favorite places in the world to dive.

This book is dedicated to my daughter,
Kayla Joy Hughes

To Kill A Diver

The Last Dive

The last thing they wanted was to get arrested. The scuba divers came to the surface as quietly as possible and each man with great intensity scanned the surrounding waters. A bank of fog was moving in slow and steady. The two of them switched from using their regulators to breathing through their snorkels and began slowly and silently swimming back to the boat. Shrouded by low-lying layers of clouds, a half moon glowed dimly somewhere up above the southern most fjord in North America during the night. Both divers were exhausted from their work and their scuba tanks were low on air pressure. It was hard to see by the natural available light, but they dared not turn on their flashlights. No one could know they were here. The first diver ascended the side boat ladder while the second diver held on to a rope tethered to the side of the white Bayliner boat. Holding on to the rope the water rippled as it gently swept past him. The diver floated and rested until his buddy climbed up and moved away from the dive ladder. The first diver made his way up the ladder with his fins still strapped to his feet. He pulled his mask up and over his head as he awkwardly stepped from the ladder over to the port side bench. As he sat down with the scuba tank still firmly strapped onto his back he glimpsed a faint silver blade swing under his jaw. The skin on his neck and chin immediately felt an infusion of warmth. Abruptly and inexplicably, he no longer possessed the ability to speak or breath. A black shadow moved away from him as he slumped forward on to the deck.

His partner climbed up the ladder just in time to see what he thought was his buddy moving towards him. How could his buddy have gotten his tank off so fast? He stepped aboard the back of the boat and as he pulled his mask over his head he felt something plunge deep in to his chest. He started to gasp, but the sound was cut off as he felt something press against him then quickly slide across the neck seal of his drysuit. His eyes began to glaze over and he dropped his fins. The fins fell on the deck. What ever pressed against his neck also pushed him backwards and he would have fallen into the water had not a neoprene glove grabbed hold of him and propelled him forward in one swift martial arts move. Across the deck he flew until he landed against his partner's limp body. His body twitched for a brief moment, then all was still as the thick fog engulfed the boat as well as the rest of the Hood Canal.

Diver Down

Two men dressed in street clothes stood in an almost empty parking lot down at Edmonds underwater park with their hands covering their ears. A train whistled then roared past them on steel rails a mere twenty feet from where their cars were parked and where they were standing. They dropped their hands back to their sides as the last of the rail cars rolled by. It was dark and the fog had rolled in early, but the streetlights in the parking lot still gave them all the lighting they required for what they were about to do. They pulled their scuba tanks out of their cars and set the tanks on the ground standing up right. They took Buoyancy Compensators (BC's), which are the functional equivalent of fish air bladders for divers, and placed them over their tanks and secured them tightly. They then attached their regulators to the tanks and turned on their air pressure was full. All they had to do now was get suited up and go get wet.

They first met each other when they took an advanced diver course offered by one of the dive club members who just happened to be a dive instructor for one of the local dive stores. Last week they planned a dive in this same location, but Carl had forgotten to bring his hood, so after they had suited up and were just about to enter the water, they aborted the dive.

Terry Fryberg and Carl Baker came from different walks of life and they were an unlikely matched up pair, but finding a buddy willing to dive at the drop of a hat was a rare commodity. Terry, who was a conservative mortgage broker, would have liked to discuss every step of the dive. Carl, a firefighter, was a take-charge type of guy with a "let's do it now" type of outlook on life. The thought of sitting down and discussing the dive in advance took all the fun out of it as he earlier told Terry right to his face. Diving was his way of relieving the stress of being a junior member of a very rigorously trained fire fighting team. To Carl, diving was the one place where he could just relax and do what ever he wanted. He tolerated having a buddy just because everyone would give him such grief if they found out that he had gone diving alone. He had also heard that diving in the park by oneself was against the local city ordinances and could get a lone diver a hefty fifteen hundred dollar fine.

—

The two of them assembled their scuba gear in silence. Once underwater, they wouldn't have to talk to each other at all. If Carl would just look back and see where his buddy was from time to time then Terry would be fine and he could enjoy the dive. The last dive of their advanced class he spent half the dive just trying to find Carl. Carl finished putting on his seven-millimeter thick wet suit and looked over at Terry. Terry was slow as usual. Terry was wearing a drysuit. He had just finished putting on his undergarment. Terry would next have to step into his multiple layered laminate outer garment. It took a few extra minutes more to suit up in a drysuit than put on a wet suit, but the extra time it took to suit up was well worth the wait. Terry would remain dry and warm the entire dive. He tried to explain the benefits of a drysuit to Carl, but Carl thought real divers only dove wet. So he told Carl that real firefighters used water buckets and horses to put out fires. Carl didn't say much after that. Terry stopped to powder his neck and wrist seals before he finished wriggling into his drysuit. If Terry could just get the lead out Carl thought, things would run so much smoother. Carl set the tank on the back end of his red Chevy Blazer, sat back, and pulled his shoulder straps over his arms and began fastening the chest straps that held his BC and tank to his back. Terry precariously set his gear on the lip of the trunk of his gold Toyota Corolla. The back end of his car squeaked as it lowered at least an inch just from the extra weight. Terry realized that he was going to have to get another vehicle better suited to his new hobby, or risk going through several pairs of shocks. He leaned back and put his arms through the buoyancy compensator vest then sat down on the lip of the trunk. The back end of the car lowered further. His tank was now wedged slightly in the trunk, but most of it rested against the underside of the lid of the trunk. He started to fasten his Velcro cummerbund and noticed that Carl was already walking towards the water. Terry finished putting his gear in place, grabbed his fins, mask and snorkel, a large primary dive light, slammed the trunk shut, and hurried down to the water.

Carl was already standing chest high in the waves and ready to go by the time Terry entered the water.

"Hey, check out the crazy fire fly display." Carl said as he waved his arms back and forth in the water.

Phosphorous green tiny spheres illuminated and left a trail in the water wherever Carl moved his hands. Abruptly Carl turned on his light and the glowing lights all but disappeared. He began to examine the surrounding bottom while Terry put on his mask and snorkel, gloves, and fins. Just as Terry finished getting his fins on, a head popped out of the water in front of him. Carl spit out his regulator.

"You ready to go yet?" Terry just looked at him and shook his head.

"What about a buddy check?" Terry asked.

"Forget it," Carl said. "That's just for newbies. Let's go diving."

It was right then that Terry realized he should never have agreed to go on another dive with Carl. Terry's instructor told him that a buddy check was the most important thing to do before every dive. How else would you know where to go to grab your buddy's alternate regulator (your spare regulator)? How would you know how to help your buddy in an emergency? Or check to see if your buddy's air was even turned on? People forget the little details. To do it right you had to check your buddy's buoyancy compensator and make sure it inflated and deflated, their weight belt easily released and fell away by the mere pull of their right hand, that you checked the other buckle releases and tank straps, air was turned on all the way; not just barely cracked open, regulators functioning properly, and only then did you give your buddy the final ok before you went underwater.

Besides the buddy check, they hadn't even discussed where they were going, at what point would they return to shore, or anything else for that matter. Carl put the regulator back in his mouth and dipped back down beneath the surface. Terry had gone to too much trouble to back out now. He put the regulator in his mouth and sunk underwater. He made a mental note that this would be the last dive he ever did with Carl. He turned on his dive light and caught up to where Carl was hovering above the sand, looking up and blowing circles of bubbles that expanded as they rose towards the surface. As Terry approached him, Carl gave Terry the OK sign with his right hand. He then turned to swim off before Terry had time to signal back to Carl.

Visibility was close to twenty feet near shore, so even though Carl quickly swam ahead of Terry, he could still see where Carl was located by following the beam of his buddy's flashlight. Terry didn't have time to really see anything. He was too busy trying to keep up with Carl. Carl made it all the way out to a spot where a large propeller laid in the sand. He turned left following some ropes that were weaved through cinder blocks, and he swam to the other side of a giant cement structure called the cathedrals. Carl had taken him here the last time they dove. Tonight Carl had a surprise for Terry. He looked to see if Terry was still following, then he swam west another hundred feet on another trail. Carl followed the trail north until he saw a smaller rope line heading west again. Ten feet past this rope line he was looking right at the stern of the Triumph; a ninety-four foot long tugboat sunk a few years back. The boat was an awesome sight. Plumose anemones lined this side of the boat. Algae hung from the cracks in the wood. A brown and white spotted Ratfish with the head of a hound dog, a pointed fin on the top, two spiky pectoral fins on the sides, and a sword blade like tail hovered in the water next to the Tug's propeller blade. On his silver belly were two claspers denoting this one was a male. Carl swam directly over to the fish. Green iridescent eyes of the ratfish reflected the beam from Carl's flashlight. The ratfish was an old breed that had separated early in history from the rest of the prehistoric shark family. A ratfish didn't have sharp teeth like other species of shark. Instead, they had a small fused plate in their mouth for crushing and grinding shells and eating soft-bodied worms. Their defense was a dorsal spine that was reported to be quite poisonous. Ratfish looked like cute little rabbits with smiling faces, and were irresistible to watch swim in the water.

Carl took his mind off the ratfish when Terry caught up to him. Terry was pointing at his air pressure gauge. It read fifteen hundred pounds per square inch or more commonly referred to most divers to just "fifteen hundred pounds". Carl didn't know what the big deal was. His own pressure read fourteen hundred pounds. If they ran low on air they would just have to swim back to shore on the surface.

He signaled ok to Terry as he swam away towards the bow of the tug. Terry was going to give him two more minutes of this whirlwind tour around the structure and then he was heading back to shore with or without Carl.

He watched in dismay as Carl swam around the bow and out of sight. Terry stopped to look at the ratfish, which was following his beam of light. Forget him Terry thought. If Carl didn't need a buddy so be it. He thought of the old Chinese proverb. Fool me once you're an idiot. Fool me twice I'm an idiot. He felt stupid for even going on another dive with Carl; it's just that he wanted to go diving so bad that he was willing to overlook his gut instincts. He was determined never to dive with Carl again.

Terry turned his attention to a cluster of leopard nudibranchs on the side of the boat. They were little white nudibranchs with little brown rings painted on their backs. This was truly a great dive site he had to admit.

Terry then heard a small motor that sounded quite close. He suddenly remembered he'd better go find his poor excuse of a dive buddy. He came around the bow of the boat and saw nothing there. The visibility was lower on this side of the sunken tug. This side of the tug was barren compared to the side closest to the shore. No anemones, no starfish, and worse, no sign of Carl. He swam up and looked across the main deck of the tug. His light shinned on a cabezon sitting on top of a hatch cover. A cabezon is a fish that looks like a bulldog with fins and dressed in green, brown, red, and purple camouflage paint. This cabezon had his mouth open displaying several sets of razor sharp little teeth. He looked mad, but that was just his permanent expression when he was letting water flow passively in through his mouth and back out across his gills slits. The eyes of the cabezon starred at Terry then suddenly the big fish swam off a few feet from where he was previously resting.

Apart from the company of the fish, Terry suddenly felt as if he was all alone in the park. He swam across the deck towards the back of the boat. Halfway back he saw a light shinning in the sand not too far from the tug. The light remained motionless. As he approached the light, he could make out Carl's outline.

Carl was resting on his back with his hands raised and floating aimlessly in the air. The light was still attached to his body by an extendible cord and lying in the sand.

The sight appeared too surreal to be true. If this was some kind of stunt, then it was the scariest stunt ever played on Terry, but deep down he knew this had all the appearance of a real life tragedy. No bubbles were coming out of Carl's regulator. As Terry swam nearer, he noticed the regulator wasn't even in Carl's mouth. Oh god. Terry thought as he reached for Carl's right arm.

13

He shook Carl's arm, but Carl didn't respond. Then he noticed that Carl's eyes were open and didn't dilate as Terry brought his flashlight up to Carl's face.

Terry quickly rotated Carl as he swam behind him. Once behind him, he reached over Carl's left shoulder for his inflator hose. This can't be happening he thought as he started to lift Carl's limp body off of the sand. He pressed the inflation button on Carl's buoyancy compensator a couple of times. He soon had just enough lift to raise Carl to the surface. On the way up he thought to himself about all the material he had read in the Rescue Diver manual.

He was planning to take the course next month. He had to call for help. He had to start mouth-to-mouth resuscitation. He'd have to ditch their gear between breaths and get Carl to shore quickly. He'd have to start CPR as soon as he got to shore and during the whole time he'd have to tell himself it's not too late and that there was still a chance to save Carl. He got them both to the surface and looked around. The fog was dense and he couldn't see shore.

He heard a small motor moving away from their direction. He screamed for help then released both of their weight belts and took off both of their masks. Carl's mask had a crack in it. Terry was too busy to see the crack or the blood running down Carl's nose. He tilted back Carl's head and gave him two long slow mouth-to-mouth breaths of air. Just like it said to do in the Rescue video. He could taste the iron from the blood mixed together with the salt water. The water was cold as it splashed against his face. There was no response from Carl. He reached for his compass so he could see which way to swim.

They were a long way out in the park, and his chances for survival didn't look good. Terry began counting between breaths as he started the process of bringing Carl back to the beach. It was hard dragging Carl against the tide. He started pulling Carl eastward as much as he could tell by using only his compass. In the fog he could see no more than ten feet in any direction. This was the first dive he'd ever made where he felt completely lost and unprepared. It was unfortunately to become the last dive either one of them would ever make.

The Old Boat

Two men wearing worn out scuba gear tightly held on to the side of a small fifteen-foot long boat. They had just towed it some two hundred yards against the current and the rest break gave them a chance to catch their breath. On the surface with their heads bobbing in the waves they looked identical. Two black hooded heads each with an oval patch of pink flesh half covered by a mask and blue lips. It wouldn't be till they got to shore before you could tell that one was really a foot taller and much heavier in weight than the other.

"I didn't expect the current to be so strong today," Paul Lybarker stated. Tom Erickson who was the unofficial leader of the team was absentmindedly looking over the load of broken concrete the small boat carried.

"Yeah, it's amazing how fast the current can pick up," Tom finally spoke up. " It wasn't bad next to the shore line, but it can be very unpredictable here in the northern part of the park." The sound of a train blowing its horn carried faintly across the water.

"You sure you still want to sink it out here?"

"Yes Paul," Tom had already answered the question half a dozen times before they ever left shore. But as if the question had never been asked before, he began his well-patented statement that held true for most of their work the last four years.

"We've got to sink it out here if we are going to attract divers. Our only goal with this project is to give the divers something to dive other than the dry dock."

The dry dock was actually remnants of an old cement and steel pier that was sunk to form a protective current and wave barrier for the new pier used for the Kingston ferry run. Over a hundred and fifty feet long and ending at the far end in a mere forty feet of depth, the old sunken dry dock was an ideal structure to dive in and around. Over the years the underwater structure had become home to some of the largest residents in the state's waterways. Three lingcod over six feet in length made their home on the south side of the elongated cement and steel structure.

Lingcod are not part of the cod family, but are a very large

15

predacious species of greenling. They have eighteen large sharp teeth that they use to grab and hold on to anything including other less fortunate lingcod before swallowing their prey whole. Males are typically smaller than females. he record catch while angling was a female weighing eighty-five pounds, and just over five feet in length. The fish in this park break all state fishing records. Brackett's Landing Park is a sanctioned marine reserve and this is the only reason the fish are so large.

The park represents what the entire Puget Sound looked like a hundred years ago before the big ones were all fished out. A small female lingcod may lay 70,000 eggs. A large one will spawn over 500,000 eggs. The larger the ling, the more eggs produced, and the more offspring, the more food available for other predators. It's hard to imagine that many eggs until you are diving and come face to face with a white ten-pound basketball size mass of what appears to be a cross between cottage cheese and Styrofoam. A mass of eggs this big rolling across the sea floor tells you that the male guarding the nest has been caught or died.

Within minutes of the disappearance of the male's protection, other fish, crabs, and shrimp, begin to gorge themselves on the little white pearls. After a female lays her eggs, a male will fertilize the eggs then guard the eggs until they hatch. He will starve himself during the process if he has to. He will defend against all intruders no matter how big and depending on his current mood. Although his teeth are sharp, his main defense is just to ram into the object of his wrath like a Billy goat. Swimming too close to a guarded nest can lead to a terrible bruise around the point of impact.

Usually what happens is that you are diving or swimming along and suddenly you feel something bang into the side of your body. You look around while half scarred out of you wits and notice a lingcod getting ready to ram you a second time. You immediately put your hand out in front you to provide a smaller target for the attacker while you make a hasty retreat in any direction away from the fish.

Out of the corner of your eye while making your exit, you may see a glimpse of a white mass hanging under a large pipe or stone. You make a mental note to avoid this spot again for the next five to six weeks until the eggs hatch and the male's testosterone level and temperament have settled back down to normal levels.

After the eggs have hatched, lingcod can be approached and you can practically touch your facemask against their snout before they get annoyed and swim off a few feet.

Divers don't scare the big ones, they put up with the gawking divers as best they can, knowing full well that we, the divers, are the most curious and potentially the most dangerous creatures underwater. It's our natural curiosity as divers that bring us down face to face with the dark green freckled fish with the big teeth.

The problem with this dive sight isn't with the fish; it's with the ferryboat that comes to rest at the adjacent ferry terminal less than two hundred feet away from the dry dock. As the ferry nears the shore ready to off load cars and reload for the round trip to Kingston, the huge propeller blades rotate through the water like a giant salad slice and dicer.

The sounds made from the ferry's blades can be heard in the northern most section of the park on any given dive. Up close, say less than three hundred feet, and it feels and sounds like the blades are moving right over your head. You don't want to be off course when you are this close to the dice-o-matic. Not only could the ferry turn a diver into ground fish food, but the officials can also fine you a considerable lump of money for swimming too close to the ferryboats. Now that some of you have sworn off diving the dry dock, let me just add, that no one has ever been sliced and diced. The ferry system shuts down when a diver can't read a compass, swims the wrong way, or forgets to check the local current conditions. This doesn't happen often, but when it does, it can keep a ferry from berthing for hours. People stuck on the ferry can't get to shore. People on shore can't cross over to Kingston. A traffic jam of hundreds of cars, trucks, and pedestrians ensues because one person can't read the signs and stay away from the ferryboats. This is the reason Tom wanted to sink the boat in the north end of the park. This is the reason they were no longer building anything south of the Jetty. One unfortunate diver would give them all a bad name or maybe even get hurt.

"Looks like we have company," Tom announced. They looked over to the stern and saw bubbles rising to the surface.

17

Vic Swenson's hood broke through the water. His gray bristly mustache and beard made it appear as if a sea lion was inside that hood. He spit the regulator out of his mouth and smiled.

"Line's attached," he announced. John Ho a soft-spoken Korean with a muscular barrel chest, surfaced right behind Vic. He didn't say anything. He just held part of the line out of the water, spit out his regulator, and smiled.

"Good," Tom said.

"How come we never use a boat to help us out?" John asked.

"For one thing, I have terrible luck with boats." Tom replied. "The last time I went on a dive boat it sunk while we were just returning from our dive. The time before that the motor went out half way out to the San Juan Islands."

"So deep down, you sink them in the park as a personal act of revenge," John concluded.

"I never thought of it that way," Tom said. "You might have something there. Tom felt the current nudge him and he quickly turned towards Vic. "Vic if you would do the honors and undo the cork."

"Aye Captain. You know I'll never get a job on the love boat when they find out I helped sink sixteen boats in the last four years." He started to swim back to the stern of the boat.

"That's almost a boat every three months." Paul exclaimed.

"Hey don't look at me, Tom's sunk over twenty by himself."

"That's because of my Freudian complex and next time you'll be saying I sunk sixty boats. You tell bigger tales than most fishermen." Tom said as he shook his head in disbelief.

"Almost sixty . . . if you add in all the concrete, rubber tires, plastic PVC tubes, steel pipes, milk crates, cement blocks, and rocks." Paul continued.

"And don't forget the miles of rope!" said Vic. "There's enough rope on the trails to go from here to Japan."

"Oh, Brother!" Tom lamented.

"What's wrong with Korea?" John asked. Paul looked at him quizzically then smiled and said, "Sorry not enough rope to reach that far John. Maybe next year after we replace the rope on Northern Lights trail." They all started laughing.

The underwater park had a grid of trails mapped out on the sea floor with odds and ends of thick ropes of various sizes, lengths, and materials. The grid pattern ran north to south, and east to west. East was shore, west out to sea, north to Canada, and south to the ferry. They were now in the northwest section of the park. Below them was thirty feet of water. On a high tide the deepest part of the park was only forty some feet deep.

Paul swam out of the way as Vic made his way to the back of the boat.

"After you sir."

"Thank you Paul." Vic reached over to the drain plug in the back of the boat. "Don't try this at home," Vic said to no one in particular. He pulled out the cork and water began to pour in the small craft. He turned and handed the cork to John. "Would you like a souvenir?" John shook his head and moved back from the boat. They all moved back from the boat and watched in silence as the boat began to fill with seawater. They all knew from experience that a sinking object will create suction and pull you down along with the object if you stood too close as it slid underwater.

"There she goes," Paul exclaimed. They all looked down in the water; they only had about ten feet of visibility due to the natural breakdown of the plant life at this time of year. The boat went out of sight quickly.

"Let's give her a minute for the muck to settle," Tom stated.

"Any bets on how she landed? Paul asked.

"Five cents says she landed upside down." John spoke up.

"Why do you say that?" Vic asked.

"Because you pulled the cork." John replied.

"Oh man, I've been set up by my own dive buddy. I'm glad you don't carry a spear gun. You'd probably use that on me too."

"Lucky you're in a marine reserve," Paul added. "No spearguns allowed."

"Ok, it's time to release the rope then head back to shore," Tom announced. They all put their regulators back in their mouths, let the air out of their buoyancy compensators, and slowly descended beneath the surface.

At first all Tom saw was a gray cloud in front of his mask. If he reached out in front of him he might touch a fellow diver, but so much sediment had been stirred up by the boat plunging down to the seabed that six inches in front of his mask was the furthest away he could see. He suddenly felt pressure on his ears. That was a good sign. It meant he was sinking underwater. He equalized his ears by making a clicking noise with his lower jawbone and surrounding muscles. The procedure only took a fraction of a second to do, provided you didn't have a head cold or sinus congestion.

He placed his right hand out in front of him hoping to make contact with the boat along the way. He kept descending slowly downward. His fins were the first to touch the bottom. He bent his legs and soon his knees were resting in the sand.

He reached forward and his right hand connected with something solid. It was the side of the boat. He could only see as far as his elbow in the swirl of debris. He ran his arm upward and found the gunwale. He grabbed the edge of the boat and pulled himself over to its side. He reached over and felt the concrete inside the boat.

The boat had landed right side up. He sighed with relief. Had the boat landed on it's side or worse upside down, he would have had to turn the boat right side up and then reload all the concrete and rocks back inside the boat.

Without the ballast, a strong storm could move the boat at will. It took several hundred pounds of rock to keep even a small boat in place. If the storms and currents got rough, they may not be able to move the boat, but they could at least ripe off the sides and leave nothing more than a pile of rocks where the boat once came to rest on the bottom of the ocean.

Tom didn't mind if this happened, because the main thing was to put rocks and concrete where before there was none and provide a new habitat for fish to call home.

Divers needed things to look at, and fish needed places to live. Food is abundant in the northwest; the limiting factor seems to be places to live. Each boat sunk gives a home to a couple hundred shrimp and one or two lingcod. This boat would be no different. By tonight, several dozen shrimp would move in and set up permanent residence. A day latter, a three-foot long lingcod would wander over and claim the territory comprising the bow of the boat. A young cabezon would claim the stern area or vise versa. Lingcod and cabezon worked together like tag team wrestlers when it came to staking out an area; where you found one, you usually found the other close by.

Besides being known as the bull dog equivalent of the fish family. Male cabezons are known to bite fins when protecting their masses of purple or greenish colored eggs. A three-pound female can lay some 48,000 eggs. A ten-pound female can lay over 96,000 eggs.

The eggs stick together and are poisonous to mammals and birds, but if that's not enough incentive to steer clear of the eggs, the male will bump against you or bite your fins as you swim anywhere near the eggs.

Cabezons have a big mouth, wide enough to swallow a good-sized crab whole. They can practically dislocate their jaws to swallow an even bigger crab and they have sharp teeth to hold a crab in place during the feeding process. They will regurgitate the crab shell after the meat inside is digested. A polished crab shell sitting in the sand is a good indicator of a former meal.

Cabezons have a short body attached to the head almost as an afterthought. Female cabezons are generally bigger than males. Cabezons can generate short bursts of speed and can take a crab right out of your hand before you barely get a chance to move your fingers out of the way. Most people don't swim holding a crab in their hands, so few are witness to the real speed and power of these creatures. The marine reserve avails itself to experiments like this. Food is abundant, and fish are not afraid of divers. After some twenty years of divers blowing loud bubbles next to the animal life, the local inhabitants have learned to put up with the gawking, poking, and prodding behaviors of new divers. Divers kick fish with their fins, disturb their eggs with careless hand motions, shine lights in their faces, and in general are just something the well to do animals living in the park have learned to tolerate.

On the other side of the equation, each diver that dives the park becomes another advocate for world wide marine reserves. They protect the local inhabitants in general, and they allow the animals to peacefully propagate. It's hard not to support the marine reserves once you see the bounty of life and the beauty marine reserves sustain and proliferate. Some sea life can be readily found nowhere else in the wild. Beside abundance and size, the marine reserves also give residence and sanctuary to other rare species. One month, skates, triangular shaped stingrays may make their way through the park. The next month they are gone and in their place two-foot long Nemertean worms are crawling on the sandy bottom looking for polychaete worms to

---

feed on. Nemertean worms don't have eyes, but they can smell a tasty feather duster worm from quite a distance away. They have a squiggly semi-flat body lined with white racing stripes. They move slowly across the sand, but they ooze slime and gyrate like a worm on a hook if you try to pick one up.

Beside different creatures living in the park during different seasons, the species will change during longer periods of time as well. Twenty years ago, the park was well known for its sea pen colonies. Sea pens are bright orange and get one to two feet long. They look like an old quill pen that Benjamin Franklin used to write the Declaration of Independence with. Most of the sea pens are gone now except for a handful living in the northern end of the park. Under the sands, huge colonies of striped nudibranchs, colorful reddish brown and white members of the snail family, but without a shell, sift through the sand until they come into contact with the sea pens. Then they emerge from underneath the sand and feast.

The park is filled with nudibranchs. Nudibranchs have learned over millions of years that you don't need a shell to hide in if you can incorporate stinging cells from the prey you eat into your own defense arsenal. Some nudibranchs incorporate or store obnoxious chemicals from the plants they eat. Other nudibranchs either make their own nasty chemicals, or just happen to mimic or resemble other distasteful species. Over twenty some species can be found in the park from the common Lemon nudibranchs down to the Shaggy Mouse nudibranchs. Most of them graze unobtrusively on Bryozoans, hydroids, plants, and algae. On the other hand, striped nudibranchs may have had one of the most obvious effects on the park in recent years, and except for the north end of the park, sea pens may have vanished from the park for good.

The silt began to settle and Tom could see Vic tightening and re-tying the line on the stern of the boat. The line had been added in case the current tried to move the boat while it was sinking. Paul and John were floating nearby him. They gave each other the OK signal.

Tom put his two index fingers together signaling for them to buddy up, and then he made a motion with his two hands like he was turning a steering wheel back and forth. Steering wheels were on cars, and cars were back at the parking lot, so the signal translated to "lets go back to shore". The others nodded and off they swam at a slow steady pace. A new diver at the park might spend twenty minutes under water before they were low on air. These volunteers had spent so much time in the park that at a slow steady pace, they could lift rocks, build structures, move boats, and still get well over an hour of dive time on a single tank of air. The divers would traverse halfway across the underwater park before they made their final ascent near shore. Along the way they checked the ropes for signs of wear and tear. They had set up small rectangular plastic signs to identify the various trails. The surfaces of the plastic signs were cluttered with barnacles, and algae. In less than six months underwater, barnacles had moved on to the glossy white plastic surfaces and smeared, gouged, and covered from sight the black lettered words. Surface area was the limiting factor for most animals out here in the park. Food is abundant and so no horizontal or vertical space of real estate remains free of life for very long. A clean surface no matter how small was a place to survive and thrive. Tom found a large flashlight out here once. The lens was covered with barnacles and small plants. He turned it on and nothing happened. He let the light soak in vinegar over night and in the morning rubbed the barnacles off the clear lens plate. He turned the flashlight on again, and a high beam bulb illuminated the room. After six months in the cold Puget Sound, the light still had a full charge on the battery.

Other divers may have found it, turned it on, thought that it was dead, and so discarded the light, but Tom knew better. Years of diving had taught him that nothing looked good under water except gold. Whatever the object was, until you brought it to the surface and spent hours trying to clean it up, there was no way you could determine without a doubt that the artifact was still good, or trashed beyond repair. The sea was filled with treasures covered with barnacles, small plants, and animals. The sea was also filled with tons of discarded trash that small invertebrates desperately, and in most cases in vain, attached themselves and used the objects for homes.

The dive group swam back along Northern Lights trail. Northern Lights had plastic milk crates weaved into the trail's rope and spaced every ten to fifteen feet. The crates themselves were homes to thousands of juvenile shrimp, nudibranchs, and other small creatures and plant life. Once the shrimp grew larger, they would migrate to join their cousins in the crevices of rock formations and around the undersides of sunken boats. Lingcod would occasionally perch on top of the crates in order to survey their domain, scare off intruders, and occasionally snack on a few shrimps that wandered too far from the security of the crates.

The group of divers swam south along Northern Lights until they reached an intersection in the rope trails. On the left and heading east to shore stood a large piece of cement pipe large enough to crawl through. It was strategically placed on top of a pile of rocks. A rope trail ran through the pipe and ended a hundred yards from shore. This trail was called Cathedral way. On the west side of the pipe and the other side of the intersection, Cathedral way passed a trail that lead to a sunken one hundred and ten foot long tug boat and the trail ultimately ended at the west park boundary. The depth out here was a maximum forty-three feet. There was nothing out here but sand and the beer bottles thrown over board by non-caring fishermen.

The fishermen would hug their boats right up to the marine reserve boundary then cast their lines into the park. Some of the fishermen were also divers, and they knew how big the lingcod get in the park. If you didn't mind risking fishing in a marine reserve, you certainly didn't mind throwing your empty bottles, beer cans, and trash over board. Most of the bottles out here quickly found tenants such as barnacles and small crabs. The cans however had a surface too smooth for much to grow on accept an occasional brown algae film so they just rolled along in the drifts of sand until the cans made their way towards shore.

From where Tom was hovering in the water next to the cement pipe he could see the first of the large cement blocks that formed the Cathedrals. The block was just south of Cathedral way and a few feet west of Northern Lights. The cement block was close to twenty feet wide by twenty feet tall. On the north end it was hollow with a square cave that went back a good ten feet and could accommodate two divers easily.

Pressed up against the ceiling of this compartment was a shinny substance that looked like a pool of mercury. It was nothing more than spent air bubbles from scuba tanks trapped against the ceiling on their quest to reach the surface. The pool of low oxygenated air waved back and forth with the currents and occasionally a bubble would reach the lip of the overhang and escape upwards. Soon, another diver would enter the man made cave, blow a few bubbles as they looked at a crab, and the ceiling pool of depleted air would swell again to its maximum allowable size.

An octopus used to live under the southwest corner of the giant cement block. Remnants of his den are still visible. That was several years ago. The giant octopus can reach a length from fifteen to twenty feet long in just five years. The record was 600 pounds and thirty feet long from head to arm tip. This particular octopus didn't even reach the age of two before a large lingcod swam by and most likely swallowed it whole.

Tom and Paul turned down Cathedral Way and headed towards shore. Vic and John swam past the giant cement block and headed south on Northern Lights. They wanted to check out a sight called the Jackson and the Boat yard before returning to shore via Jetty Way trail. On a good day of visibility you could see the Jackson from the southeast corner of the Cathedrals. The Jackson was a white forty-five foot boat sunk just a few years ago and hadn't taken the beating by the storms and currents like some of the other boats in the park. As a rule, the more north or west you went, the tougher the conditions were on a boat.

South in the boatyard a dozen fifteen foot long boats had survived the ravages of the sea for close to ten years. A few looked almost even sea worthy. At the north end of the park though, a boat called the Hiccup was sunk less than four years ago and all that remained of it was pieces of material still held down by rocks and chunks of cement.

Three other boats placed by the Hiccup were also being systematically torn apart by the currents and tides. Like the houses of the three little pigs, nothing survived in the northern end of the park except for stone and the sturdiest of construction material. But what the northern end of the park lacked in construction sites, it made up in unusual animal life. This was also the area where you could expect to see an occasional harbor seal.

Harbour seals couldn't resist swimming around the former bow of the Hiccup and looking inside the cabin. They were curious and had to check out everything sunk by humans. The north end is the area where great numbers of white spike fringed

Alabaster nudibranchs gathered in huge congregations. The Northern boundary of the park is also where squid come in at night. Males with red arms hold on to female squids with clear bodies as they copulate. The males inject packets of sperm into the female's mantle where they will soon explode into clouds of sperm. At about the same time, females release eggs from the oviducts that are gathered and coated with mantle secretions. The secretions contain chemicals that have antibiotic properties and they are also chemically unsavory to other invertebrates and fish. On contact with water, the eggs begin to swell up and the secretions turn to jelly with the outside layer of the egg mass secretions hardening enough to form a spindle shaped sheathed capsule. Each capsule can contain up to two hundred eggs and can swell in size until the capsules appear almost as big as the female herself. A single female can lay twenty of these capsules in a single night before both she and her male suitor die of exhaustion. The eggs develop and the squid larvae are released in about three weeks. In approximately two years, these squid will be back in the park to repeat the whole mating cycle.

Sticking out of the east end of the pipe was a small cabezon. Tom kept one eye on him as he swam by. The cabezon fidgeted as if deciding weather to fight or flee. Paul swam right behind Tom and the sight of two of these noisy bubbling creatures proved too much for the Cabezon and so he swam off a few feet and landed on a nearby milk crate. Paul waved goodbye to him as they continued swimming along on a parallel course with the trail.

On Cathedral trail there used to be an empty discarded scuba tank stuck strait up neck in the sand, one every hundred feet. The tides and currents had taken their toll over the last three years and currently most of the tanks were missing. Tom swam close to one of the tanks that laid flat in the sand some five feet off to the side of the trail. A hold fast, the exposed roots, of bull kelp had attached to the side of the tank. The long rope like stalk of the bull kelp ascended from the hold fast up to the surface some eighteen feet above and ended in a group of long leathery leaves that were held together and remained afloat by a central gas filled bulb. The bull kelp leaves break off during the winter storms and are back in full force by next spring. If the weather was good, some kelp could grow a foot in one day. The stalk of the bull kelp can live for seven years or more. With all the additional underwater structures to hold on to, it's no surprise that the in the last four years the bull kelp had become more numerous in the park.

Nothing the divers built so far could stand up very long against the elements. It was more of a challenge to sink and build structures just to see how long they would last. Tom kept on his course. Over to his right was a tall metal work art object they erected last winter. It stood over ten foot high and four foot wide on each of its triangular sides. A couple of months after they installed the structure a female lingcod laid her eggs right in the middle on the structure and around the base. A male lingcod that Tom didn't see rammed into the side of his body and put a good bruise on his hip. Not to mention the water he accidentally sucked down as he tried to figure out if he was being eaten alive by a great white shark or just mauled to death by an angry polar bear.

It's ridiculous or should one say uncanny how much fear a three-foot fish can instill when you're not prepared for the sudden bump.

There were no lings hanging around the structure today. At the end of the trail, a huge six-foot diameter piece of cement pipe lay on its side on top of a pile of rock. One side had sunk into the sand so the structure leaned a bit. A large lemon nudibranch lounged on top of one of the rocks. The group of divers was still ten feet underwater. Without looking at their compasses, they turned southeast and crossed the ripples in the sand towards shore.

A couple more minutes passed by as they swam through water less than four feet deep. When the water depth became shallow, they signaled each other with a thumb up gesture, and slowly stood up in the sand. The first thing Tom did when his head was above the surface was spit out his regulator, remove his mask, and blow his nose into the ocean. The cold temperature of the water had stuffed his sinuses way past his comfort level. He almost sneezed on the dive, but reframed due to fear of permanently obscuring his vision for the rest of the dive and he didn't like having to clear his mask during a dive on cold days. Paul surfaced and looked over at Tom.

"Do you mind doing that in some other body of water? I have to swim here you know."

Tom just smiled at Paul and used his hand to churn the surface of the water and scattered the surrounding surface debris.

"They're all gone. Just like the bird crap and all the fish poop."

"I try not to think about that when I dive," Paul said.

"Whether you want to or not, you're diving in seal dung and fish sperm. Not to mention the bacteria you sucked in down your snorkel."

"I think I prefer you better underwater. You're not as gross down there." Paul began to unsnap his fin straps in order to remove his fins. Tom wiped his face with his hand. "It's all good." Tom said. "This is a great way to build your immunity system."

"Well anyway. Are we going to take the blocks out now?" Paul asked.

"No, let's move them down to the edge of the water tomorrow at low tide. I don't think the boat will be going anywhere with these tides." The two of them waded to shore and approached a collection of used cinder blocks lying on the beach. They had dropped off the cinder blocks before they went out on the dive. Tom got the blocks from a construction site last Monday. By Wednesday he had hauled them down to the local dive shop where they sat until Friday next to the rinsing station and the wet suit rack. It didn't matter what he collected or how long he collected it. Most of the material made its way down to the dive store before it ever made its way to the park.

A derelict boat might take up all the parking spaces in front of the shop and even make it hard to open the front door, but it was still good for business. Divers knew that the shop and the volunteer crew who helped Tom work on the park were dedicated. Divers knew that by buying at the shop and buying dive maps made by the volunteers and were sold to support the volunteer activities, they helped make the park the most interesting and diverse underwater reserve on the west coast. The best part was that the twenty-seven acre park was all shore entry diving. No boats, kayaks, or canoes, were allowed in the park. You didn't need anything except the will to keep your hands to your sides and kick in a slow steady pace. A new diver could make it out to the boat yard on a single tank of air. A good diver could make it to the far end of the park and back on one tank of air. There was so much to see that a photographer could make it halfway down one of the trails before running out of film and it was a long way back to shore just to reload the camera.

Tom and Paul walked by the collection of cement blocks. They had used an old wooden wheel barrel to cart the blocks from their trucks. The front rusted wheel didn't move that well in the sand. The front wheel had a tendency to sink into the sand and so it required more of a push/pull technique to get the blocks moved right down next to the waters edge. When the water receded at low tide, they would carry the material down to the low tide mark. When the water flowed back in at normal levels or better still, the high tide mark, the blocks would be submerged. Once underwater, the blocks were easy to pick up and put in a cargo net strategically place on the adjacent sandy substrate. After the cargo net was filled, a barrel with four hundred pounds of lift capacity was attached to each of the four corners of the square cargo net and each barrel would be filled with enough air so the blocks could easily be lifted off of the sandy bottom and readily moved to wherever desired. The team of divers could float up to sixteen hundred pounds of material this way and sink it anywhere in the park.

Tom and Paul headed for the shower next to the restroom to remove some of the sand and salt off their dive gear before heading over to their trucks. The water from the faucets was cold, but not quite as cold as the water they just surfaced from. As they left the shower they walked over to a picnic table and looked out into the water.

A group of divers were just entering the nearby water. They looked like a small group of four students from a dive class, one instructor, and one dive master.

Tom recognized the instructor. He worked out of a Seattle dive shop. His name was Don and he was down at the park at least once a month. He'd seen the dive master before too, but couldn't remember his name.

It appeared that they were just starting dive one of the PADI open water dive course. They were adjusting weights and taking turns descending below the surface in about four feet of water. The task at hand was just to put on enough weight to allow one to sink beneath the waves without putting too much weight on the diver. Too much weight could make a diver unable to float on the surface at rest. Don was standing near a diver as the diver released air from his buoyancy compensator. The diver let the air out of his BC and slowly went underwater. The books said if you deflate a BC and float holding you breath, then you should be able to exhale and descend beneath the surface. In the real world though, you had to count on the fact that the aluminum tank on your back would become lighter during the dive as more air was used from the tank. Therefore, by the end of the dive, a diver needed an extra five pounds of lead to compensate for the increased buoyancy of an empty aluminum scuba tank.

Don reached down in the water and pulled the diver to the surface. The diver looked at Don with the regulator still in his mouth.

"Take the reg out. You're good to go." Tom heard him call out.

"There they are." Paul pointed out towards the water. Two divers surfaced half way down Jetty Way trail. Vic and John surfaced next to one of one of the park's orange floats. The float was weighted down by all the mussel and algae growth around its chain and subsurface areas. The two of them started removing barnacles, mussels and the plants growing on the float. They had to be careful as they pried off the barnacles, as the edges were razor sharp and could rip right through a good set of thick neoprene gloves.

Within minutes the buoy floated higher in the water. In another couple of months they would have to be back out here removing new growth all over again.

Tom and Paul didn't wait for the task to be completed; they went over to the trucks to discard their gear. The gear tends to get heavy after awhile. Both were wearing twin tanks on their backs. Tom wore steel twin seventy-two cubic feet tanks that by anybody's count were more than fifteen years old. Paul had new twin aluminum eighty cubic feet tanks. You could go through a lot of air underwater when you were moving concrete onto cargo nets, moving it to dive sites, and then lifting and placing the cement according to plan.

Tom opened the back tailgate of his 1981 Toyota truck. It was rusted through in a couple of spots and the original orange paint had faded. The tailgate creaked into place and he sat down. Paul went over to his 1999 Silverado with the rubberized truck bed coating. He opened the back tailgate and carefully sat down. As soon as he got out of his scuba unit, he laid it down on a large 4x4 one-inch thick rubberized truck mat. Paul thought nothing was too good for the overall care and longevity of his gear.

Tom felt his back was suddenly a hundred pounds lighter as he leaned his tanks against a pile of rope. Tom didn't have much room sitting on the back of his truck for the back end was filled with four faded yellowish white fifty gallon plastic buoy barrels, a 16 x 16 foot military style cargo net, a dilapidated wooden wheel barrel, and the odds and ends of plenty seaworthy rope. He sat for a moment while he caught his breath. Paul was doing the same. They looked over at each other and smiled. The day's work went as planned. Tom felt tired yet his mood was upbeat and carefree, but all that was about to change.

Finders Keepers

Dave and Ben had just finished setting their first crab pot. They wanted to set a few crab pots before all the good spots for the day were gone. Ben, the taller of the two had a family get-together this weekend and wanted to collect as many Dungeness crab as he could before Saturday. Dave was glad to help out being he was also invited to the family reunion. For the two of them the plan was simple. Place the crab pots before they went to work, and haul them in before they went home. They had four double-ring crab pots in the twelve-foot aluminum boat and placing the crab pots was a chore that wouldn't take long. Besides, it was nice to get out on the water now that the fog was starting to lift.

Dave idled back on the motor and Ben got ready to toss over the second pot. A piece of frozen chum salmon head was attached to the middle of the smaller inner ring. With one heave, the two rings and netting material went overboard and sank quickly from view. A long rope and an old orange float was all that remained on the surface to remind them of the pot's location. Ben started to tie another frozen fish head to the next pot when he noticed Dave was staring at something. He looked over and saw a white Bayliner boat gently coming out of the fog and drifting sideways right towards them.

"Hey, anyone on board?" Dave yelled. Both of them stood silent as they waited to hear any sign of life from the vessel.

"What do you want to do?" Ben asked.

"Forget the pots. Let's go check it out." Ben dropped the fish head, rinsed his hands over the side of the boat and then wiped his hands on his jeans.

"Now I know why your pants always smell like salmon," David uttered sarcastically. Ben reached over and wiped his hands on Dave's pants.

"Ok, Ok, you win Ben." Ben laughed while Dave turned on the small outboard engine. They made a circle around the drifting boat and approached cautiously. There appeared to be no signs of any movement or sound coming from the boat. Dave motored behind the boat. The name "Misty Fog" was painted on the back of the boat. Dave slowly pulled up next to the left or port side of

---

32

the boat. The aft deck contained two benches, one on each side of the boat. Each bench had several semi-circular wooden support brackets complete with bungee cords to hold three or four scuba tanks. However, there were no immediate signs of any scuba equipment on board.

"There's blood on the deck," Ben said with a quiver in his voice. They both looked in at the aft deck and saw the splatter patterns on the gun rails and a pool of blood and saltwater lay on the deck itself.

"It could be Salmon," Dave said. He didn't believe it. He said it just to reassure his buddy. Ben looked closely at the red droplets.

"I don't think so."

"Hey, anyone on board?" Dave yelled. Both of them stood silent as the waited to hear any sign of life from the vessel.

"Doesn't seem to be anyone on board," Ben said.

"Ok," Dave began. You stay here. I'm going to check it out." Before Ben could say a word, Dave was out of the boat and standing on the deck of the Bayliner. A pink liquid sloshed around his boots, but he didn't give it a second thought. It could have been salmon or seal blood for all he knew. He stepped over to the cabin door. The door was unlocked. He opened the door and peered inside, there was a container of dry suit powder on the table next to some discarded clothes. It looked as though the owners had just stepped off the boat for a dive and would be returning any minute. But if that was the case, then why were all the lights off? Dave hit the light switch and the cabin lights came on. He hit the switch again and turned the lights back off.

"Find anything Dave?" The boat was giving Ben the creeps.

"No," Dave replied as he backed up and shut the cabin door.

" I don't see an anchor line," Ben stated. "That's probably why the boat was drifting."

"It must have happened while the divers were underwater." Dave added. He stepped over to the starboard side of the boat. A line was hanging over the right side of the boat.

"Those poor bastards could be drifting out there right now," Ben lamented. Dave pulled up the rope and found a mesh bag filled with half a dozen "Geoduck" clams. He knew they were geoducks by the long muscled necks and the fleshy bodies that never would quite fit between the shells. But since geoducks buried themselves up to three feet deep in the mud, geoducks had little risk from exposure to predators.

"You mean poor poachers," Dave smiled and said. He lifted the mesh bag up to show the contents. He handed Ben the bag as he saw another line on the port side next to their own boat.

"Hey," Ben exclaimed. "Some of these guy have to be over a hundred years old." Dave lifted the other rope and hauled up another bag full of geoducks.

"There's got to be several hundred dollars worth of meat here," Dave gasped.

"You want to keep it?" Ben asked.

"Hell yeah. We'll call it a finder's fee for bringing in their boat. He handed the second mesh bag to Ben and Ben set it down in their aluminum boat right next to the other mesh bag of geoducks.

"We've got a years worth of clam soup," Ben proudly proclaimed. Dave smiled at him and turned his attention to the stern of the Bay liner. He noticed that the galvanized dive ladder was still down in the water and the extra drag would slow them up as hey brought the big boat back to the pier. He reached down and pulled on the ladder. The ladder seemed to be stuck in the down position. He got down on his hands and knees at the back of the boat and reached his hands in the water to pull on a lower rung of the ladder. He figured the extra fulcrum would make it easier for the ladder to swing up into its sea going resting place. As he pulled with all his strength, the ladder started to move up and outward. Through the water at the end of the ladder he saw a familiar outline.

"Hey Ben, I think we got some more geoducks!" Ben leaned back in the small boat. He couldn't wait to see for himself. Dave was about to tell him how many the bag contained, but instead of seeing a mesh bag full of clams he saw what appeared to be two human heads, each severed at he neck, and one of them staring glassy eyed right back at him. Dave gasped and dropped the ladder back into the water.

"Let's get out of here," he said with his voice trembling in fear. He jumped aboard the little boat and started up the engine. He almost knocked Ben overboard trying to move past him. Ben barely caught himself before he fell over.

"What the?" Ben looked at Dave and wondered why his eyes had become so large and his face so white.

"Sorry Ben," Dave choked out. "We gotta get out of here now." Dave floored the engine and the tiny boat headed back in the direction they came. Ben held on for dear life. Something got to Dave worse than Ben had never seen before, and now Dave was running the boat like a freaking maniac. Ben hoped to god he would make it back to shore alive. Dave didn't dare speak to Ben until he had put some distance between the boat and themselves. His only thought was to try and make it back to shore in one piece too.

The Ferry

Tom looked over at the water and saw two divers swimming out on the surface. They were headed right for Delion Way. This was the most southern trail in the park and ran east from shore out west. A large metal pole held a two-sided signboard that stated, "Warning Restricted Ferry Area. Do not dive south of this point." The divers were swimming right for the sign.

In theory, you were permitted to dive here and see the remnants of a ninety foot long tug boat called the Alitak and just west of that lay the submerged dry dock that was sunk in 1935 to make a breakwater for the Kingston ferry. Not much was left of the Alitak. The sunken dry dock was another story. The dry dock gave a diver something large and long to dive around, through, over, and peer underneath. The further most west end of the dry dock lay in approximately forty-three feet of water on a high tide.

On a good day you could see from the north side to the south side less than forty feet across. Plumose anemones lined the sides of the derelict. Giant rock scallops attached to the inner ribs of the steel joists. But the best-kept secret was on the south side of the dry dock; the side nearest the ferry. On this side huge lingcod take up residence under the dry dock; two lings over six feet long and one slightly bigger. The fish that live on this side put state fishing records to shame. Lingcod this big usually dwell several hundred feet deep in the ocean, especially females who rarely come near shore except to breed with the smaller males. So these fish are not only an exception, but also the main attraction at this dive site. It gives a diver a different perspective on life when coming face to face with a fish bigger than a fellow diver. The location was the only flaw of this dive site. Divers saw the park on the web, came from around the world to see and experience the beauty of nature, but failed to plan for the dive.

Tom looked off towards Jetty Way. A tall light blue pole tilted into the wind on top of a float. The pole leaned in the direction on the prevailing surface current flow. By his best guess, right now the current was running south at one and a half knots.

He took off his gloves and checked to see how big the holes were becoming in the glove's fingertips. Not bad he thought, only a few of the fingers were directly exposed to the ocean. He set the gloves down next to his mask, snorkel, and fins. He wanted them ready just in case the divers needed assistance. You didn't want to dive Delion Way unless the current was going north. Right now the current was nonexistent which was the same as saying the tide was slack.

There was no reason to kick against a current unless you were going to use the current at the end of your dive to take you back to your entry point. Here, a southbound current could only sweep you right in the path of the Kingston ferry. Being that close to one of the most giant slice and dicers was a rude awakening to the ever exciting and heart-pounding world of miscalculations. Just the thought of being close to the ferry's giant propeller blades and hearing the loud resounding thump thump thump emanating from the blades churning up the water would be adequate to scare to death any right minded diver.

The two divers reached the pole and hung on to rest as the current pushed by them and headed south. A black cormorant stood on the sign directly above one of the divers. Cormorants do not secrete their own oil to make their feathers water proof. Instead, they are constantly preening their feathers and hanging their wings out to dry between dives. This bird was one of the best divers around. She could swim using her wings down to a hundred feet underwater, catch a fish in her mouth, swim past one group of divers, and surface by another group of divers all on one breath of air.

The bird peered down on the two divers and gave its profession opinion of their diving skills. A glob of white residue landed on the hood of one of the divers. The diver wiped clean the front of his mask with the surrounding water then displayed an arrogant gesture with his gloved hand back towards the dirty bird. The bird looked quizzically at him for half a second then resumed preening her feathers. A loud horn blew suddenly announcing the arrival of the ferry. The divers looked south at the giant dive-o-matic turning into position to dock so close to where they were momentarily planning to dive.

Tom could see them talking to each other and shaking their heads. The horn blew again and the divers let go of the pole.

They started swimming on the surface northwards against the current. It looked like they had a sudden change of plans. Tom watched them swim. The movement was slow considering the current they were trying to go against. They were quickly becoming tired. If they stopped to rest, or to fix anything, they would be swept right back towards the ferry. Sure enough, one of them ran out of steam and stopped. The other diver stopped when he realized his buddy was falling behind. The lead diver shouted to his partner and they began swimming back towards shore. They found a spot where the current wasn't so bad and both descended beneath the waves. More than likely the surface currents were worse than the currents below. If the divers were smart, they would follow a northbound compass course, do a dive around the boat yard and then return via Jetty Way. This way they could still have a good dive and, if nothing else, be a little wiser next time around.

"That was fun to watch," Paul said as he walked over to Tom.

"I think I would get an ulcer if I sat around here all day." Tom replied.

Paul looked at Tom already enjoying what he was about to say. "You think those guys are from Oregon?" Tom just rolled his eyes. He knew what Paul was insinuating. Divers that came from out of state were usually the ones connected more often with local accidents. They didn't know the local conditions. They didn't own their own gear, didn't get to dive often enough to keep their skills up to par, or if they did have gear it was years old, out of date, needed repair, or worse yet, they got certified twenty years ago in Hawaii wearing nothing more than a tank, swim suit, and a smile.

All it took was a documentary on the Discovery Channel on sea life of the Puget Sound and on a whim people thought they would go diving in the northwest to see for themselves what the diving here was like. Divers that earned an open water diver certification card sometime within the last thirty plus years could technically go rent or use their own old gear and take a plunge in the cold Puget Sound waters any time they felt like it.

Diving is a relatively safe sport providing you keep in good physical condition and you keep your dive skills up to par. National statistics do show that diving is safer than many other sports. The reason for the good safety record could be due to good initial training supplied by good self-regulating diving agencies.

The problem is that in diving, you're not required to keep your skills fresh and honed in; you should, but there are no rules that say you have to. It's all up to you and at your own discretion. Your tank may have to be visualized annually to check for rust. Your tank has to pass a Hydro test once every five years to make sure it can hold pressurized air, but a long time inactive diver isn't required to do anything including even the minimum of passing an occasional refresher course. All a certified diver has to do is put the gear on their back any which way they can possibly remember, and off they can go for a fun dive in hopefully warm water.

Fortunately, diving accidents are very rare. Although, Tom felt the way the government declared an incident as a dive related accident was more than a little unfair. If a person had a heart attack in a bowling alley, you didn't call it a bowling accident, but if the same person had a heart attack while wearing dive gear, it was ruled as a dive related accident. In addition, even though more people died in bowling alleys in North America per year than all the diver related accidents in the entire world, diving was still a young mysterious sport to millions of people and therefore scarier to read about when something unfortunate happened.

Most of the out of state license plates at any given dive site in Washington read "Oregon". A few plates read "Idaho", and once in a great while a plate read "Montana". Because of sheer volume and wild speculation, the rumors often spread about divers from Oregon being involved in the local diving accidents. The problem was, Tom was from Oregon and this leap to twisted logic really bugged him. To make matters worse, he was fourth generation Oregonian. If they had any diver friendly locations along the Oregon coastline he might still be living down there, but Washington had the Puget Sound, the San Juan Islands, and the diving off the coast of Canada was less than six hours north.

Tom was a permanent Washingtonian transplant and cringed every time he heard something sour mentioned about his former home state and this had bugged him nonstop for at least the last twenty years.

Incidentally, Paul was from Detroit Michigan. He had little

room to talk about outsiders even if he had lived in Washington close to thirty years.

"My bet would be on New Zealand." Tom said. "Give them a black hood and they look just like us, but wait till they take the reg out of their mouth. I bet they've got an accent you could cut shrimp brine with." Paul laughed at Tom's suggestion.

"That was good Tom. I'll go check and see if they have any sheep in the back of their truck."

"I thought you were into llamas?" Tom sarcastically remarked.

"Hey, leave my preferences out of this. We were talking about your friends from down south."

"There you go again," Tom countered. Talk anymore like that and I might have to open up a can of redneck on you." Tom stood up and straightened his back. He was still almost a foot shorter than Paul. Paul probably out weighed him by eighty pounds too.

"You know it's lucky I don't pick on former football players." He told Paul.

"Yeah, it would look real bad me getting beat up by a former chess club member."

"Hey, I was third in state." Tom replied.

"Where . . .in Oregon?

"There you go again."

Paul put his stretched hands out in front of him. "I can't help it if New Zealand and Oregon are both down south."

Vic and John shook their heads as they approached Tom and Paul.

"Do we have to separate the two of you again?" Vic interrupted with a loud shout.

"Maybe we should just put them on separate beaches." John added.

"No, better to keep them on the same beach. Then their more contained…you know like sequestering noise pollution."

"Very funny guys," said Paul.

"So you want some help tonight moving the blocks?" Vic said shifting the conversation.

"Tonight?" Tom asked without comprehension.

"Tonight at around seven we have a minus point six tide." Vic said.

"We should be able to move the blocks down the beach quit a ways." Paul agreed. Tom shrugged his shoulders. At first he didn't know what to say.

"Believe it or not, my mother set me up with a blind date. If I don't go, I don't get homemade spaghetti for a couple of weeks."

"Sounds like your mother has you by the meatballs."

"Very funny Vic." Tom said.

They all knew Tom's mother lived with him. He remodeled the ground floor of his split-level house to give her her own living quarters four years ago after her husband died. Tom was divorced with no kids and didn't need the extra space anyway so at the time it didn't seem like a bad idea.

Vic smiled and said, "I'm sorry. We all know you can't build a park if you don't take care of home first." They all nodded in agreement.

"Tell you what," Tom spoke up. "Three feet is all we really need. Maybe I could swing by around six thirty. Move some blocks half way down the beach, and then go to the movies. That should submerge them deep enough for tomorrow."

"Six thirty it is then," Vic stated. "I'm going to go remove my gear." Vic suddenly realized that the tank and weights were still on his back.

"I'm with you," John added. Both of them were wearing single eighty-cubic feet tanks, but they still felt heavy after awhile, especially when you added on forty some pounds of weight just to make you heavy enough to move you down the water column. Dive gear was intensive in the Northwest. You could get away with a twelve to eighteen pound weight belt in the tropics. Here, that would be considered a pool belt. Tom had an integrated Zeagle Ranger BC. The same buoyancy compensator used by the military for the past twenty some years.

His Ranger BC had side pockets that held additional weight when he dove with just a single tank. The contents of the pockets could be jettisoned in an emergency.

Two large side pockets usually held fourteen pounds of weight each. He also wore a twenty-five pound weight belt around his waist. He could have put all his current weight in his BC pockets and then some. He had a Tech Ranger with sixty-five pounds of lift. The Ranger was built to take the load, but he preferred to separate the weight; that way he could jettison weight in stages. His Ranger had over four hundred dives on it and still worked as good as the day he first bought it. When he mounted his dual tanks on the Ranger he left the weight pockets empty. Instead, he used the weight of the steel tanks along with the weight from a fifteen-pound lead bar screwed in place between the tanks to compensate for the empty pockets. With extra stage bottles to further weight him down he had gone down to a hundred and seventy five feet deep. On the surface with that much gear on it took everything he had just to cross the parking lot and plop himself into the water. Needless to say, divers in the northwest have strong back and leg muscles in addition to an even stronger desire to dive in cold water with sometimes very limited visibility and swift currents.

Paul walked over to his truck and took off his wetsuit top. Tom unzipped his top piece and then pulled his hood over his head. He laid the wet suit top and hood on the tailgate. A small green shrimp fell off his suit and landed in a puddle of water. It tried hopping around for a brief moment, and when finally exhausted, it became motionless. Tom picked it up and went down to the water's edge and tossed the shrimp back into the ocean.

The wet suit top was ripped and glued in several locations. Working on the park took a terrible toll on dive gear. He put his first big gash in his new wet suit a week after he'd first tried it on for size. He still felt plenty warm wearing the 7mm farmer johns so after returning from shore he went around to the passenger side of his truck, got his dry clothes, a towel, and tennis shoes and headed over to the men's changing room.

Tom opened the door to the restroom walked by the urinal and stall and into the adjacent room. The changing room was cold and damp, but it sure beat changing his clothes in the parking lot any day of the week. Vic and John were already changing. There was water on the floor and Tom looked around for a spot on a bench that was still dry. He set his clothes down in a reasonably dry location. He started peeling of his farmer johns and a small cloud of steam escaped from his upper chest region. The rubber from the suit clung to his legs and didn't want to peel off. It took a moment of frenzied energy to push the suit down his legs and step out of it one leg at a time. A puddle of saltwater formed around the base of his ankles and a thin stream of water trickled in the direction of a half rusted out floor drain. Tom quickly grabbed his towel and dried himself off. His bare feet were getting cold on the concrete floor. After drying his hair he threw the towel down and stood on it as he put his clothes on. His toes felt frozen by the time he got his socks on, but they would warm up considerably within the next hour or so. He had a dry suit at home, but he would rather save that for when he didn't have to risk ruining the material during heavy labor and underwater construction.

Paul came in the changing room and looked around for a dry location.

"We got a lot done today," Paul said as he found a spot.

"One boat down, thousands to go," Tom stated. Vic and John were getting ready to leave the changing room.

"How many boats do you want to sink in the park?" John questioned.

"There is no magic number." Tom began. "And we can't possibly compete with mother nature. We just do what we can and hope for the best."

"Well, it's been fun. See you tomorrow." John turned and left the room.

As the door shut behind John, Paul turned to Tom and a concerned expression appeared on his face.

"You heard what happened last night?" Paul asked Tom. Tom quickly lost his smile. He looked over to Paul and then to Vic.

"I heard rumors. I'm sure Steve knows the details." Tom said. As soon as we get dressed I guess we better go down to the shop and find out."

Out Of The Bag

A car marked Mason County Sheriff turned off the main road and down an embankment. Dennis Windred drove across a road made entirely from oyster shells and pulled his car to a stop next to two fishermen standing beside their twelve-foot long aluminum boat. Their boat was tied down to a rusted out trailer and hooked to the back of an old ford truck. Just beyond where they were standing and tied to a make shift dock was a twenty-six foot long Bayliner boat. Behind the white boat was the county sheriff's aluminum boat. Deputy Sheriff Willey Short walked up to the car as it came to a stop. Willey ran his hand through his short black hair and tried to straighten his pressed uniform shirt. Dennis turned off the engine and opened the car door.

"I didn't want to say it over the radio unless anyone was listening, but these two found two severed heads tied on good to the dive ladder." Dennis nodded as he walked past the deputy.

"Morning," he said to the fishermen. He knew both of them for more than the last twenty years.

"Morning, Dennis," they both spoke up. Dennis pulled out a cigarette and matches. He lit the cigarette and took a big puff.

"Where did you find the boat?" he finally asked.

"We found it just drifting along." Dave, the shorter of the two, spoke up.

"We thought it was coming right at us until we saw no one was there," Ben added.

"No one on board?" Dennis asked.

"No one," Ben answered.

"Did either of you two go onboard?"

"I did," Dave sheepishly replied. "But I didn't touch a thing."

Dennis took a few more puffs, and then he threw the cigarette on the ground. He looked over to their boat and saw the two mesh bags of geoducks sitting in their boat.

"That's good." He said. "Now let me see the sole of your boot." Dave looked at him quizzically for a second, and then lifted up his shoe. Dennis leaned over and examined the sole of Dave's boot. As he rose up he took a glimpse inside their aluminum boat. "Anything else you want to tell me?"

"Do you mind if we stick around?" Dave asked.

"If you want. Why?" Dennis asked.

"We want to know who the poachers were." Dave replied.

"How do you know they were poachers?" Dennis asked. Dave took a second to swallow and then Dave said.

"I've seen the owner of this boat down at Bill's. He looks like he'd kill his mother if the price were right."

"Do you know his name?" Dennis asked.

"No. He wasn't the kind of fellow you wanted to know either."

"When did you last see him?"

"Not sure, maybe a year or two ago."

"What about you Ben?" Dennis asked.

"No Sir, I've never seen either of them."

"What about the owner?"

"Haven't seen him either. Sheriff." Dennis wondered why Ben was suddenly so formal.

"Have you boys been poaching?" He already knew the answer judging from the clothes they were wearing and lack of dive gear present. You can't get geoducks that big unless it was a record low tide or you went diving for them. The two crab pots more than explained what the two of them were up to.

"Do me a favor and empty out those mesh bags." Dennis asked them. Dave and Ben stepped over to their boat with Dennis and Willey right behind them. They opened up the bags and emptied them on the floor of their boat. Geoducks tumbled out on to the aluminum boat's deck.

"Well, I don't see any fingers or missing hands," Dennis casually commented. Ben's stomach rolled over and Dave felt a shiver go through his body. "If you don't mind, I'll take the mesh bags with a geoduck in each one. We'll need them for evidence." Ben reached for one of the clams and started to put it in the bag.

"Not the biggest one." Dave rebuked him. "Put the smallest one in the bag. Like me." Ben realized his mistake and exchanged the clam for a smaller one. They each held out a bag toward Dennis.

"You can set them by my car. On your way our out." Ben and Dave glanced at each other then disappointedly looked at Dennis. Dennis waived his hands as a sign of exasperation.

"No, you don't have to leave right now. Just stand back a

little, while we check the boat out."

Dennis and Willey walked past the two men and over to the white Bayliner boat. Before seeing anything else Dennis noticed a smear of diluted blood on the aft deck of the boat. Foot prints matching Dave's made a path towards the closed cabin door and then back out again. Drops of blood were sprayed on the sidewalls as well as the side benches. Small holes at the base of the sidewalls occasionally let some of the pooled mixture of blood and saltwater escape back into the sea. Dennis climbed on board and gently stepped over to the cabin door. He opened the door and peered inside. Two big bags lay on the seats next to a small table. Some scuba diver labeled non-scented talcum powder stood upright on the table. Nothing in the cabin seemed missing or disturbed. The scene was as if the occupants had just left the cabin to go for a dive. He stepped out of the cabin and back over to the aft mounted dive ladder.

"Ok Willey. Show me what you got." Willey cringed as he reached in the water and pulled the ladder upward. Dennis watched as the mesh bag approached the surface. The end of the ladder cleared the water, but the contents of the bag at the end of the ladder made it too heavy to raise the ladder any further. Dennis bent down and grabbed hold of the ladder. With the strength of both men they were able to pull the ladder up and out of the water. The mesh bag, tied to the edge of the ladder, came up out of the water and swung right at Willey as the ladder reclined to its normal resting position. Willey didn't have time to move as the bag smacked against his left shoulder.

"Son of a," was all Willey could mutter as he stepped back and peered at the water logged remains. He wiped his shoulder off with his right hand and he felt an uncontrollable chill sweep through his body.

"Good Job Willey." Dennis eyes quickly moved from the contents of the bag over to rope that tightly secured the bag to the base of the ladder.

"You recognize the knots used?

"Yeah," Willey responded. The one that loops over the bottom rail is a bowline. The side tied to the bag looks like a double half hitch. Looks like they were done in by a demented boy scout," Willey said jokingly.

"Or any of the other locals that know how to tie a common

fishing knot," Dennis added. I'd say that narrows it down to a couple of thousand suspects." They both stared at the contents for a moment. Dennis took out another cigarette. He lit it and took a few puffs then said, "Judging from the colors, I don't think they've been dead long." Willey was starting to get sick as Dennis spoke. Dennis could see the green expression on his deputy's face.

"Should I cut it down?" Willey asked in attempt to retain his composure. He needed to keep busy and keep his imagination at bay.

"Yes, but wear gloves. The killer may have left DNA on the rope."

Dennis stepped off the boat and went to reach for a cigarette, when he suddenly realized that he still had a lighted cigarette pressed between his lips. He made a quick attempt to make it look like he was just rearranging the pack of cigarettes he had in his shirt pocket. Ben and Dave didn't seem to notice his actions, as they were standing nearby looking up at the bagged remains.

"So where are the rest of the bodies?" Dave asked.

"My guess is that they are tied to the anchor or an empty scuba tank or two." Dennis walked over to face Dave and Ben. "Look, I wouldn't go bragging about what you found here."

"Why not?" Ben asked. Dennis exhaled a big puff of smoke.

"Because whoever killed them really enjoys his work."

"Look Dennis," Ben began. "All we did was find the boat and that's all." Dennis looked over towards the back of their boat. Then I guess it'll be easy telling everyone how you came into possession of all those fine looking geoducks using nothing more than baited crab pots." He inhaled another great puff and the end of his cigarette burned bright red.

"You know those cigarettes are going to kill you."

"Thank you Dave, I appreciate your concern." Dennis replied. "And I was sincere when I asked you keep this out of the local gossip for awhile. Like you said, you found the boat. I wouldn't feel like I was doing my job effectively if all this came back and did worse than haunt your dreams."

"You can't scare us Dennis." Ben angrily stated.

"No I sure can't. But if you're like me, whoever did this sure does."

"Ok. We'll stay quiet," Dave replied. "But only for awhile.

If you don't catch this nut soon, we aren't going to keep it to ourselves. Dennis flung the half finished cigarette down to the ground.

"Seems fair. That gives us some time to work with."

"Come on Ben, I can see we aren't wanted here any more." Dave and Ben got in their truck and drove off. They left disappointed that they couldn't stay and gawk at the crime scene all day, but at the same time they drove away excited about all the clam meat they'd managed to keep. The meat they could sell easily to friends and neighbors and make a little money for their efforts.

"You let them have the geoducks?" Willey asked as he walked over to Dennis. He was holding the bag of heads in his gloved left hand and a knife in his right hand.

"Aren't you a sight from Hell," Dennis couldn't resist saying.

"Yeah, I've got that Freddy, Jason, Halloween, Elm street thing going on strong," Willey said "You mind opening the trunk and handing me a plastic bag or do you want to see what happens when I get upset?"

"Here Willey, allow me to help." Dennis rummaged around in the back end of his car until he came across a role of large black trash bags. He opened a bag and Willey set the mesh bag inside.

"You check out the boat registration like I asked?"

"Sure did," Willey replied. "The boat is still registered to Claus Richter. No one has seen much of his widow lately, but by word of mouth she put the boat up for sale about a month ago."

"So we got some moonlighters just helping themselves." Dennis said more to himself than to Willey.

"That's the way it looks chief."

"They've got rigor mortis and cloudy eyes. I bet they've been dead for less than twelve hours. Looks like they were decapitated with one sharp knife. I bet autopsy says they were dead before the heads were severed. Take some blood samples off the boat for lab analysis. Put a tarp over the boat and wrap some crime scene tape around it. We don't need any looky loos."

"Oh, and wait for someone from CSI in Olympia to get here and check the boat out. I'll have the head in the fridge waiting for them."

48

"I'll get right on it chief, but can you tell me why you gave those two clowns the geoducks?"

"Well Willey, I needed the Geoducks to pay off our new recruits."

"So you consider Ben and Dave informants?"

"Willey, this here isn't the big city. We need all the help we can get. And if giving them clams gets them to join our circus, then I consider we've already moved a little closer to solving this case."

"I see, but what about the other two geoducks?" Willy asked.

"Oh those. They're for Bill."

"The bartender?" Willey asked. Wondering what Dennis was up to.

"That's right. Seems we never have any money, but we always have a few extra clams at our disposal."

Who's Down For Lunch?

The Roadside Café & Bar was only a few miles down the road from where the Bayliner was being covered with a giant blue tarp and wrapped up with crime scene tape. A portly man with thinning white hair and a thin mustache wearing an extra large chef's apron was standing behind the counter. He smiled as Dennis opened the door and came inside.

"Afternoon Bill." Bill pushed his big black glasses back up the bridge of his nose. He noticed Dennis was holding a black bag.

"What you got in there Dennis? More road kill?" Dennis strode over to the counter.

"Better than that, take a peek." Bill opened the bag and found himself looking at two good sized geoducks. He picked one up. He gave it a closer inspection then he set it back down in the bag.

"Is this the best you could do?" Bill snarled as he tried to portray the aggrandized actor.

"Without getting my pants wet. Yeah."

"Very nice," Bill smiled and said.

"How come you're cooking today?" Dennis asked. Bill sighed.

"Ed called in sick again. I think he has a touch of hangover's virus."

"You should fire him."

"Now you know I can't do that Dennis. He's my son in law. If I fire him, my daughter and kids will move back in my home, and if they do that, I'll have to shoot myself. So you see, either I let Ed have the day off or you get stuck filling out a homicide report."

"I guess I owe you a favor Bill."

"So how can I help you today?" Bill inquired. He grabbed a towel and began to wipe his wet hand.

"Do you know who's been working the Misty Fog?"

"Clause's old boat?" Bill quizzically cocked his head to the side.

"That's the one," Dennis replied. "Seems he may have

had some silent partners. I was told they might have frequented your bar. Do you mind coming outside and identifying them?"

"What's the matter? Bill asked. "You can't get them to talk?" He sat the towel down on the counter.

"You could say that," Dennis replied. "Are you sure you don't mind?"

"Sure I'm Sure," Bill said. A skinny gal stepped out of the back room holding a bundle of table napkins. "Florence, watch the place for a moment would you?" She nodded yes without slowing down her stride. Dennis and Bill walked out the door of the restaurant. Bill stopped as he looked out at the sheriff's car. There was no one in the car.

"Where are they?" Bill inquired.

"They ah . . . are in the trunk." Bill quizzically looked at Dennis wondering what kind of game he was up to.

"You don't have to look if you don't want to."

"No. I'll look," Bill said. "Can't look worse than anything I've ever cooked." Dennis shook his head as he walked over to the trunk of the car. Bill followed him. He opened the trunk and Bill peered inside. Neatly placed between all the sheriff's job related paraphernalia was a black lawn bag held shut with a twisty tie clip.

"That's them?"

"What's left of them. You sure you want to look?"

"Yeah, open the bag." Dennis undid the tie clip and opened the bag wide enough to expose the two heads. Bill jumped back as the heads came in to view.

"Holly jeas. . . What happened to them?"

"Boating accident." Dennis stoically answered.

"Boating accident?"

"Yeah, a bad one. Do you recognize them?"

"I do. The brown haired one is Larry . . . I mean was Larry Johnson. The black haired one was Frankie Stratton."

"You know them well?"

"No, not really. They come in for drinks sometimes. Frankie liked to hit on the women. He didn't care if they were married or not. Larry was a real jerk after he had a few drinks. They must have really made someone mad to end up like this."

"Maybe not," Dennis softly remarked. "Maybe they were just in the wrong spot at the right time . . . Anything else?"

"Yeah, I think they may have worked for Wilson brothers. I overheard them talking about framing and sheet rocking down by Sund Rock." Dennis closed the bag, replaced the tie clip, and shut the trunk.

"Well thanks Bill. I hope you didn't mind it too much."

"On the contrary," Bill said. "It wasn't half as bad as some of the things I serve."

"You're a sick man Bill."

"Thanks Dennis. I better get back inside."

"Yeah, and I'm off to Sund Rock just as soon as I put these two on ice." He got back in his car and waved goodbye. Bill stood in the doorway of the café and waved back at him.

The Dive Shop

Tom pulled up next to the local dive shop. A big red and white sign read "Underwater Sports." Underwater Sports had eight stores in Washington State and was arguably the largest dive store chain on the entire northwest coastline. It was quite a feat considering that it was still family run and operated. The Edmonds Underwater Sports shop was just a few blocks from the underwater park. On the weekends the small white painted building was busy with divers who had congregated from literally all over the world, and were currently trying to get their air filled before they went to the park. This was the closest location to buy a pair of gloves, rent a hood, replace a worn hose, or purchase some mask defogger if you left yours at home. Sometimes it was just nice to stop by and see what the latest and greatest underwater gadgets looked like. Sometimes it was just relaxing to stand around and talk about diving with other divers. Steve Kemplin, a tall muscular man with short blond hair, was the shop manager. He had over twenty years of diving experience, but was so busy lately that the only way he could find time to dive was by taking a trip to the Caribbean, and so he did; ten days a year he dove in warm tropical water, and the rest of the year he explained to people how to get the most out of cold water diving. Besides his own extensive knowledge of dive gear and local dive sites, most of the employees had logged hundred of dives in the park. A large map of the park hung inside above the entrance door. The staff could tell you about anywhere in the park with information that was updated daily.

Tom parked on the street in front the shop. He opened the door to his truck and saw Steve standing out side over by the wet suit rack. He was rinsing off a couple of rental dive suits. Behind him were two blue fifty gallon plastic barrels. One was marked "Weight belts here", the other was marked "Regulators Here. Dust covers on Please!" He sprayed the suits trying not to get too much of the water on the shops windows or on himself. He noticed Tom right away.

"How's the diving?"

"Good," Tom replied.

"You sink the boat?"

"Yep. Right where we planned. We'll put some weight on it tomorrow."

"Good." He stopped spraying and hung the hose up. "Do you have a moment?"

"Sure," Tom replied. He followed Steve inside the shop. A group of divers were waiting around the cashier counter and talking to one of the shop employees named Jim. He was explaining to the unfamiliar divers how to get to Tube Henge. Tube Henge was a dive location off of Centennial Way in the northern section of the park. Most likely Jim would describe the whole park provided the divers had enough free time to listen to him.

Steve and Tom made their way through the shop back to the classroom. This was a large room with white walls and carpeted like the rest of the shop. On the high overhead ceiling three tracks of phosphorescent lights illuminated the room. Maps hand drawn and signed by Divemasters were placed above two four by eight feet long white boards. Two rows of tables that could hold sixteen students faced one of the white boards. Behind the seated chairs and on various walls stood an assortment of dive pictures taken by several former and current divemasters and instructors. The white board facing the entrance of the room was not for writing on; instead, this board was a giant three-dimensional map of the underwater park. Little wooden objects represented replicas and locations of every boat and every structure sunk in the park. White pieces of clothesline represented the dive trails and boundary lines. Photos of actual dive sites filled the open spaces between sites and trails.

Tom entered the room and took the nearest seat in the second row. Steve entered and shut the door behind him. He took a seat in the front row and leaned back in his chair.

"You heard about the accident the other night." Steve asked.

"Not really. Just rumors."

"A diver died in the park last night. Police said he looked like something hit the side of his head. They pronounced him dead about an hour after his buddy called 911."

"When was this?" Tom asked.

"Around nine last night. The buddy said one minute he was there swimming and the next he found him unconscious on the bottom."

"And what do you think happened?" Tom questioned him.

"I don't know, but it doesn't look good for the park anytime something like this happens."

"Was he local?" Tom asked hoping it wasn't another guy from Oregon.

"He was local. You'll find out his name soon enough, but I will tell you he was Rescue Diver qualified and he had recently joined the dive club."

"And his buddy doesn't know what happened?"

"Not a clue. He's pretty shook up about the incident. He was new to the dive club too. Apparently they meet at the last meeting. They dove together the last two Friday nights. Both times at the park, both night dives with the last one fatal."

"So what are you thinking?" Tom knew Steve too long not to know he already had a few ideas and opinions. Sure enough, Steve got a real stern look on his face.

"Could a ling hit a diver so hard that it knocked him unconscious?" Steve asked. They both remained silent for a moment to speculate the idea. At first Tom couldn't imagine a lingcod killing a diver. "I guess it could happen." He finally spoke up. "But it would have to be a big ling. The diver would have to be hit right on the head, and he would have to be hit hard at high speed."

"So you think one could do it?"

"I guess anything's possible." Tom reluctantly replied. "Where did the buddy say he last saw him?"

"They were out at the Triumph."

"There's only one ling out at the Triumph." He's about three feet long and lives under the stern on the right side. There's a small cabezon on the bow with a cluster of purple eggs, but that's the only egg mass on the boat."

"So you think the ling could of done it?"

"I highly doubt it. With out any eggs to guard he doesn't have the hormones racing through his body that tells him to attack anything near the eggs. Besides, I've been hit head on by a lingcod that size. The one that hit me knocked off my mask and almost tore the regulator out of my mouth. I'll never forget it. He gave me a red mark on my forehead for a week where my mask was. He stunned me for a moment, but didn't put me unconscious. To do that, a ling would definitely have to be a lot bigger."

"Could a large one have been passing by . . . looking for food when it happened?"

"It may have," Tom countered. "But back to the point, without the eggs, there's no reason to attack."

"I see," said Steve. "Well, what about the wreck itself? Could something have fallen off the wreck and struck him?"

"What are you getting at?"

"I'm just questioning the safety of the boat."

"Well, the steering house caved in six months ago. It's an old tug and there's not much left to fall on anyone any more. Maybe if you were on the bottom with your face pressed against the sand and piece of solid steel fell on you, but the viscosity of the water would reduce the rate of decent and leave you with little more than a bruise and shaken up emotionally."

"I'm just trying to figure out what happened. I'm not trying to fault you guys."

"I don't think he got hurt by any of the structures, but I don't think it was a lingcod either. Unless . . ." Tom stopped to think about what he was going to say. "If he was spear fishing. That would explain it. A speared ling could beat the crap out of a diver, especially a big one, but he would have to be hunting in the park for that to happen."

"No, they weren't hunting. Just swimming around."

"Then I can't help you." Tom said felling the futility of the conversation. They both stood up and looked at the park map on the wall.

"Thanks for you input. I just want this thing put past us as soon as possible. The longer it lingers, the more bad publicity we all get." Instantly a horrible incident with the diver from Oregon came back to mind. It happened over two years ago, but it was still fresh in his mind. A group from Oregon came up for the weekend and was completing an advanced course in the park. A nineteen-year-old football player in top shape had just gone out with his buddy into the water. They were both wearing rental gear including rental dry suits. They swam out on the surface and were just getting ready to go underwater when they started having problems.

The current began to separate them from one another as they started their decent.

The young football player began to get freezing cold ocean water coming inside his dry suit as his head went underwater. He yelled to his buddy and waved his hands frantically. He had let all the air out of his BC in order to descend and now his legs quickly became tired as he desperately tried to hold himself up out of the water as much as possible. He was still shouting when his legs gave out. The cold water entering his suit helped him tire at an accelerated pace and he quickly slipped back underwater. He didn't think of inflating his BC. No attempt was made to release his weight belt. Either of these actions could have kept him floating on the surface. He didn't even consider putting the regulator in his mouth so he could breath while underwater. He did none of the above. He panicked and drowned in twelve feet of water. It was a tragic accident that could have been prevented. Panic had killed him and left a group of fellow divers with feelings of despair and disbelief, and affected the local diving community for months long afterwards. Diving is a safety conscious sport. Divers train to avoid panic. Divers learn to stop, think, then react. Divers know that panic can kill anyone, anywhere, and at any time.

Tom wondered if the diver last night panicked. What could have knocked him unconscious forcing him to drop his regulator and coming to rest in the sand? The whole scenario made little sense.

They both left the room with solemn expressions. Upon opening the door Steve noticed a young guy looking at the dry suits. He got a big smile on his face and went over to him. "So you're still comparing the dry suits?" The guy looked at Steve and smiled back at him.

"I'm getting close to a decision. I hate wearing my wet suit anymore." The guy answered. Tom walked passed both of them as he headed back outside to his truck. He pulled his twin seventy-two's out of the back end of the truck and carried them into the shop. The group of divers he first saw when he entered the shop had vanished. They had been hanging around the shop waiting for air fills so they could go dive the park as soon as their tank's air pressure were topped off. Now that they were gone the air station was empty.

He carried his tank over to the air station and hooked his tanks up. He saw Steve still working with the young guy over by the dry suits. Jim the other employee had gone back in the rental room to retrieve something. Tom slowly started to fill his tanks. He thought about what Steve had said as he filled his tanks. By the time he was done more people were coming into the shop to get their tanks filled. He walked past the group of people as they clustered around the counter.

"Hey, did you hear anything about that diver last night?" Tom heard one of the divers say in a deep voice. The shop became quiet for a second.

"No, nothing yet." Jim nonchalantly replied. "Just the air fills today?"

"I guess that's it for now. We're going out for one more dive tonight." The diver stated.

"The weather's good. You should have a good time." Jim said as he took the man's money and put it in the cash register.

Tom went through the front door and headed over to his truck. For a split second he had thought about telling the group of divers not to dive at night. For the first time in his life he thought about closing down the park until they at least figured out what had happened to the diver the previous night. Then he thought about all the volunteer labor he and his friends had put into the park just to attract more divers, even more work to make the park safe, and the continued struggle against mother nature to try to maintain their past efforts. All he could really do without going crazy was wish the visitors a good dive and hope they had fun.

Over twenty thousand divers dove in the park each year. This group was no different from the rest. If they practiced their basic diving skills on a regular basis and didn't panic, they should have a great dive, see lots of animal life, and make it back to shore safe. Giant lingcods attacking without provocation sounded like the making for a low budget monster movie, but had nothing to do with reality . . . or could it?

Chilling Reception

Dennis pulled out of the parking lot and headed back towards his office. He parked in the back of the building. The building was a one-story brick structure that had been painted white six or seven years ago. He took the black plastic bag out of the trunk and went thru the back door.

"What's inside the bag?" asked Mary. Mary was the receptionist, radio operator, secretary, accountant, coffee maker, office coordinator, and technically third in charge of command. She was a short blonde gal with light blue eyes who loved being in charge of the office. She had previously worked as a corrections officer for King County, but moved back to Hoodsport after her marriage ended in divorce.

"You don't want to look," Dennis replied. She knew from experience that when the chief said this, it was best to take his advice.

"I'm going to put it in the fridge. Don't open it unless you want to loose your breakfast."

"It's that bad?" she asked as she stepped back.

"Worse," Dennis replied. "This is all that's left of two victims." Mary stepped back even further, turned, and left the room. Dennis set the bag in the fridge and shut the door as quick as he could. He went down the hall and found Mary at the front desk. She was scrolling through the J.C. Penny catalogue online while eating an apple. On a note pad he wrote down the names Larry Johnson and Frankie Stratton.

"Do me a favor and find out everything you can about these two. He jotted down the two deceased names on a note pad. "Some one should be over from Olympia to pick up the remains. I'll be back in a few hours."

"Where are you going?" Mary asked between bites.

"Sund Rock. I've got Willey staked out at the dock, so call me if anything comes up." He then handed her the note pad.

"Will do chief." She took the notepad and set it down next to her computer. She recognized Frankie's name right away.

Sund Rock

Driving down the highway it was hard to see where to turn off on the road that lead down to a few houses nestled on the southern end of Sund Rock. Highway 101 sloped up and down over and over again as it curved and whined around and repeatedly butted and hugged the fringes of Hood Canal. Dennis was just starting to go up a hill when he noticed a familiar stand of trees. The slope of the turn off onto the gravel road was too steep to peer over and look down in advance. You literally had to turn off the main highway and if you drove slowly and guessed accurately enough you could soon find your car tilted and heading down an unmarked gravel road. Over the side of the embankment Dennis drove. He turned to the right as he headed down the now visible gravel road and parked his sheriff's car behind a Toyota pickup with the words "Wilson Construction" printed on the side panels. The sun was shinning down here. He reached over and put on his sunglasses. As he opened the car door the strong scent of fresh sawed lumber mixed with sea breezes filled his nostrils. He took out a cigarette and lit it. A circular saw could be heard cutting through two by fours somewhere on the far side of the house. The house in front of him was in the process of being remodeled. The north half of the house looked old and needed painting. The south side exterior was wrapped with an undercover layer of white Ty-Vek. It looked like they were in the middle of doubling the square footage of the house. Dennis took a few puffs off his cigarettes then shut the door and headed around to the back of the house.

Jack Anderson, a short husky guy with long black hair tied neatly behind his head and a member of the Skohomish Indian tribe as well as one of the founding partners of Wilson Construction, was just finishing sawing through a two by four. His sawhorse was set up behind the house inside what looked like the unfinished framed area of a future sunroom. The view from this waterfront home was spectacular. A mere seventy feet away and down a gentle slope of soft sand and pebbles lay the clear saltwater of Hood Canal.

Five other boards lay on the saw horse already cut. Jack cut thru the board and then set the skill saw down. It took a few seconds for the high-pitched roar of the circular saw to dwindle down to a stop. Jack picked the board up and scrutinized the end. He turned and was startled when he saw Dennis out of the corner of his eye. He cringed as he pulled his safety glasses up onto his forehead.

"I don't drink anymore," Jack said with a hint of disgust in his voice.

"That's good," Dennis said. He flicked the remainder of the cigarette on the ground.

"And I don't do drugs anymore either."

"I heard," Dennis said.

"Then what are you here for?"

"I had heard rumors that Larry Johnson and Frankie Stratton were doing some sub-contract work for you?"

"Yeah, Sheet rocking. They didn't show up today." Jack started to walk away from Dennis.

"They're dead." Dennis said coldly. Jack stopped and set the board down against the wall. He turned to face Dennis.

"What happened?" Jack asked.

"Boating accident." Jack looked at him suspiciously. He walked over to Dennis, and put his hands on his hips.

"What kind of boating accident?"

"Not sure yet. Do you know what they were doing out there?"

"They were talking about catching clams. They said they were going out last night for a few hours. I tried to ignore the details.

"Anything else? Dennis enquired.

"No."

"Have they ever done that before?"

"I don't know." Dennis was thinking of what to ask him next when a boat drifted in to view. "Excuse me." Jack stepped thru the framing and quickly strode down to the beach.

"Hey," Jack yelled at the drifting boat. The occupant turned to face the man on the shore. "You can't fish here. This is a marine reserve." Dennis noticed the fishing pole hanging over the back of the boat.

"You can't fish here." Jack repeated. "This is a marine reserve." The boater waved a hand at him.

"I'm just passing through," The boater yelled back. He just stood there defiantly ignoring Jack. The boater then saw Dennis move out into the open on the beach with his full uniform badge reflecting the rays of the sun. The boater immediately reached over and gunned the engine. He didn't even bother to reel in his fishing line first. He just fled the area as fast as he could.

"Does that happen often?" Dennis asked.

"Way too often. They don't think it counts as fishing if they're drifting through the water. They think it only counts if they're moored. Guys that dumb are a dime a dozen round here.

"I didn't know you cared so much about the environment," Dennis said.

"I didn't when you first met me, but I'm older now and got my act together. If we let them fish in the reserve, then the divers will stop coming and stop spending money and then the local economy will just get worse for us Indians.

"You mean for everybody, don't you?"

"No . . .us Indians always feel it first and longest."

"From what I've seen it would be hard to disagree with you." Dennis quietly added. "So what can you tell me about Larry and Frankie?"

"Larry and Frankie were always planning some big scheme to make it rich quick. I over heard Frankie talking about some boat they could get for a song and how they could make some good money collecting Geoducks."

"Poaching?"

"I didn't ask. I didn't want to know. My record has been clean. I'm making good money, and I didn't want to get involved.

"Did either of them mention the name of the boat?"

"No."

"When did you last see them?"

"They left here around three thirty yesterday."

"Do you know anyone that would like to see them dead?"

"Yeah, half the town."

"Well, thanks Jack."

"No problem Sheriff." Dennis pulled a business card out of his shirt pocket and handed it to Jack.

"Give me a call if you think of anything else." Jack gave him a look as if Dennis was out of his mind.

"Sure, and if you know anyone that can sheet rock tell them to give me a call." Dennis shook his head. This meeting seemed to be pointless.

"I'll see what I can do Jack." Dennis turned and started walking back to where he had parked his patrol car.

Back inside his patrol car Dennis thought about what Jack had said. He felt that Jack had given him very little new information. He was either concealing information so he couldn't be linked with any involvement, and he knew more than he was telling but there was no way he was going to help out Dennis, or Jack just didn't care what happened to his former sub-contractors. Maybe that's all he wanted; warm bodies to sheet rock, and that was it. But that couldn't be it, because if he wasn't concerned about what happened to two unfortunate humans, why would he bother yelling at the fisherman to protect some defenseless fish in a marine reserve?

He started the car, drove up the gravel road, turned on the main highway and headed back towards his office. He was sure that by now either Mary had already solved the crime, or she would at the least have some leads he could check up on.

Returning to the Sheriff's office he entered the back door and opened the fridge. The black bag was just as he had left it. A box of baking soda in the fridge seemed to be keeping the smell in check. He closed the fridge and then made his way down the hallway to the front desk. There he found Mary looking up some books on a web site. She turned and handed him some paperwork the minute he came into view.

"How did you know it was me?" He asked her as he took the papers and held them in his hands.

"Because Willey thumps when he walks."

"It could have been one of the other deputies."

"With keys to the back door and that heavy foot step?" She shook her head. "I don't think so." Dennis looked at her and smiled.

"So what do you have for me?" he asked. She smiled and stood before him. She then pointed at the papers.

"These will tell you where they lived, but you won't find any leads in there." She smiled like she was in control of the world.

"And you have a better source?" He didn't know how she did it, but he was ready to play the game.

"As a mater of fact I do. I just spoke with Kim at the gift shop in Hoodsport. She dated Frankie a few times after her divorce. Well, Florence told Kim that she saw Frankie's pickup truck parked up by Nancy Richter's place."

"The widow?"

"Yep."

"How long ago?"

"A couple of weeks ago."

"So Frankie's been using the widow's boat as sort of a fringe benefit."

"That's the way I see it," Mary said with a smug look on her face. "Good work Mary. See what else you can dig up." Dennis held the papers up to examine their contents. The top one was a copy of the Misty Fog's boat registration. Claus Richter's name was still on it even though he died close to a year ago. Dennis read the address and absent-mindedly started walking away.

"Where are you going Chief?"

"I'm going to pay a visit to the widow," he replied as he kept walking down the hall.

The Homestead

More than half a mile from the Richter residence he could already see the outline of the front yard. Two rusted out trucks sitting on makeshift blocks of old cracked rubber tires and the remnants of four moss encased passenger cars blocked the view of the doublewide trailer home better than any natural occurring hedge ever could. The yard hadn't been mowed for quite some time. This would have looked like any other beautiful piece of heavily forested property except for the collected trash, the discarded metal, and the derelict shelter.

As he neared the worn out residence he could see that the lights were off and the drapes were closed. There was a good chance that the power had been cut off for quite some time. He lowered his window as he slowly pulled up the gravel driveway. Stopping next to a dilapidated front porch he turned the motor off. An old real estate sign lay over on its side not far where he parked. He sat and just listened for what seemed a good five minutes. A few birds flew overhead. Other birds chirped and whistled in the nearby trees. A squirrel scampered up a tree and he could hear the wind blowing through higher branches. Suddenly the birds became silent. The wind picked up and knocked a few branches into one another. Then it became silent again. Something was not right. He could feel it, but he didn't know what it was. Dennis was getting the creeps. He opened his car door slowly. As he stepped out of his car he drew his gun out of his holster. He held a silver .357 magnum revolver with a black rubber grip handle in his right hand. The gun was so big and impressive that just the sight of it was enough to intimidate most of the local hoodlums. The birds were still silent. Dennis was just about to close his door when Mary's voice came over the radio.

"Sheriff are you out there?" Dennis sighed and put his gun back in his holster. "Sheriff, this is Mary over?" He reached across the seat and grabbed the mike.

"This is Dennis over." He sat back down in the car.

"Sheriff, I just got word that Gordon is on his way down to the boat. And I also found out that Nancy Richter left town for good early yesterday."

"And how do you know that?"

"She stopped by the grocery store to fill up her car. She had a black eye and a suitcase packed full. Sue said she'd never seen her look so out of sorts."

"Sue the manager?"

"That's affirmative."

"Is there anything you don't know?" he jokingly added.

"That's a negative chief."

"Roger that." He set the mike down. So the house was empty. He wondered if Frankie was the one that hit Nancy? But if that were the case, Nancy didn't even have to leave. For as of last night, all of Frankie's relationships had abruptly terminated. There was nothing else for Dennis to do out here so he shut the door and turned on the car. That was strange, he thought. Dennis noticed the birds were chirping again. The uneasy feeling he got earlier had vanished too. He backed down the driveway in reverse and then turned on to the main road. Traffic was clear in both directions. He turned his lights and siren on then gunned his engine. He wanted to hear what his detective, Gordon, had to say about all this.

It didn't take long for him to arrive at the boat launch. It was only a few miles south of the Richter residence. But then again, everything seemed to be close by once you were on this side of the canal. He drove in the parking area and parked behind a White van marked Mason County Sheriff's Department. The tarp had been pulled back and Willey was standing guard next to the boat. An older man with gray hair wearing blue jeans and a Pendleton shirt was just stepping off the boat. In his left hand he held a large black tackle box with the letters CSI printed on the side.

"You mind if I go get some lunch chief?" Willey came up and asked before Dennis even had his door fully opened.

"Sorry Willey. I forgot all about relieving you. Go ahead and go." Willey walked quickly over to his car and drove off in a hurry. Willey had an appetite that was insatiable.

"I thought you retired Gordon." Dennis said as he approached the man who just stepped off the boat. They shook hands and exchanged smiles. They had first met over twelve years ago when Gordon was called out to investigate a diving accident.

A woman in her early forties had had a fatal heart attack as she was surfacing from a dive. If it had happened in a bowling ally they might have just pronounced her dead and shipped her off to a funeral home, but because it happened in water, they did a complete autopsy on the victim. They found major heart tissue damage and no water in her throat or lungs. Her death was out of the blue and relatively painless. Gordon had worked the scene for other mysterious deaths over the years, but as far as Dennis could remember, this was the first multiple death he had had to examine that didn't involve drugs, guns, or automobiles.

"I tried to retire Dennis, but they keep on calling me."

"You should change your number."

"I will, just as soon as I get back." Dennis knew he never would. Gordon loved doing what he did too much.

"So what do you think?" Dennis asked. Gordon hesitated as he took one look back at the boat. He set the big plastic box he carried by his left hand on the ground.

"Off the record, I think you have one serious wacko on your hands. Whoever he is, he left no fingerprints. I think he waited for his victims to emerge and then he did them in one at a time. He may have had military training; he might have even known the victims. That would help explain how he got so close to them. I don't think he came out with them for all the indications show that two men ate sandwiches and crackers, two men drank a bottle of beer each, and two men were found dead. I think the third man joined the party while the other two were underwater."

"And the heads?" Dennis asked.

"That's his way of saying stay off my boat or this is what will happen to you . . . Have you spoken with the owner yet?"

"She's unavailable."

"She?" Gordon asked.

"Her husband died at sea almost a year ago."

"I would bet you a nickel a man did this."

"A whole nickel Gordon?"

"Yeah, two cents doesn't get you much any more." Gordon proceeded over to his van. He opened the back door of the van and set his plastic toolbox inside next to a big cooler chest.

"Are you staying long today? Dennis asked.

"No, I've got to get back to Olympia just as soon as I pick up the heads. We are swamped." Olympia had a big crime lab that cooperated with Mason County when need be.

"Oh, something unusual happen?"

"No different from any other big city." He closed the door of the van.

Dennis followed Gordon back to the Sheriff's office. Gordon opened the door to the refrigerator and was in the middle of pulling out the black bag containing the two heads as Dennis entered the back door. Dennis watched as Gordon set the bag on a nearby table where the department usually sat down and ate their lunches. Gordon opened the bag and peered inside.

"Well?" Dennis asked. Gordon looked at him and shook his head.

"They're dead alright." Using the plastic bag as a barrier, he manipulated one of the heads to turn it upside down.

"Anything else?"

"I would say this one was severed from the victim by a large knife. He probably used just a few back and forth motions to cut it off, so the victim was probably lying flat when he did the cutting. Which means he was probably already dead. This guy did a neat job. To him it was probably just like taking the head off a salmon. I think you got one sick bastard on the loose."

"You think he'll kill again?" Gordon wrapped the bag back up and resealed it.

"Don't know. What ever set him off could possibly happen again. I'll let you know more about what happened after the autopsy."

"That shouldn't take too long considering how little you were left to work with."

"Any ideas where the rest of the bodies are?" Gordon asked.

"Since we didn't find any dive gear on board, my bet is that they're still under water."

"Give me a call if you find them."

"Will do," Dennis replied. Gordon picked up the bag and went out the back door.

The Home

Tom left Edmonds Underwater Sports and headed back home. It was raining now. A deep dark cloud has descended over the bowl. The bowl was the area of Edmonds closest to the water. A ridge of hills circled the down town area. High priced view houses lined the hills and expensive condos filled the bowl. Edmonds was mostly comprised of senior citizens or more mature people with money to spend on the view. The view itself was worth the high prices they got for the properties. From your living room or terrace you had a panoramic view of the Puget Sound. Those on the hills could look down on down town Edmonds. Main Street ran right down to the Kingston Ferry dock. Only the last four or five blocks had any commercial interest. The town was mostly set up for visitors, people using the ferry system, divers eating out after the dives, and retired people strolling the streets looking in shop windows, admiring the flowers hanging or planted around main street, and senior citizens walking along the many beach access paths.

On the other side of the water you could see the Olympic Mountains with snowcaps on most of the peaks year round. Light blue skies, white peaks, green forests and the dark salt water combined to make the Puget Sound a picture perfect habitat for humans and fish alike.

If all this wasn't spectacular enough, you could sit at your table and watch sail boats tack back and forth across the water. Ferryboats left Edmonds on a regular schedule and made a quick trip over to Kingston and back. At times ferries would pass one another or even bigger ships from the navy yards would grace the view. There was nothing like seeing an aircraft carrier and it's entourage of support vessels to remind you of this country's military power. The Puget Sound was even deep enough for the large class nuclear submarines. With only an occasional ripple on the surface, they were hard to detect. All this action on the surface of the water was just a precursor for the main event. What everyone opened their curtains for and every waterfront restaurants waited for was the daily arrival of sunset. Colors of red, orange, yellow and blue filled the sky as the sun began to set in the west. To eat, drink, and relax while you watched the sun descend below the horizon was a very popular pastime in this sleepy little town. Edmonds had by far one of the most beautiful sunsets on the west coast; weather permitting. The problem was that for most of the year, clouds hung in the sky and every once in awhile they decided to let down a torrent of rain and spoil the view. Twice in the last couple of years so much rain had poured down in the bowl with such speed that it flooded out the dive shop and most of the other properties close to the edge of the shoreline. A new drain had been installed in the adjacent parking lot last year with a greater pumping capacity. So far the system was working fine, but they hadn't had a real bad storm since then to test the system to its full capacity.

At the moment the rain was coming down so hard Tom had to turn on his windshield wipers. This was something a true Washingtonian didn't do unless the rain was really bad. It was a matter of pride not to turn on the wipers when it was merely drizzling. Besides, the blades were worn out and left big streaks across the windshield. Sometimes it was just easier to see through the droplets without the wipers. He was going to change them just as soon as he could find some spare time.

The constant use of the worn out blades made a noise similar to chalk across a black board. Right now the blades were bugging Tom, but not as much as the sheets of rain on his windshield. He drove up the hill and out of the bowl on highway 104. A few cars passed him on their way to the ferry. It was Saturday afternoon. On Friday the ferry lanes would be full with everyone trying to get over to Kingston. Kingston was the gateway to the Olympic Mountains, Long beach and the Pacific Ocean, and one of the top sites for divers. Hoodsport was less than two hours away on the other side of the fjord like waterway. After a brief drive inland you turned south and soon found Hoodsport nestled along the shoreline near some of the best diving locations in the entire Puget Sound.

At Hoodsport Tom liked to stay at a place called Divers Inn. It was a private residence turned into a bed and breakfast inn. The house was built by divers, operated by divers, and catered to divers. The only thing divers had to do was make their own meal in a very large and utensil filled kitchen. It was a two-story house that could house an entire dive club comfortable for the weekend. Across the street from Divers Inn lay the mild tidal exchange salt waters comprising what was called the Hood Canal. Keep in mind that even though it was termed a canal, the waterway was as wide as the fjords in Norway. It was deep enough for nuclear submarines to navigate frequently, and the area contained enough animal life to keep tribal and state regulated fishermen busy most of the year.

Across the street and thirty feet underwater laid a boat upside down where two giant octopuses resided. Dungeness crabs crawl all over the substrate in this particular area. An octopus doesn't have to travel far to dine on the sweet meat of Dungeness crab. A giant octopus can grow to twenty feet in length in less than five years eating local seafood. Octopuses are such skilled hunters that they spend only seven percent of their time hunting. The rest of the time they remain in their dens, and watch the fish go by or fall into a deep sleep similar to humans who fall asleep in front of the TV. Octopuses at this site are currently less than ten feet in length, but their cousins down the road at a spot called Octopus Hole are already at maximum size. Eight long coiling and slithering arms extend from a tough skin casing of the soft rubber like body structure called the mantle. All their internal organs are hidden inside the mantle. The giant octopus is a creature of beauty and immense brainpower. Out of one hundred and seventy million nerve cells in the brain, they use one hundred and thirty million nerve cells just for seeing their environment. Another three hundred and fifty million nerve cells, which are part of the central nervous system, are located in the arms. Their brains have distinct centers for tactile and visual memory. The cranium has folded lobes for producing higher intelligence in a confined area. They can distinguish shapes and problem solve such as unscrewing a jar to get at the contents such as a crab. They recognize, and act physically and emotionally different to different human individuals. In laboratories they have shown traits of deception, planning tasks, and covert operations. At the Seattle aquarium, octopus have slithered out of their tank, crawled into another tank to eat a crab or two, then crawl back into their own tank when no one is looking. Only cameras and an accumulative wet spot on the floor can be used as evidence to catch them in the act. Recent research suggests that unlike other invertebrates, octopus may have distinct and individual personalities. Scientists are still studying the octopus in order to figure out why the octopus has evolved such enormous brainpower and how this has made the octopus unique in the world of invertebrates. It's interesting to note that we are doing the same research on humans to determine why we as humans are so much more intellectually advanced than our own ancestors and other living primates.

Octopus unlike humans, live in a water world where legs and arms may not be the best way to get from point a to point b. Over millions of years they have evolved and perfected a funnel that gives them the equivalent of jet propulsion. This modification makes them faster than most prey over short distances. The jet propulsion system also doubles as a powerful blower when they are cleaning out their den.

Their arms are very sensitive to touch with two rows of suction cups running down the length of their arms. The suction cups closest to the mouth can be larger than a salad plate while the suction cups at the tips of the arms are very small. Chemical receptors also line the length of each arm. This gives an octopus eight noses to use to sniff the local environment and this helps make them a deadly hunter in pitch-black conditions.

In lighted conditions the position of sensory cells in their retina makes their eyesight keener than that of humans; they have no blind spot and although they have monocular vision, the position and size of their eyes lets them see three hundred and sixty degrees around the surroundings and them selves. They can observe and learn from one another, but they wear their emotions on the out side of their skin. A dark red body color signifies they are mad at you. An all gray color denotes they are close to death. All the colors and combinations in between help them blend into the background so well that most divers swim right past them without ever seeing them.

The mouth is shaped like a parrots beak. Octopus can bite into a crab's shell, inject a poison, and suck out the contents in a matter of seconds. The small blue ringed octopus of Australia is deadly poisonous to humans. The giant octopus is very gentle and rarely is provoked to the point of biting a diver. They would rather move away or get lost in a cloud of ink before ever inflicting a wound. This makes them easy targets for human poachers. If they do bite however, the bacterial infection accompanying the wound could be the main concern for the transgressor.

Males differ from females in that a male's third right arm is cup shaped at the end. The arm is modified to place sperm packets inside the mantle of the female. In some species, this tip of the arm can break off and is occasionally found in the mantle of females. Scientists thought this tip of the third arm was some type of parasitic worm and called it a *Hectocotylus*. The name stuck so now many people still call the third arm of the male the hectocotylus.

Old age sets in fast after they mate. The male dies soon afterwards while the female stops eating and spends the rest of her days defending and carrying for her white eggs that usually hang like tight rows of grapes from the ceilings of crevices and caves. To see the rice grain size young maturing inside their cavernous chambers is a wondrous sight.

Besides octopus, Hoodsport is known for one of the most ugly fish in the ocean. The wolf eel to some people looks like an old bald headed man with big gummy lips. On the inside of those lips are several sharp and powerful teeth. When a wolf eel opens its mouth to sweep oxygenated water across its gills, it looks like a wolf ready to attack. Nothing could be further from the truth. The gray and white spotted adult is very shy and at most will only come out of the hole if you offer it something good to eat; half a sea urchin works best. Their gummy lips protect them from the spiny thorns of a sea urchin. Wolf eels prize the soft yellow gonads of sea urchins just as much as people do in Asia. The brown juvenile wolf eels prefer to hide in kelp blades and seaweed until divers move on.

Back at Divers Inn after a dive, groups sit around eating oysters, clams, and Dungeness crabs; all fresh and locally caught. The group rarely takes red rock crabs. Their shells are harder to crack and the meat tastes bland in comparison to the sweet meat of a Dungeness crab. People ship Dungeness crabs all the way to Portland Maine to enjoy the exquisite flavor of Dungeness crab. People from Portland Oregon in return receive shipments of Maine lobsters. The lobsters may not be quite as flavorful as a Dungeness crab, but they are easier to peel and retrieve the meat. Eating a Dungeness crab and cracking all the legs open to extract the meat can be a very messy process. The meat is worth the effort, but the romance of the moment can be lost with just one unfortunate unexpected flick of a leg, and so lobster will always win out on formal occasions. Besides Dungeness crab, the local wine is nationally recognized and good too. Just thinking about Hoodsport is enough to make Tom's mouth dry and his stomach grumble.

On Sundays, on the other side at Kingston, cars would be lining up to come back from a weekend of fun and adventure. The lines would be long and chances are, you would have to sit there and watch a ferry or two sail back to Edmonds fully loaded before you got a chance to board. The trip over however, was definitely worth the effort.

Tom turned off the main road and drove into a town next to Edmonds called Ferndale. Near a grocery store and small mall was a speed trap that he new intimately. He slowed down to pass through the area then turned on his home street. His house was at the end of a cul-de-sac. The split-level was in need of a new coat of paint. His father, before he died, had helped him paint it last time. Pieces of yellow paint were now flaking off and lining the cracks in the cement stairway that led to the front door. He backed into the driveway, angled his truck, and parked in the gravel in front of a wooden gate that led to the back yard. The gate and fence were silver with age, but cedar was a sturdy wood in the northwest. It would be another ten years before he would have to replace the fence.

Last year he finished remodeling the down stairs so his mother could move in. The studio project worked out fine. She had her own little kitchen, bedroom and living room. She still cooked most of her meals upstairs in the main house, but Tom was fine with that. She always prepared too much food and there was always something left over to snack on. All the fuss with cooking kept her busy and content.

Tom left the truck running, got out, then went back to open the gate to the backyard. He latched the gate in the open position, got back in the truck, and put the truck in reverse. He backed up a good twenty feet into the back yard before he killed the engine. He got out of the truck and took two steps towards the tailgate.

"Hey, how goes the park?
He cringed when he recognized his brother's voice. He looked up and there on the patio was his brother Kevin. Kevin had a beer in

his hand; most likely one of Toms. He was dressed in an old tee shirt and jeans. He hadn't shaved in several days.

"I didn't know you were coming over," Tom said. He walked back to the tailgate and started to unload the gear. He hadn't seen much of his brother since Kevin was released from prison over a year ago. He only served a year behind bars, but the time had changed him, and apparently it had changed him for the worse.

Kevin pointed with a sweeping motion with a beer can in his hand to all the clutter that lined the fence line perimeter in the backyard.

"You sure store a lot of junk back here."

"Well Kevin, it takes a lot of "stuff" to make a park." Tom stopped and looked at his brother. "What brings you over here... Money from mom?" Kevin shook his head.

"No, I just brought over some fish. Thought it might give us a chance to get together and have a family meal." Kevin took a big swig and emptied the beer can. Tom returned to his task of unloading the lift barrels.

"Well, I've got a date tonight, so it's just going to be the two of you here." Tom started to laugh to himself.

"You got a date? No way."

"Yep, mom called and set it up." Kevin slammed the empty can down on the wooden porch rail and looked at his brother in awe.

"How come she doesn't set me up with a date?" He fumed.

"Probably because you don't have a phone." Tom said. He was in the process of pulling the loose pieces of rope out of the truck and throwing them into a pile next to the left side property fence."

"I'm going to get a phone, it's just that I can't get any credit till next season." Tom had heard a variation on this theme for quite some time.

"You still going back to Alaska this spring?"

"Maybe, if I can find another boat to work on. The last crew sucked." Tom shut the tailgate and looked around. The backyard looked like a dump yard for construction companies. Bits and pieces of marine hardware were haphazardly strewn about to give the place a proper motif.

"Nice collection of cement you got going there," Kevin

quipped.

"It's gett'n there. I seem to bring more in than goes out to the park."

"I think your nuts for even trying." Kevin said. Tom put his hands on his hips and looked up at his brother and shook his head. Pity, not anger, filled his voice. "That's the difference between us. You don't try." Kevin turned and stomped back in the house. He slammed the glass patio door behind him.

Tom parked the truck back out front. As he shut the gate to the back yard the front door opened. Kevin stepped out and slammed shut the door behind him.

"Off already?" Tom asked.

"Going to get some beer," came the reply. Kevin was already walking towards the curb.

"There's a couple in the fridge."

"Already drank them," Kevin said without even bothering to turn his head.

"What happened to your truck?" Kevin stopped in the street and looked back at his brother.

"I'm having trouble with the bank. Ok? I'm parking it where they can't get their hands on it." He then turned and walked off.

Tom went in the house and up stairs. He found his mother sitting at the dinning room table. She was a frail seventy six year old white haired lady who loved to spend all day reading.

"Hi mom." Phyllis put the book down and looked up at him and smiled.

"Your brother was here."

"How much did you give him?" Tom went over to the sink and poured himself a glass of water. The water was light brown and tasted funny. Twenty years ago the Seattle area had some of the clearest water in the nation. He needed to get a water filter next time he went to Costco.

"I gave him fifty dollars . . .but he did bring over a lot of fish!"

"That's great mom. What did you do today?" He drank the rest of the water and set the glass down on the counter.

"I started this new book." He looked at the book raised in her hand. The cover was worn and the pages looked yellow.

"I thought you already read that book?" She looked at the

cover in earnest.

"Dr. Jekyll and Mr. Hyde. . .hmm. . . I don't believe so. I just found it on the book shelf earlier today." Tom had read the book as a boy. They printed this edition a few years before Hitler invaded Europe. His mom was beginning to forget things.

"Well anyway, what time was I suppose to meet my blind date?" He thought the whole thing was amusing. Here he was divorced, forty-eight years old, and getting ready for the big date. He wouldn't have even considered doing it, but his mom seemed to be having fun setting it up.

"You're not." She said disappointedly. "Her child got hurt so she had to stay home." Tom looked at her incredulously.

"You tried to set me up with a woman with children?" She set her book down on the table.

"All single women your age have children. This is Seattle. Hello! We're number one in the nation in single mothers with kids. That radio shock jock said so on the air yesterday."

"Mom, you're not seriously listening to him again are you?" Tom's jaw almost fell off his face.

"I can't just sit here and do nothing all day. Who do you think you got your urge to keep busy all the time from? Your father? I highly doubt it." She picked her book back up and thumbed through the pages to find where she left off.

"Ok I'm sorry. If you don't mind I'll be out in the shop." He turned around to go down stairs.

"Supper'll be ready by five thirty." She spoke into the book.

"I have to be back at the park by six thirty," he said at the bottom of the stairs.

"You'll have time." He heard her reply.

He opened the door to the garage, turned on the lights, and went over to his workbench. The garage smelled like diesel fuel mixed with mold. Boxes of electric motors and construction equipment lined the far wall. A shop bench ran the length of the back wall. Pieces of dive gear were lying scattered across the bench; dive lights without lenses or bulbs, regulators without face coverings or hoses, pressure gauges with corroded spools, and a wide assortment of fin straps and buckles. Hanging nearby on a rack next to the furnace was a selection of wet suits that were guaranteed to leak on any given day. Someday he was going to combine pieces from each outfit and make one single outfit that would still work. He'd already bought the glue for the project. The glue was sitting on the bench with a sales receipt that was turning yellow and the can of glue was gathering dust. He bought the can right after he got divorced five years ago. In the middle of the bench was the only semi-cleared spot. Here with the light right above his bench he was busy working on making his own oxygen analyzer. He got the kit off the Internet. It only took two nights to put together. One night he drilled holes in the proper spots on the plastic outer casing. The next night he soldered the resistors and connected all the wires. All he had to do now was set the electronic parts back inside the plastic case, screw it shut, insert two AA size batteries, and it was ready to go.

It took him less than ten minutes to put the oxygen analyzer together. When it was done he just set it down and looked at it. He didn't have a tank filled with nitrox to test it. Nitrox is the term divers use to denote oxygen-enriched air. Instead of breathing 21% oxygen and 79% nitrogen found in normal outdoor air, divers bump up the oxygen concentration to say 36% oxygen, which lowers the nitrogen concentration to 64%. By boosting the oxygen concentration you reduce the nitrogen concentration. The lower the nitrogen concentration, the lower the amount of nitrogen that builds up in your body during a dive. Nitrox essentially allows a trained diver to extend the length of time at certain depths without increasing the amount of nitrogen accumulating in their body. This means that under certain conditions you can extend your dive time and stay down longer than you could by using regular compressed air. The reason why you have to be trained to use nitrox is that too much oxygen at too great a depth can lead to a seizure underwater. Pure 100% oxygen at little more than twenty feet can be fatal. There are tank and regulator issues to deal with as well. There are stories told of titanium regulators igniting due to extremely high levels of oxygen.

On the plus side, Nitrox training usually can be completed in a day and is relatively an uncomplicated subject. Most divers read a short book or watch a video, and then receive some hands on training from an instructor in the course of two dives. Nitrox is just becoming popular on the west coast. Most tropical destinations have already caught the wave and extol the virtues of nitrox. Some live aboard vessels use it as their primary source for filling tanks. Tom just liked the refreshed perky feeling it gave him at the end of a dive. Within moderation, increased oxygen percentages made a sick patient feel better at the hospital and likewise made divers feel more invigorated at the end of a dive.

He set the analyzer down on the bench and admired it. It would have cost him three times as much to buy one commercially built. He would put it to use just as soon as he got his tank sporting the green and yellow "Nitrox" sticker refilled. He had to send the tank out to get it filled. He would have to take it to a shop twenty miles away and leave it for a few days. No one filled Nitrox while you waited around here. Besides, you had to let the tank sit for at least six hours before you could get an accurate reading on the percentage of Oxygen in the tank according to some dive agencies. Also, there weren't enough people qualified as gas blenders on duty at the nearby dive stores. Most of the local dive profiles such as those in the park didn't warrant a preference for nitrox. The park was just too shallow. You needed more than forty feet to extend your dive time by using nitrox. As an example, using normal air, 21% oxygen, a diver could stay at sixty feet for fifty-five minutes before reaching the no decompression limits on a standard set of dive tables. Using a mixture of 32% oxygen the same diver could stay down ninety minutes before reaching the no decompression limits. If your tank held only sixty minutes worth of air/gas mixture on a typical dive you would only benefit by five minutes by using enriched air, at 32%, in your tank. Where nitrox wins out over air is on dives deeper than seventy feet, or when you just want to reduce your accumulated nitrogen level in your body in general. A diver on air can only stay down at seventy feet for forty minutes before reaching the no decompression limits, but a nitrox diver using 32% oxygen can stay down for sixty minutes. So you can see that for deeper dives nitrox gives you more time to check out fishes and swim around. It's not until you get down to deeper depths does diving with nitrox raise another complete different set of concerns and that is why one should take a nitrox course before using any enriched air on a dive. At the park most dive tables give you hours to play underwater. The limiting factor with diving at the park is the size of your scuba tank, or tanks, if you don't mind the extra weight.

Tom tinkered with some items and moved other things back

and forth across the bench until he heard the front door open and close. The heavy footsteps could only belong to his brother. He left the garage to go see what he was up to now. As he came up the stairs he could see Kevin sitting at the table. Kevin had a beer in his hand.

"Want a beer? Kevin asked.

"No thanks. I still have to drive back to the park."

"It's ok. A couple of beers won't affect you. It takes two six packs to affect my driving."

"You should know. You got the two DUI's." (Driving under the influence).

"Whatever man." Kevin grasped his own neck and acted as if he was choking. Phyllis came out of the kitchen and sternly looked at both of them.

"Can you two be nice for just a moment."

"Sure mom," Kevin quickly spoke up.

"We're going to have a nice dinner and I don't want either of you spoiling it. You both understand?"

"Fine mom," Tom said. Kevin shook his head. Phyllis went back to the stove.

"So what's for dinner," Tom asked.

"Lingcod," His mother proudly announced. "Your brother brought over six nice fillets."

"Whoa, must have been good sized."

"Not bad. Put up a good fight though," Kevin added.

"I'm broiling three of them in the oven. I put the other three in the freezer."

"Sounds good mom." Tom came into the kitchen and opened the fridge. He took out a diet Dr. pepper. He didn't bother asking his brother if lingcod was in season. Phyllis came over and set silverware down on the table. She turned and went back to a cupboard.

"Hey, sorry to hear about that diver the other night." Kevin said right before taking another sip of beer.

"News sure travels fast." Tom exclaimed.

"Yeah, Ian told me. Nothing happens in this town without him knowing about it." Ian Grebonski worked down at the marina. Ian spent all day loading and unloading boats from the water. The corporate businessmen taking a few hours off from their stressful lifestyles confided in him as he lowered their boats into the water. Self-employed people told him the rest of the story as he lifted their boats out of the water. People looking out on the dock or walking along the main path would stop and tell their life history while he swept debris off the walkway. He made everyone feel better after they had a chance to vent their frustrations. He always agreed with them no matter which side they took. He would look interested and smile just enough so you could see where two front teeth were missing. He lost his teeth ten years back when he was sleeping on the streets of Seattle. Sleeping under an overpass could be a dangerous thing if someone deranged wanted the possessions of a middle-aged man. They robbed him and took his rusted out shopping cart along with a worn out sleeping bag. He lost his two front teeth during that exchange. He hadn't been beat up since he sobered up and left the city. Tom first met Ian down at the park. He would come over every once and awhile and help them carry something heavy down to the beach. He probably knew more about the underwater park than any other non-diver. Ian's only downfall was his habit of chewing sunflower seeds and spitting them out the gap between his front teeth.

Tom came over to the table and sat down. He would have helped his mother set the table, but she liked to do everything herself.

"So how is Ian?" Tom asked.

"Fine. Just fine."

"I haven't seen him down at the park lately."

"You know how he is," Kevin began. "Always working around the marina."

"Sounds like a nice man," Phyllis commented.

"For a reformed alcoholic." Kevin spoke up. "He gives me the creeps when I'm drinking beer. He just stops and stares at me." Kevin took another sip.

"He makes you feel guilty?" Phyllis asked.

"No, I just don't like the way he looks at me." Kevin crushed the empty can in his hand and set it down on the table. "So what's new at the park?" Tom ignored the question. He knew Kevin really didn't care.

Phyllis brought over two plates full of food. Broiled lingcod, green beans and mashed potatoes covered with cream of mushroom gravy.

"This really looks good Mom." Tom said.

"I ought to bring fish over more often," Kevin said as he picked up his fork.

Phyllis brought over a plate with a much smaller portion of diner for himself. By the time she had sat down Kevin already had a mouth full of food.

"Mmmmhh" Kevin smiled and moaned with a full mouth. They sat silent as they ate for the next few minutes. By the time Tom was half way through his meal, Kevin's plate was empty.

"Any more mashed potatoes mom?"

"I made extra just for you." She started to get up, but Kevin stopped her.

"Just stay there mom. I'll get it." Kevin got up with his plate and his crushed beer. The rest of the potatoes was all his. Tom never had seconds. He went over to the stove and scooped the rest of the potatoes in the pot and made a mountain of mashed potatoes on his plate. He poured the remnants of the mushroom gravy over the top of the stacked high white pile. He got another beer out of the fridge and made his way back to the table.

"I still don't know where you put it," his mom said in amazement.

"If I tried that, I'd need a bigger wet suit." Tom said. Kevin took a bite then swallowed.

"You know it isn't easy being me. I'm hungry all the time." They both watched as Kevin devoured the tower of food.

"Mom, that was great. You mind if I do the dishes?" Tom asked.

"You go ahead and do whatever you were going to do," She said to Tom. "I don't mind doing the dishes." Tom got up and put his dishes in the sink.

"Where are you going?" Kevin asked while finishing up his plate.

"Down to the park. Were going to move some blocks while the tide is low. Why? You want to come?"

"Hell no. I was just wondering. Does that diving accident affect the park any?"

"Like what? Tom asked.

"You know, close it down or anything like those ferry commissioners suggested?"

"No, our safety record is too good for that. Besides, the park generates too much business for the city to shut it down. The park puts Edmonds on the worldwide map. A lot of people would rather move the ferry than mess with park.

"I wouldn't be so sure about that brother. Most of us fishermen couldn't care either way."

"But don't you see, that the lingcod we ate tonight could have hatched right in park," Tom said. Kevin laughed out loud.

"I don't doubt it did, but park or no park, fishermen need to fish." Tom could see where this debate was going. They had been here many times.

"Well, I prefer to be proactive. I'm going to the park and work no matter what. I can't change the world and I can't change the fishing regulations, but I can build a park and that's what I'm going to do. I might never have my name in the paper or read about it in history books, but at least I feel better about how I spent my time on this planet." Tom turned and headed for the front door. Kevin came to the rail and looked down the steps.

"Whoa, nice speech. Think I'll get a beer and drink to it. Having a beer might not be considered saving the world, but it at least it gives me something meaningful to do on this planet," Kevin growled. Tom sadly looked up at his brother.

"I'm sorry you feel that way," Tom replied. He shut the door behind him. He stomped his feet as he went over and got in his truck. Kevin watched from the window as his brother drove down the street. To Kevin, the park was like his life, a waste of time and energy. He hated his brother for trying to always prove him wrong. Oh well, at least Tom liked the fish. A devilish smile suddenly formed on Kevin's face.

The Beach

Tom's return trip to the park was quick due to the lack of weight in the back of the truck. Seeing his brother was always a stressful situation. He wanted the best for him, but his brother's lack of motivation ticked him off, but the family eating and spending time together made his mother happy and that had to be worth something. Coming down the hill on Highway 104 the sun was beginning to set in the west. Within the hour it would be pitch black this time of year. He drove down past the ferry waiting area. The ferry lanes were empty. The policemen that were usually on duty directing traffic during peak periods had all gone home. The coffee bar was closed and the only person visible was the man at the ferry tollbooth. He was reading a paper. Tom crossed the intersection and turned left towards the empty ferry dock. He got in the right hand lane, crossed the train tracks, and entered the park.

There were at least a dozen other cars in the parking lot. A few of the occupied cars belonged to people who were just looking out at the water. A group of divers were gearing up for a night dive. It looked like they were just unloading their gear from their vehicles. He recognized one of the trucks. It belonged to Sherry Silverton, a heavyset woman with long black hair. She was a dive instructor down at the local dive shop. Ten years ago she was one of Tom's open water students. She was a lot thinner when she took his class. Just about the time she was ready to take her advanced diver course Tom quit as an instructor. He found there was no way to work on the park and teach at the same time, so one of the best instructors on the west coast packed up his student slates, set aside his classroom slides, and gave his full attention to the underwater park. That decision is what has made the park what it is today. The world would always come up with good dive instructors, but very few people had the dedication and determination to change part of the world; even if it was just a small insignificant shallow spot on a water covered planet. Tom never thought that hard about what he was doing. He remembered that old Chinese fable that said if everyone threw just a tiny pebble into the lake, it wouldn't take long for the lake to fill in. He was just throwing his pebble out into the park. He didn't care who was next or how long it took. It was the process he was going through that made him feel good about his own life.

Tom drove to the open parking spot closest to the restrooms and changing area. As he pulled in he remembered that he had forgotten his wheel borrow. He knew it he forgot it because he was preoccupied thinking about his brother. He had let Kevin get to him and it was his own fault. He got out of the truck and slammed the door. He could hear the nearby divers talking out loud, but he ignored them as he walked back behind the restrooms and down to the beach. The cinder blocks were now a good fifteen feet from the water's edge. He picked up the first one on the sand and carried it to the water's edge. As he came back for the next block, he saw Paul walking in the sand towards him. Vic was right behind him.

"Hey, didn't think you were going to enjoy this sunset by yourself did you?" Paul stated more than asked as a question.

"Don't you guys have a life?" Tom asked half-heartedly.

"No need to rub it in," Vic said. They both reached down and grabbed a block. They all carried blocks down to the beach and dropped them next to the edge of the water. They had carried no more than twelve blocks when a train sounded two large blasts and the noisy cars rumbled by. They abruptly heard the voice of a woman shouting, but barely audible over the train. They stopped and turned to see who it could be. The train rumbled on.

"Is one of you Tom Erickson?" They heard her ask. They all stood there with blocks in their hands. They were too stunned to move or do anything else. She was a brunet in her early thirties. She was tall and had slightly almond shaped eyes. She wore blue jeans, a cotton shirt, and a very charming smile.

"Hello? Can any of you talk?" She laughed at the three Neanderthals holding their stones. Tom dropped his block and wiped his hands on his pants.

"Sorry, the trains here made us deaf. I'm Tom. What can I do for you?" He watched as she approached them. She looked a good two inches taller than him. He straightened his back, but it had little affect in raising his stature.

"I'm Gina Belloni." Tom just looked at her not realizing the significance of her name. "You know, I was supposed to have the blind date with you tonight?" He suddenly got a big smile on his face. Vic and Paul resumed their task. Tom stretched out his hand and shook hers.

"Nice to meet you. I thought you were at home with a sick child." He said. She instantly started to laugh.

"I probably told my mother that and she told your mother, but I don't have any real children. It was my new horse. I just paid a lot of money for a horse that needed tendon surgery."

"Is it ok?" Inside he was sighing with relief.

"Oh yes, the stitching didn't take as long as we thought. I just have to make sure he doesn't move around too much and open the sutures."

"Well that's good. Listen, I've got to help move these blocks before these guys do all the work."

"We don't mind," Paul said as he carried another block towards the water. Gina quickly surmised what they were doing.

"Here, let me help." Gina grabbed a block before Tom could say a word. She hauled it down to the water's edge and let it fall in the sand next to the rest of the pile.

"So what's all this for?" she asked.

"Tomorrow, when the tide is high, we're going to float these blocks out to a boat we sunk this morning. The added weight will keep the tides from moving the boat around, and piles of blocks make good living spaces for little creatures."

"Sounds interesting," she said while carrying one of the last blocks. "Mind if I join you?"

All three men looked at her as if she was crazy.

"Are you a diver?" Tom asked incredulously.

"Certified last year."

"Great! We're meeting here tomorrow at nine." Paul and Vic got the last two bricks. Tom suddenly felt like a slacker.

"Well that didn't take long," Tom said. They all looked at the beach and their random pile of blocks. The sun was still setting. The skies were bluish purple with hues of orange close to the sun.

"It's beautiful isn't it?" She was standing close to Tom when she said it. He was looking right at her when he answered. "Yes it is." She looked back at him and neither one spoke.

"Well, Vic and me have to go," Paul stated.

"Yeah, we got stuff to do that can't wait another minute." They both grinned and left Tom and Gina standing alone on the beach.

"Your friends seem nice." She said as Paul and Vic turned around the corner of the restrooms.

"Oh they're great guys." Tom was trying to think of something to say, but he was suddenly having a mental lapse. "Would you like to get something to eat?" he finally came up with.

"No thanks, I had a sandwich while I was waiting for the vet."

"We could go out for coffee. This is Seattle, and you have to drink a cup every hour or the local economy will take a slide."

"Seattle needs a new past time." She replied. "I'm all coffeed out. But I do have some wine some of my friends left at my place." She smiled and looked at him. His throat suddenly became dry and he had to fight to get the words out.

"That sounds better than coffee any day." All he needed now was a pod of killer whales to start splashing in the water to make this sunset complete.

He was ready to leave that instant, but he took his time to walk with her along the beach and then over to their cars. She opened the door of a red Nissan Pathfinder and wrote something on a piece of paper.

"This is my address, In case we get separated. Otherwise you can just follow me."

"Should be fine." He took the piece of paper just the same. He put it in his pocket and got in his truck. He followed her out of the parking lot and didn't even once look back at the group of divers getting ready to go in the water. He had no idea that these divers were about to encounter a clue to what incomprehensible transgression struck the life of the unfortunate night diver named Carl.

The Night Dive

Sherry Silverton stood on the walkway adjacent to the beach. She was getting ready to take her advanced open water class out on their first night dive. A tall twenty-year-old student by the name of John was fifteen minutes late. She could only guess what he forgot this time. Four other students, three males and one female, and her divemaster, Tina, were just finishing setting up their gear and had already changed into their wet suits. Sherry and Tina were both wearing dry suits. Tina had been helping Sherry with her classes for the last two years. They had been living together for the last three years and it was nearly four years ago when they first met on capital hill in a trendy little same sex bar.

Sherry and Tina were one of the most efficient instructor teams around. Both men and women felt comfortable telling Sherry and Tina about their diving concerns or personal problems. There also never seemed to be an incident involving male pride. The best feature of this team was that they worked together so well that things got accomplished with few words being said. Student gear configuration got checked, dives were planned, and signals underwater were few because they sensed what the other was about to do next.

Tina had the group come up and stand near Sherry once the group including John, who was getting his gear together ever so slowly, was ready to go diving. The sun was just in the final stages of sunset. Sherry liked to go in right at sunset, because there was still visible light they could use to set their gear up properly. Nothing worse than trying to hook up a regulator in pitch black darkness and have a rubber O-ring the size of a nickel fall off the tank and roll on the ground right before you attached the first stage of the regulator to the tank valve. It could take a military size searchlight to find the missing O-ring; it was bad enough just finding all your loose hoses and release points in the dark. The gear was finally set up and ready to go. John was still putting on his wet suit jacket when the train came roaring by and the engineer honked twice before passing through the railroad crossing. The students held their hands over their ears. Sherry waited for the train to go by before she began to talk.

"Ok listen up. Tonight we go on your first night dive.

You've all been diving in the park, so you know what it's like during the day. At night, some of the fish go to sleep. Others come out to look for food. Some just change their personality. The best part about diving here has to be the bioluminescence. I already discussed this in the classroom. Now you are going to witness it first hand. A couple of things I want to mention before we go in. We all have a primary light and a back up light and everyone has glow stick on the back of their tank. If the primary dive light goes out, you end your dive. Use the alternate lights to guide you back to shore. We are going to dive as a group, remain as a group and comeback as a group. We turn back to shore when we get down to fifteen hundred pounds of air. We surface when the first person gets down to five hundred pounds of air. If for some reason you get lost, look around for no more than one minute then surface. The rest of the group will do the same. Once on the surface we will discuss what to do next. If you look at your compasses, you will see that out is west, back to shore is east, the ferry is south, and Canada is north. Remember swimming south will lead to a fifteen hundred dollar fine for interrupting ferry traffic. If you swim north you need a passport. Swim west and you'll find yourself in Seattle. Our cars are east. When I make this signal."

She took her hands and made it look as if she was steering a car. "That means we are going back home to our cars. Everybody got that so far?" They all nodded their heads. "Now about the dive lights. A few simple rules to follow: Never shine your lights in someone's face. Light in the eyes will cause night blindness. You'll see nothing but white dots for several minutes. Keep your lights aimed low; around the waist works best. If you want to signal to someone, aim the light low and put your hand in front of the light. I'll demonstrate in the water. To point out something to another diver just slowly paint a circle of light around the object. If you want to say something's wrong or make a distress signal wave your flashlight back and forth or up and down in a quick repeated manor." She demonstrated by moving her flashlight from side to side. "Remember, a dangling flashlight left in the on position can flash in other divers eyes and looks like a call for help. Everyone with me so far?" They all shook their heads. "Good. Now on this dive we are going to take our time and slowly swim out to the boat yard. On the way I will have everyone drop to the bottom and sit in a group. I'll turn my light on and off several times. That will be the signal for you to turn your lights off. I want you to look around in the dark and see just how much light there still is from the moon. I'm going to let your eyes adjust and then I'm going to swim around the group just above your heads. You'll see my silhouette and a cloud of bioluminescence trailing behind me. Then we'll turn our lights back on and go look around the boat yard. Everybody clear with this?" They all muttered yes.

"Good, then lets get the gear on and do a buddy check waist high in the water." The students went back to their cars and helped each other gear up. Sherry and Tina were already in the water as the students stepped on to the beach. It was all about how fast you could get in waist deep water as far as they were concerned. You had to let the buoyancy of the BC lift some of the weight off your back. Putting on your mask and fins on afterwards was a breeze. "Go ahead and do your B.W.R.A.F buddy check." Big white rabbits are funny, she thought in her head and she watched the students check their BC's, weights, releases, air, and signal each other a final "ok", before they put on their masks and fins. "Put on your masks first, then put on your fins. That way when you drop something in the water you already have your mask on and can immediately start searching for it." Sherry saw John suddenly drop his mask. "Or not," she quickly added.

Tina reached down underwater and grabbed hold of John's mask. She handed it back to him before he realized the mask was no longer in his hand. "Like I was saying," Sherry continued, "If you have to wait to find something while you put on your mask, you're too late. It's probably already drifted away." They all put on their masks then their fins. "Mask seals in place?" A mask seal partially overhanging the outside of a hood worked like a gutter spout during a rainstorm. "Buddy's glow stick on? Good. Now everyone move your hands in the water and see the light trail behind them. Cool isn't it? Ok, primary lights on and lowered? Good. Let's swim out a few yards then do a five point decent like we did earlier today." They all followed Sherry out into the water. Tina stayed behind and close to the right side of the group. The visibility was over twenty feet. Down below Sherry, the depth ran about six feet.

"Let's drop down here," she stated. They all signaled each other ok to go down, used the shore as their reference point, put the regulators in their mouths, checked the time on their watches or pointed to their computers, then slowly let out little bursts of air from their deflator valves on their BC's. The back of her neck felt icy cold the as water seeped into the back of her hood as they sunk below the surface.

The object was to slowly sink underwater so you could see where you were going and more importantly know what you were landing on. Sherry could see John plummet like a rock to the bottom. Tina caught him just before he hit his back on the sand. He still had the deflator button pushed down all the way. His light dangled and flashed every which way and the light beam momentarily caught his buddy Ted right in the face. Ted put one of his hands up to cover in front of his face as he tried to readjust his night vision. Ted closed his eyes and saw a big bright sun burned in each pupil. It would take a few seconds before he could regain his vision and see the blurry outlines of his surroundings.

John managed to put some air in his BC and right himself in the water. A cloud of sand whirled around where he stood. Over by Ted and the rest of the group the water was clear. Tina knew that John was nervous and that's why he blundered so badly on the decent. She moved over by him just as a safety precaution.

Sherry waved at everyone to swim closer to her. She pointed at Ted and put her two index fingers together. She was telling Ted to get with his buddy. There was no blame intended, just a signal for the two of them to pair up. The group reorganized and Sherry signaled each one of the divers asking if they were ok. They each responded with the ok signal back to her and she turned to slowly lead them out into the park.

After kicking out past the end of the jetty, Sherry turned sixty-degrees and headed out for the boat yard. She felt a slight current going south, but nothing these divers couldn't handle. She looked behind her and counted six glow sticks, including one rescue strobe light on Tina, and six different flashlights waving in every conceivable direction. The students looked ahead at the fins with the neon yellow bicycle tape, the flashing rescue strobe light, and the powerful twelve-watt light that lighted up their way.

Sherry stopped swimming when she found a sandy spot.

She pointed to the spot then signaled by bending her right index finger and middle finger half way and turned her hand downward. The students swam to the bottom and came to rest on their knees. They formed a circle and Sherry clicked her light off and on several times. The students turned off their lights. She then rose above their bodies and swam right above their heads. Sure enough, they could make out her silhouette against the surface and hundreds of small objects gave off a yellow greenish glow as they were disturbed by her turbulent wake. It was cool to reach out at the little points of light.

After circling the group one more time she turned her flashlight back on. The students turned their dive lights back on. She held up the palm of her hand and with her other index finger she pretended to draw a circle on her open palm. The group reached for their pressure gauges and read how much air they had. Dan, a stocky student who she saw smoking before putting his dive gear together, had the lowest tank with twenty two hundred pounds of air. Divers who smoked were a rarity now days. She knew how it felt to be always low on air for she was a smoker too when she first started diving. She didn't like the coughing spell right before a morning dive either. Her lungs cleared up fast after she quit cold turkey and her ability to breath easier and do longer dives improved dramatically. Dan would probably stop smoking too if he continued diving. Now if she could just stop her craving for food. Tomorrow was Sunday. The local Indian restaurant would be open with an expanded all you can eat buffet and individually cooked and plated appetizers by the owner himself. She was doomed already.

Sherry waved for the student to follow her. Right before reaching the Boatyard they came across a Sailfin Sculpin. Sailfins are pinkish orange colored with vertical stripes running along their body. Their dorsal fin looks like a sail off a boat followed by a long short ruffle. In the daytime they are very shy and run before you can get three feet from them. At night they are out on the prowl and they will literally let you set a camera inches from their body before they turn skittish and move away. They all tried to get close to the sailfin. Sherry soon felt claustrophobic with all the divers pressing against her, so she moved on to show the group some nearby shrimp.

Coonstripe Shrimp with translucent bodies with reddish

brown wavy strips come out of their hiding spots at night and fan out across the sand. It's like a convention without a theme; mingle and eat, mingle and try not to be eaten; safety for them is in numbers. The students poked and prodded the shrimp with the knowledge that their fingers were safely covered and protected by their thick neoprene dive gloves.

As Sherry neared the boat she pointed out a geoduck clam with it's neck sticking out of the hole. The word 'Geoduck' comes from the Nisqually Indian name, which means, "dig deep". Geoducks grow rings on their shells like rings on a tree for every year they live. At four years they weigh two pounds. At fifteen years they are full grown. The oldest geoduck ever recorded was 168 years old. They can weigh over ten pounds and the fleshy neck can be several feet long. The main white shell of the clam can be over three feet deep under the sand. This is the largest burrowing clam in the world and all you will ever see of it is less than a foot of the neck with its two openings on top: one for siphoning water and food in, and the other hole for pushing filtered water and debris out. They are usually found close to shore, but have also been found three hundred and thirty feet deep. All in all, they are amazing creatures. The shadow of a diver or pressure waves generated by a diver makes them retract their neck and hide in their deep burrows. Because of this, most divers swim over geoducks without ever seeing them.

As the divers came near the hole the geoduck did as expected. Two of the student saw a glimpse of something protruding from the hole. The other three students saw nothing but and empty hole. Suddenly Sherry saw a large lingcod over three and a half feet in length come towards her. She held out her arm so that the point of contact would be on her fist and not on her body. The lingcod veered at the last moment and swam away. The students all witnessed the event. A fish that big was hard to miss. That was odd she thought to herself. She swam over the top of a small boat and found the reason for the ling's expression of aggression. On the other side of the boat was a mass of white eggs resting in the sand. Hundreds of shrimp were eating the eggs. The egg mass was teetering back and forth as the currents gently moved it along. The lingcod still felt the need to guard the eggs, but he also felt the futility of this exercise without the egg mass being firmly attached to a steadfast object. A Dungeness crab was on the far side of the egg mass feasting on the eggs. It wouldn't take long for these eggs to be devoured. Sherry reached for the egg mass and held it up in the water for the rest of the students to see. The crab took a few side steps backward across the sand. The crab was familiar to divers in the park and didn't see them as much of a threat; divers were more of a nuisance. Another large male crab holding on to a smaller female against his raised chest ran away before anyone in the group saw him. He was holding the female crab in his arms until the female's new shell had a chance to fully harden. Female crabs will send out chemicals in the water a few days before they are ready to molt. After they step out of their old body shell, they are soft and vulnerable. It's at this one time when the male can deposit his sperm in her special receptacles. After mating the male will hold on and protect the female while her body pumps up and enlarges her size and after a few days her new outer shell hardens. The male and female will then go their own separate ways. The male will go off in search of another receptive molting female.

Months later the female will allow the sperm to make contact with some two and a half million eggs and she will then keep the sponge mass of fertilized eggs attached to her abdomen. After the eggs hatch, the larvae may take up to a year before they go through several stages and finally molt into the first juvenile crab stage. After two years of growth, the females slow down their growth rate. Both females and males are sexually mature after three years. Males will be over 6 ½ inches in shell width after four to five years of age. Dungeness crabs may live between eight to thirteen years and exceed ten inches across in shell width.

Some shrimp remained on the clump of eggs as Sherry raised the mass of eggs off the sand. The shrimp were oblivious to all except the eggs. The student divers shinned lights on the egg mass and passed it around to one another for a closer look. The lingcod made another close pass by them and then swam off. Sherry then took the eggs mass wedged it back between two rocks. She turned to the students and gave the palm and index signal for "pressure gauge". Wayne a tall skinny student was down to fourteen hundred pounds. The excitement of the night dive had been too much for him. Dan was relieved that he wasn't the only one breathing hard. The group wasn't that far out in the park, but Sherry knew they probably wouldn't make it back to shore without surfacing when they got down to five hundred pounds.

Sherry made the signal to return towards shore. The group swung around the boat. They could see some other twelve boats in various stages of decay in the nearby area. They all wanted to spend more time out there, but when one diver was down on air, all the divers were considered down on air. Sherry took the lead and soon realized she was out pacing the rest of the group. She stopped and waited for them to catch up. She counted flashlights trailing her while she waited. She could only see five flashlights and her heart began to race. She saw Tina's strobe so she knew the missing light belonged to one of the students. She immediately started swimming back to the group. What on earth happened? She thought to herself.

When the group swung around the boat John found himself on the right hand fringe of the group. Being alone felt a little freaky. If some giant sea creature attacked the group, he would be the first on this side to be devoured. He shined his light out to the right. The water was relatively clear. A few shrimp played in the sand. The area was almost as deserted as the surface of the moon. He began to relax a little. Then after moving his flashlight slightly forward he caught a glimpse of something lying in the sand. Something man made. He swam away from the group to investigate what the object was. Wayne, his buddy stopped to see where John was going. The rest of the group were now stopped, but didn't know why.

Tina saw John swim away from the group and immediately swam around the group. She stopped ten feet short of John when she noticed he had stopped too. He had picked up something and was looking at it. His back was to her and she couldn't really see what was going on due to the debris that swirled up in the water by his fins.

John swam over and found a mask and snorkel half buried in the sand. He scooped the mask up and then shook the sand off. The sand immediately clouded his vision, but he could still make out that the mask had a crack in the glass and the snorkel was cracked too. The initials C.B. were marked with yellow ink on the top of the seal on the mask and on the side of the snorkel. If he hadn't swirled so much silt in the water he would also have noticed red streaks of paint imbedded in the side of the partially crushed snorkel.

John turned and threw the mask down in the cloud of silt. He suddenly got panicked when he realized he didn't know where the group was. He looked around in his cloud of silt and saw Tina's light and quickly swam towards her. The water was clearer around her. She signaled asking him if he was ok? He signaled back ok? He wondered if she was mad at him? He was only gone a second, but he still got freaked out by being alone. From now on he wouldn't venture out with out his assigned buddy even for a second.

Sherry had only gone a few feet when the other flashlight swung into view. Her heart was still thumping loudly when the group reunited. She gave the ok signal to everyone in the group including John. They all signaled her back and the group swam back towards shore. This time however, Sherry kept very close to the group and took special care not to take her eye off of John. She wanted to ring his neck when they got back to shore, but she knew she couldn't do that. He was a customer of the shop first and her dive student second. She couldn't remember how many times Steve had driven that into her head. Don't let a customer do something stupid in the first place. He'd told her. She was mad at herself now for getting too far ahead of the group.

They stopped again when they were close to shore. She had them hold up their gauges. Dan was down to five hundred pounds. She signaled for the group to go up to the surface. Dan hit the surface and yelled out. "Sorry, I'm an air hog'"

"That was sweet!" Wayne exclaimed. The rest of the students agreed. Sherry was too busy blowing her nose to comment. She did notice that they were close to the end of the jetty.

"Ok." Let's inflate and surface swim over to the beach. Rinse your gear in the shower, then we'll go over to the cars and break it all down."

"Did everyone have fun?" Tina asked out loud. A resounding yes filled the air. The group had a lot of fun and a great dive. Sherry had a moment of terror, but all in all she had a good time too.

The group showered off while wearing their equipment. They then went over to their cars and trucks. Sherry opened the tailgate and she and Tina both sat down. It felt good to get the weight off their backs. Sherry had parked her truck across from the students and next to the fence by the railroad tracks. In a low voice she whispered to Tina. "What happened out there with John?"

"I don't know, one second he was with the group and the next he took off to go look at something."

"I think I better go have a talk with him." Sherry removed her tank and BC and went over to John. He was in the process of removing his regulator from his tank.

"John can I ask you why you left the group out there?" she whispered.

"Oh, that." He said out loud. "I found a mask and snorkel in the sand. I was going to bring it back and show everybody, but the glass was cracked and the snorkel broken. I silted the water pretty good and I panicked when I couldn't see anyone. I guess I learned my lesson the hard way about staying with my buddy."

"Are you all right now?"

"Yeah, Tell Tina thanks for keeping and eye on me."

"Not a problem," Sherry replied. She was sure Tina could hear his deep voice even if she was a mile away. Sherry turned and started to walk away.

"Oh by the way, you now anyone with the initials C.B?" Sherry stopped and slowly turned towards him.

"I found those initials on the mask."

"No," She lied. "We find lots of discarded gear in the park." She turned again and walked to her truck. She could see Tina staring at her. They were both thinking the same thing. Carl Baker, the guy from the dive club who died in the park the other night. Not the best information to pass on to a student. The police found both sets of tanks, BC's, and regulators right after the accident occurred. They found one tank and BC floating in the water column near the Cathedrals and the other tank set close to shore. Terry had to keep his gear on longer than anticipated because his compass was attached to the tank set and without the compass he couldn't find his way back to shore in the fog. He never thought of ripping the compass out of the console and holding it in his hand. He was already over burdened and too task loaded to think any clearer.

Police found the jettisoned weight belts right by the Triumph, but they never found Carl's mask. Sherry wished she could have seen the mask or better yet, retrieve the mask and examine it on shore. Tomorrow she would go look for the mask while the students worked on their navigation skills. A loud horn blasted. Then the railroad crossing chimes began signaling the approach of another train.

The Oil Dock

It was now Sunday approximately seven in the morning. A little more than a mile south of the underwater park is a place where divers like to do advanced diver training as well as technical diving. There's a narrow road adjacent to a small city park where the divers like to park and set up their gear. Other people like to park on the narrow road to quietly read, look out at the waves, have a quiet lunch, or just to forget about the rest of the world and just relax. The park itself, which has it's own parking lot and is just on the other side of a small mound, is set up for kids and their parents who want to play in the sand, walk along the beach, climb on the driftwood, or play on the plastic jungle gym.

South of the narrow road large oil pipes ran from the top of the hill, down along the shore, crossed over a hundred yard long pier that ran perpendicular to shore, and ended at a "T" shaped dock. A tall fence ran the length of the oil pipes and kept the public away from the pipes. Large wooden creosote soaked posts suspended the pipes twenty feet in the air at the point where the sloping shore met the water line.

Dave Benson and Mark Webber were both experienced divers and Master Instructors. Today they had no students to look after. Today it was all about fun. Today their plan of attack was to film all the creatures that lived on the pilings. They figured that on a high slack tide they wouldn't be down more than fifty feet. The poles that made up the support legs of the dock rose twenty feet above the water line, forty feet below the water line, and no telling how far beneath the substrate. Hundreds of large round treated logs made up the framework of the pier and dock giving countless thousands of sea creatures a place to call home. Dave and Mark planned to swim through sections under the T shaped dock and then make their way around the entire dock perimeter.

Dave and Mark were "Dogs". Both wore DUI dry suits. DUI stood for Diving Unlimited International and not the DUI you receive for driving under the influence. The black and blue suits they both owned were made in San Diego with specially crushed neoprene material. Their suits automatically entitled them to membership in the DUI's owner group or Dogs.

Dave and Mark got their gear ready in a rather casual fashion. They paid extra attention to their camera. Dave was using an old Nikonos 4-A underwater camera and an SB 101 strobe. Mark was using a SeaMaster Pro ex camera with a YS-60 strobe. The difference between the two cameras was that Dave could always get good pictures, but he was limited to the size of the creatures he could frame. Mark had extra lenses strapped to the side of his strobe arm and he could change from Micro to Macro while swimming through the water. Marks preferred method was to start the dive with the wide-angle lens attached to his Seamaster. If something big came along he was ready to snap away. Small subjects didn't usually move far fast so in case he had to take pictures of small animals; he had time to switch to his close-up lens or his macro lens, then all he had to do was just move a few buttons and he was ready to shoot. Dave liked Mark's camera system a lot, but he wasn't going to give up his twenty-year-old buddy until digital cameras got just a little bit better and a little bit cheaper.

The two dogs got their gear on, did their buddy checks, and then headed down to the water. They had planned the dive so that the current was almost nonexistent, but because of the high tide, they would have to swim a hundred yards before they could drop under the surface. On a low tide they could walk out to their start of decent point.

On a low tide, the area next to the pier formed a shallow bay with a sand bar separating the beach from the open water. On the other side of the sand bar the bottom sloped by approximately sixty degrees until you dropped down to a hundred and ten feet at which point it sloped less than thirty degrees past the one hundred and thirty feet depth mark. That's if you went straight out to the T-dock. Some of the other directions put you a lot deeper and a lot quicker. Some divers didn't realize this until they were close to one hundred and thirty feet and low on air. Each thirty-three feet of depth adds another atmosphere of pressure on a diver. On average, a scuba tank filled with air lasts a diver around an hour at thirty feet of depth. Thirty feet has a pressure equal to two atmospheres pressing against your body; (one atmosphere for above the surface and one for thirty feet). A diver at one hundred and thirty feet has five atmospheres of pressure on him or her, and for this particular deep diver, that same previous tank of air will last less than twenty minutes at 130 feet. This only considers pressure and doesn't take into account drag under increased pressure, or even raised anxiety levels due to just feeling out of your normal element. In addition, we haven't factored in the extra air utilized for buoyancy control at that depth. We haven't taken in to consideration the temperature change with depth, the workload by swimming in currents at depth, the reduced vision due to lack of light penetration, or even gas effects on physical and mental performance at depth; the most important factor, nitrogen narcosis. Someone not familiar with all these factors could drain their tanks low or empty before realizing it was time to ascend. On a deep dive you really need to factor in a third of the air to get down, a third of the air to get back, and a third of the air for reserve. Having pony bottles and extra tanks are what they teach and practice in the more advanced diving courses. Diving deeper than your training and experience permitted, was a risky endeavor to say the least.

Ascending is another important issue. Any recreational dive over a hundred feet according to most dive tables requires a safety stop at fifteen feet for at least a minimum of three minutes. Technical divers start their safety stops by as deep as eighty feet with several other gradual stops along the way to the surface. Just the time interval of their safety stops may require more time than a recreational diver spends under water on a dive. This safety stop or stops, gives your body time to off gas the majority of the nitrogen your body tissues absorb when you go on your dive. The deeper you go, the more nitrogen you retain in your tissues, and the more you need to get ride of the nitrogen by passively exhaling it out at shallower depths. If your bottom time exceeds the dive table limits and you don't do a safety stop you could get too great of a gas build up and end up getting the bends. Symptoms of the bends can range from a slight simple pain in your shoulders, complete immobility of joints and appendages making it excruciatingly painful or impossible to move or bend appendages, or even death. You choose the level of severity by depth and time you exceed established dive table limits. You can even increase your risk by drinking alcohol the night before a dive and/or by being dehydrated. Caffeine and carbonated drinks help add to dehydration. Smoking and heavy exertion while diving in cold water also adds to the possibility and/or amount of the negative side effects.

In diving the negative connotations are stressed at the beginning of your dive experience so you'll be aware right from the start and not become one of the statistics. In the end, it doesn't matter if you are told that out of millions of divers each year only a few people around the entire world get the bends. The only thing that matters is that you plan each of your own dives to insure that you never become a statistic and get the bends.

Now that you've planned your dive and you are ready to go, let's not forget to mention another important quality of nitrogen. All new divers are told that nitrogen at depth will make you happy, giddy, and euphoric to the point you want to take the regulator out of you mouth and try to make the fish breath off of it. Yet, if you ascend just a few feet, those effects and symptoms vanish. The words to describe this phenomenon is Nitrogen Narcosis, also called being "narced", or if you have a good French nasal accent you can call it "Rapture of the deep" as coined by Jacque Cousteau and the Calypso crew. The words sound silly, but the symptoms for some people can be quite scary.

Divers who have been diving awhile say they don't get narced. They've been there, done that, and built up a tolerance level to the effects of Nitrogen. That's simply not true. Consider a gentleman that drinks twelve bottles of beer a day. If he drinks a six-pack and then drives home safely he believes he's not drunk. He may not even know he's impaired unless something out of the ordinary happens to him on the way home. Say a child on a bike crosses his path. He swerves, but his reflexes are slowed and he can't quite think as fast. He misses the child on the bike, but ends up driving up on the curb. Unless a policeman comes up to him and gives him an alcohol test, there's no way you can convince him that he's legally drunk, his reflexes are slow, and that he can't add, multiply, or reason in English, but he might even consider drinking another six-pack before he wouldn't dare drive home.

If you reason that nitrogen affects you the same way as taking another glass of champagne every thirty-three feet then at ninety feet you may feel intoxicated. At one hundred and thirty feet your reflexes slow down and your problem solving abilities dwindle sharply. You may not notice any of this, but your buddy might if he or she writes a question on a slate or watches how hard it is for you to perform a simple task like opening a goody bag to catch a shrimp. They best way to handle being narced is to keep your tasks simple and familiar when diving deep. There are wrecks and animals down in the deep regions worth visiting, but only after proper training. The oil dock is a good place to learn to dive deep.

Dave and Mark swam out until they reached the ledge of the sand bar. As they descended underwater Mark unscrewed his wide-angle lens so water would fill in between his wide-angle lens and the camera's main lens. He then screwed the lenses back together. They turned on their strobes and both were ready to go. They headed down to sixty feet and came around the large mound at the backside of the T-dock. Several ratfish were hovering near the upper slope. The poles and pilings were distinctly visible and directly behind the ratfish. Both of the divers aimed their camera up to take a few pictures of the ratfish. Dave spotted a large flounder resting between the pilings. He went over to take some pictures. Mark kept his camera pointed up and took pictures of the crabs and plumose anemones that lived on the wooden structures. A small-emaciated spiny dogfish with its great big eyes swam by to see what they were up to. It was the first time in three years Mark had seen a shark south of Canada. Up off the Campbell River and next to the fish canneries you could spot hundreds of well fed spiny dogfish on a single dive. He hand fed them salmon heads and watched them fight over who got the choice morsels. Sometimes sharks would bump into him to test him. A four-footer bumped him in the shoulder and his shoulder hurt for several hours afterwards. He cussed in his regulator as the shark leisurely swam away. They got some good pictures that day. He even tried his wife's digital camera, but the sharks kept swimming either away too fast or through his legs before the shutter opened and the flash went off. It was hard trying to take digital pictures while you were preoccupied with protecting your crotch. After a few minutes this anemic poor excuse for a shark also swam away.

Dave and Mark spent forty-five minutes taking pictures before they ran out of film. Mark took several pictures of every subject. Each time he changed the f-stop on the camera, changed the aperture setting, and changed the picture speed from 1/125th to

1/60th of a second. With all the different settings there had to be at least one picture that would turn out better than the rest. Getting one or two good pictures was what the dive was all about. They each had thousands of pictures at home. Now days, a shot had to be truly spectacular to stand out from the rest. Mark signaled to Dave he was down to one frame. Dave signaled back the same. As a photographer you always kept one frame until the end of the dive. If you shot your whole role, that's when never before seen sea creatures swam right in front of you and posed for pictures. If you kept that last frame ready until right before you surfaced, you could get the shot of a lifetime. If you didn't bring a camera on a dive it was a given that a baby gray whale would look you right in the eye and then spout right next to where you surfaced. Mark knew this theory well for it's exactly what happened to him on a trip to Canada. That whale's eye staring right at him would stay fresh in his mind and not in a photo album for as long as he took pictures. The problem with Canada and the northern Puget Sound region was that there were just too many things to take pictures of. It didn't matter if you didn't dive on one of the famous wrecks, even on a mundane dive, scallops fly in front of your face, or a giant Puget Sound king crab will pose right in front of your camera lens. Puget sound king crabs can have a shell width almost as wide as your chest, but they possess short stubby legs. They can be yellow on their abdomen. Their back can be colored purple, red, orange, and other iridescent colors. Their huge claws make them look like some monstrous creature that stared in a Godzilla movie.   Although their looks are intimidating, they are very slow moving hunters who prefer to snack on starfish, spiny sea urchins, anemones, and other echinoderms. Juvenile Puget Sound king crabs are completely red or orange in color and have little cones on their heads. Both the adults and the juveniles make great photographic models.

The two divers swam around the remainder of the T-dock then swam towards shore. They surfaced close to shore and took off their fins and shut the cameras off. Mark was standing near one of the pilings that held the oil pipes up in the air. He saw the broken end of a small red wooden rowboat paddle floating in the water. He didn't think much of it because there were lots of strange artifacts comprising the flotsam and jetsam of the Puget Sound. What Mark thought was an elderly man reached in the water and picked up the red colored piece of wood. The man examined the piece of debris for a moment then stuffed it inside his jacket. Mark didn't think much about it because people always collected driftwood and other weird souvenirs they found at the beach.

The Cargo Net

Tom woke up to the sound of his mother knocking on his bedroom door.

"Time to get up. I've got breakfast ready."

He looked over at his nightstand and saw that it was already seven thirty in the morning. He had set the alarm for seven. He wondered why it hadn't gone off. He got out of bed and put on a robe. He walked out to the kitchen and saw his mother sitting at the table drinking a cup of coffee. She had a big smile on her face.

"Good morning mother." He saw that she had made him a couple of over easy eggs and two pieces of wheat toast. He had gained ten pounds since she moved into her studio downstairs. He gave her a kiss on the forehead and sat down.

"You smell good today. Are you wearing a new perfume?" she asked him.

"What?" He realized Gina's perfume last night must have rubbed off on him.

"Would you like some decaf coffee son?"

"Sounds good." He took a bite of eggs while she poured him a cup of coffee.

"I heard your alarm go off but you didn't wake up so I thought I better wake you."

"Thanks mom." He had no idea that the alarm had gone off. He didn't hear a thing.

"I guess that's to be expected when you only get three and a half hours of sleep," She added.

"I was busy," he said as he took a sip of coffee.

"No doubt, I hear she's a regular nymphomaniac." Tom suddenly choked on his coffee then started coughing.

"Do you mind mother. You almost killed me."

"Good, I have to do something to wake you up. Did you like her?"

"Yes mother she's very nice." He ate the last few bites of egg.

"That's good. Maybe I'll have some grandchildren before I die after all."

"Don't start with that again mom." He finished his cup of coffee and took his empty plate over to the sink.

"Just leave it in the sink, I'll do the dishes. With no grandchildren it's not like I have lots to do anyway." She added.

"Thanks mom, I feel better already."

Tom headed for his bedroom and took a quick shower. He knew he was running late, but there was no way he was going to show up at the park smelling like last nights perfume. He felt tired, but in a good way. He got dressed and packed up his truck as fast as he could. The lift barrels felt cold to the touch and were wet with moisture as he put them in the back of the truck. He threw in the cargo net in one big lump and tossed some ropes on top and threw the wooden wheelbarrow on top of it all. It was the worst packing job he'd ever done, but there was no way he was going to loose a day at the beach just because he lost a little sleep. For a moment he wished he were eighteen again that's when his body didn't fight against what his mind wanted to achieve.

Tom pulled into the parking lot of the marine reserve and shook his head in disbelief. Because he was running late, all the good spots next to the restrooms were taken and he had to settle for a spot next to the park entrance. A few minutes more and he would have had to park on one of the side streets over a block away. The park filled up fast on the weekends. As Tom pulled in and turned off the engine, Paul, Vic, & John, approached his truck.

"You got a late start," Paul stated.

"I'm sorry, I over slept." Tom said as he got out of the truck.

"I guess there's a first time for everything," Vic added.

"There's another surprise for you too," John said. Just then Gina walked around the van parked next to Tom. He was surprised to see her.

"Hi Tom, You mind if I help today?" He turned a slight shade of red then regained his composure.

"No, that would be great. We never turn down volunteers." She looked into his eyes, trying to see if he would be able to keep last night confidential.

"Well good, where do we begin?" She asked.

"Well, first we have to haul all of this down to the beach on the other side of the restrooms." Tom pointed to everything in the back of the truck. "Then we lay out the cargo net and fill it with the blocks of cement. Then we'll attach the barrel floats to the corners of the cargo net, inflate the barrels, and then swim everything out to where we want to sink the blocks."

"Sounds simple," said Gina.

"In theory it is simple, but the blocks have a way of tearing up wet suits, and the currents sometimes make it hard to swim in the right direction." Tom said.

"Do you ever use boats?" She asked.

"Tom doesn't do well with boats," Paul interjected. "He has a tendency to brake them." Tom gave Paul a disgusted look even though he knew Paul was right.

"We do everything with our own bare hands and fins. It keeps things simple, safe, and more self rewarding." Vic stated. Besides, Tom doesn't have very good luck with boats. He works best with them if they are already sunk."

"Thank you Vic, I couldn't have stated it any better." Tom said proudly.

"We used a boat on the Triumph, but that was over eighty four feet long," Paul added. "We made Tom stay in the water so the boat wouldn't sink or anything."

"Actually, our fins give out when a boat's anywhere over twenty feet long." John pointed out.

"So much for making us look like super human studs John." Paul grimaced.

"But that's the whole point," Tom smiled and added. "None of us have super powers or Olympic athletic abilities, we're just normal people trying to do our little part in changing the world. It doesn't take a rocket scientist to either do what we've done or to see what we've accomplished. We see what we've done every time we dive the park and we do it all on donations and volunteers. No government has done anything quite like what we've done in the entire world."

"What about the wrecks in Canada?" Gina asked.

"Those wrecks are beautiful," Paul had to admit. "But first of all you can't just swim out from shore and see them. You need to take a boat. Here you just walk in the water and start swimming around."

"Not only that," Vic piped in. "But those million dollar warships would stick out of the water over forty feet high if you put them here in the park.

"And you can't swim them out with your fins." John added. They all laughed at the absurdity of his comment.

"That would be our main concern John," Paul said as he slapped John on the back.

"Hey, are we going diving or not?" Tom asked as he tried to suppress a yawn. The group started removing the equipment from the back of the truck. Gina, Vic, John, and Paul each took one of the float barrels and slung it over their shoulders. The guys were immediately impressed by how strong Gina was. The four of them walked away leaving Tom with the cargo net. There was no easy way to carry the cargo net. The ten-foot square net was always heavier when it was wet. It usually took a week for the flat one and a half inch wide netting material to dry out. Tom just grabbed it in one big damp bundle and carried the mass in his arms to the other end of the restrooms and down to the beach. The group was standing around and waiting for him by the time he got there. He had to walk slower than they did because the net kept hitting against his legs. If the net dropped any further, he risked stepping on it, stumbling, and landing flat on his face. Over time he had learned to gauge this phenomena quite accurately. As soon as he could, he dropped the net in the sand and stopped to catch his breath.

"What's next?" Gina asked. Tom looked at her and smiled.

"We usually bring our tanks down to the beach then change into our wetsuits. Then we'll hook up the barrels and load the blocks. "

"It might take me a little more time to get ready, I'm diving in a Dry suit," she said.

"No problem," Tom told her. It takes us awhile to get ready just because of all the talking we do. He looked at Gina and smiled again. He wondered if she was as tired as he was. If she was, she sure didn't show it. She turned and walked away from the four men. She was sure they would talk about her the minute she left the beach, but if Tom was as smart as she thought he was, he wouldn't mention a thing about last night.

The four men absentmindedly watched her walk away. As she got to the corner of the building Paul said to Tom, "I guess you found a new dive buddy."

"Don't take it too bad Paul, but she does have better legs." Tom said. Paul rubbed his eyes and pretended to hold back a tear.

"You know, I work out, but it's never enough," Paul countered.

"Hey where's the fill tank?" Vic butted in.

"I left it at home," Tom said. "I figured we could just use my tanks since I'd have to come in when Gina runs low."

"Oh she's only got one tank?" Vic asked.

"Yeah, so you three will have to go without us after we drop off the blocks."

"Not a problem," Vic replied. They all started walking up the beach to go get the rest of their gear and then change into their wet suits. A sudden wind came from the south and they all smelled the aroma from the local Indian restaurant.

"You smell that Paul?" John asked.

"Yeah, we might have to get out of the water early too." Paul answered back.

"Are you two going there again?" Vic asked.

"Yeah, you want to come along?" Paul asked him.

"No, my wife made me sandwiches," Vic replied.

"Lucky you. What kind?" John asked.

"I didn't look, I want to be surprised." Just then they heard the train-crossing signal begin to chime. They looked over and saw the train coming from the south. It sounded its horn three times as it neared the railroad crossing. They all cupped their ears with their hands as they walked towards their trucks.

When the train had passed by, they lowered their hands.

"Hi Tom," A deep female voice called out. Tom turned to see Sherry Silverton walking towards him.

"Hi Sherry. Out with a class?" Tom stopped in the middle of the parking lot. Paul, Vic, and John kept on walking. Tom saw Tina standing over by Sherry's truck. He waved hello to Tina.

"I saw you last night, but you went right past us," Sherry said to him.

"Oh sorry Sherry, I guess I was a little preoccupied."

"I understand. I just wanted to tell you someone ran over the north boundary line near Telegraph Way."

"How bad is it?" he asked.

"Don't know. Couple of former students told me. They said an anchor caught the park boundary line and dragged it several yards into the park before the anchor line broke. They said the anchor is still out there but it's not worth salvaging."

"I'll have a look at it after we drop a load of cinder blocks."

"Oh, you sink another boat?"

"Yesterday. Just north of Tube Henge."

"Good, I'll have the class look for it. We just finished the navigation dive. We're doing a wreck dive next."

"Sounds good." Tom started to step away. Sherry moved closer to him and grabbed his arm to get his attention and started to speak using a low soft voice.

"I almost forgot, one of my students came across Carl Baker's mask in the park last night."

"Where is it?" Tom asked.

"I don't know," she said. "My student said it was broken so he left it drifting in the park. I just wanted to tell you so you could keep an eye out for it."

"Thanks, Sherry I will." Tom turned when he saw out of the corner of his eye Gina walking towards him. She was fully dressed in her dry suit and he hadn't even made it back to his truck yet.

"I see why I didn't have to hurry," Gina spoke up.

"Oh Gina, this is Sherry Silverton. She's one of the best instructors around here. Sherry stuck out her hand and the two women shook hands.

"Hi Gina, I had a good instructor who taught me."

"Ok," Tom said. "It's starting to get thick around here.

"Nice to meet you Gina, but I better get back to the students."

"Bye Sherry," Tom said. Gina just looked at her.

"So who is she?" Gina asked. Tom started to walk again towards his truck.

"No need to worry about Sherry. I'm the wrong sex."

"Oh, I see."

"Go ahead and carry the rest of your gear over to the blocks. We'll gear up over there."

Gina went over to her Pathfinder and started putting her gear together.

Tom hooked up his regulators to his tanks then wheeled his tanks over to the dive site. On the way back he stopped in front of Gina's SUV.

"You want to wheel your tank over there?"

"No, I'll just put it on and carry it over there."

"Suit yourself," he said. It'll be another twenty minutes before we get in the water . . . More if I don't start moving quicker."

He went over to his truck and collected his wet suit. He waved at Gina as he took his wet suit over to the changing room. She was dressed, geared up, and ready to get in the water.

Tom went inside the changing room. He saw Vic sitting down and putting on his farmer johns over his swimsuit.

"The other two leave you again?" Tom asked. Vic looked around. They were alone.

"Grab a seat. This place doesn't get as crowded now that everyone is wearing dry suits."

"I know," Tom replied. "Why come in here when you can change right down to your long johns in the parking lot?"

"These new divers wearing their fancy dry suits are a bunch of spoiled babies."

"I know what you mean Vic. Staying warm is for the wimps."

"So where's your dry suit Tom?"

"I left it at home. Those cinder blocks can rip right through my dry suit." Vic held up a pair of torn and tattered neoprene gloves.

"I've had these gloves for little over two months." For added effect Vic inserted his hand into a glove and poked his fingers out of two holes.

"Those are in good shape." Tom countered. You've still got a while before you break'em in." Tom pulled on his farmer johns and he looked at all the holes in the material.

"You know what Vic? I think my suit is past the break in stage."

"Right with you."

"Next year I say we get new wetsuits."

"It leaks a little, but next year works for me." Vic was just finishing putting on his hood. Tom looked at Vic's outfit. He had rips, tears, and black rubber glue patches all over his wet suit. Vic smiled as he headed for the doorway.

"Be there in a minute." Tom called out after him. He quickly got dressed and left the changing room. He returned back to the bench and placed his clothes on the floor of the front passenger seat. He never ever locked the truck. On dive days he rarely carried more than five dollars and a driver's license.

The parking lot was over flowing now. People were pulling up to the curb, dropping off their dive gear then leaving the beach to park on a side street. Most of the cars and trucks belonged to divers or beach goers, but a few he suspected belonged to people who parked stealthily in the park and walked on the ferry. The park sign read maximum parking three or four hours depending on what time of year or when you last read the signs. Ferry passengers tended to park all day. If they parked illegally and tip toed on the ferry, they could save some money as the ferry charged more for cars than walk-ons. One single ferry passenger could block a spot for three or four shifts of beach goers and there was never enough local police to hand out parking limit violations on a regular basis. It was usually left to the public to make a ferry passenger feel guilty for violating the local traffic codes. The violators were easy to spot. Beach clothes, dive gear, or a kid with a bucket meant you were staying at the beach. Someone with a briefcase or backpack quickly walking from his or her car towards the entrance of the park was most likely trying to ignore the signs and on their way to catch the ferry. In a way you couldn't blame people for trying, because Edmonds has beautiful beaches, million dollar parks, and little if any nearby parking. There was parking of course, but only a local would know where to look for it.

Tom grabbed his mask, snorkel, and fins out of the back of his truck. On the way over to the dive site he recognized some of the divers. He said hello to a few of them as they recognized him. There were at least three different dive shops with students in the park today. The trails next to the jetty would soon have low visibility and would be filled with particles stirred up by the fins and the waving of hands, called "sculling", of new divers. He made a mental note to be sure to come back to shore following one of the farther north park trails at the end of his dive.

He saw some divers rinsing off at the open shower station next to the bathrooms.

"How was the vis?" Tom asked them. The divers turned to face him.

"Excellent!" one of them exclaimed. "Over fifteen feet at least."

"More like twenty out by the Triumph." The other diver chimed in.

"Sounds good. Thanks." Tom said. He started to walk away.

"Did you see the size of that lingcod?" He heard one of the divers exclaim over his shoulder.

"Dude that was sweet." The other diver replied. Once he turned the corner of the building and moved across the sidewalk he could see over the beach on the other side of the jetty. He looked down at the beach and could see Paul, Vic, John, and Gina all working as a cohesive unit. They were all dressed down to their wetsuits and Gina in her dry suit. They were hauling cinder blocks over to the net. The net was laid out under water in about three feet of depth. The buoy barrels were hooked one to each of the four corners of the net and partially floating. A tire inner tube wrapped around a red milk crate and attached to a dive flag was connected to one of the barrels. By the time Tom reached the beach, they were moving the last of the blocks over to the net.

"I guess I could have stayed home today," Tom said to no one in particular.

"I thought you did?" Paul said jokingly. The group went over and started to put on their weight belts and tanks.

"We were just trying to keep up with Gina," John stated.

"Make me out to be a slave driver." She said as she began to laugh. Tom just looked at her in admiration as she sat down and put on her tank and BC. Last night was fantastic, and today was even better. She seemed to be the perfect woman.

"Well Tom, are you going to stand there and day dream, or are we going to get going."

"Oh," Tom exclaimed. "I'll get my tanks." He went over and sat down to put on his own twin tanks. Talk about feeling stupid.

"See what you did Gina?" John comically pointed out. "You've taken our fearless leader and turned him into Jell-O."

<hr>

"I'm not your leader." Tom interjected. He strapped his tanks in place then carefully rose to his knees.

"But you did know who he was talking about," Paul remarked. Tom ignored him and walked into the water holding his mask and fins in his hands. As soon as he was waist deep he placed the fins in the milk crate and proceeded to put on his mask. The others put their masks on too.

"I'll be right back," he said to Gina. The others already knew what he was going to do. With one of his regulators in his mouth he dropped below the surface and landed on his knees. He extended his alternate regulator just beneath the opening on the underside of one of the barrels. He pushed the purge button on the regulator and air began to bubble up inside the barrel. When the section of the net connected to that barrel began to lift he moved on to the next barrel. When he had done this with all four barrels, the rocks in the net were now a lot more buoyant. Only the center of the net was currently resting on the bottom of the sand.

" That's probably good enough," Paul said as Tom was resurfacing. "We can pull it out from here."

Tom turned to Gina. "We'll put our fins on now and take the load out to the dive site. Once their fins were on, Vic, Gina, Paul, and John grabbed onto a short rope connected to each one of the barrels. Tom grabbed on to the side of the net facing away from shore. While walking backwards with their fins on, they all began to drag the bundle of rocks away from shore and out deep enough so that the net no longer dragged across the sand. They walked backwards a little further until the water was up to their shoulders. Now they could inflate their BC's enough to float and begin to swim with their fins.

The net, barrels, and rocks, made up a bulky mass that glided through the water as slow as an ocean going ice burg.

"Now we just sit back and swim." Tom told Gina.

"It sure is a beautiful day," John said. He was swimming on his back with his eyes closed. It appeared as if he was trying to get a suntan, but the only part of his body that was exposed, was the oval hole in his hood that exposed his face; and his mask obscured even half of that area.

"You guys do this every weekend?" Gina asked. Her legs were already beginning to tire. Tom could see the churning movements of her fins just below the surface.

"Slow your pace down Gina. Most people tire out because they kick too fast. We've got a long way to go and only a turtle can win this type of race." She did as Tom suggested and her legs immediately began to feel better.

"How far are we going?" She asked.

"Out towards that white buoy," Vic said. Vic was at the back right corner of the float. Gina looked straight ahead and saw a little white buoy. It looked far away from where they were presently paddling in the water. She looked behind her and saw they had moved quite a ways from shore. Both distances appeared far away; she couldn't gauge the distance at all.

"About ten more minutes of swim time," John stated. He was still lying on his back while holding on to the left front corner buoy. He was soaking in the sun as he kicked with his legs.

"How could you tell with your eyes closed?" Gina asked him.

"That's easy, after working a while out here you begin to see the park in your dreams. He opened his eyes and looked across at her.

"He's right," Paul said. Paul was swimming and holding on at the back left corner buoy. "We should be there in less than ten minutes." Suddenly the buoy next to Paul shot half way out of the water brushing against the side of his face. At the same instance, the lack of buoyancy on the back left corner propelled the cargo net to sink and fold inward. A few cinder blocks tumbled out of the freed corner of the net. The other three buoy barrels started to sink below the surface.

"Drop the lines and back away from the barrels." Tom barked. Vic, Gina, and John let go and regrouped way behind d the barrels. Paul had his hand up by the side of his face. He looked like he was in pain.

"You ok Paul?" Tom asked.

"Yeah, just feel like someone hit me." He moved his hand away from his left cheek and a few scratch marks were visible on a reddened patch of skin.

"Nice bruise Paul," John commented.

"What now chief?" Vic asked Tom. Tom was looking at Paul's exposed cheek.

"You ok Paul?" Tom asked again. Paul rubbed his sore jaw.

"Yeah, it just nicked me. I'm fine. Just didn't expect that."

"Ok then, you guys stay up here. I'll go down and access the damage. Be back in a few minutes." Tom shoved a regulator in his mouth and went under water. Ten feet under he saw the three buoys holding up the net and it's contents. It was drifting lazily in the water. The structure of the net and blocks looked so sturdy that he figured all he would have to do is add more air to float it all back up to the surface. He could re-attach the fourth barrel on the surface once they figured what had gone wrong with the buoy barrel.

Tom swam up to one of the barrels and took out his spare regulator and positioned it under the barrel like he had done near shore. This time however, he had plenty of room to look up and see what he was doing. He was about to press the purge button and fill the barrel, when he saw something odd that caught his attention. It was the material that made up the net. The loop of material that went through the carabineer and connected to the buoy barrel was torn. More likely the material was cut by something sharp. If he filled the barrel with air, this loop could fail from the induced stressed too. He moved back and swam over to the other two buoy barrels. The loops in the net were cut partially on both of them. If he filled them, they would be a disaster waiting for a place to happen. Especially if anyone was directly below or above the barrels when they gave way.

Tom grabbed the closest barrel and slowly opened up the valve on the top of the barrel. As the air crept out of the hole on the top of the imbedded PVC plastic pipe, the barrel began to sink and one by one, cinder blocks began to fall out of the net. The net became lighter and the remaining barrels and net began to move upwards towards the surface. The other four watched what Tom was doing from the surface. By the time the barrels reached the surface all the cinder blocks had fallen out of the net. Vic had never seen Tom do anything like this before in all the years they had dove together. Tom cleared his head out of the water and took the regulator out of his mouth.

"What happened?" Paul called out. Tom took off his mask and blew his nose.

"It seems we had a problem with the net, so I let the blocks go."

"You want to re-attach the barrels and try again?" Vic asked.

"No, I was planning to build a teaching platform out here for the instructors, so we can just leave the blocks here.

"What about the boat?" John asked.

"It should last another week or two without moving much." Tom turned to Paul who was hanging on to the other floating buoy barrel. "Paul would you mind tying that barrel to the others?" Paul swam over and quickly tied it off as the others watched.

"I don't know about you guys, but I'm getting cold just bobbing on the surface." Gina interrupted. Tom looked over at her and smiled.

"Here's the new plan. We go down and lay the blocks down flat and make a big square, then Gina and I will bring back the net and barrels."

"You sure you want that much drag with you." Vic asked Tom.

""Gina's a good swimmer, we should be all right. Let's go down."

They all descended slowly and landed close to the blocks. At first the water felt cold, but as they started moving the blocks around they all began to warm up. When they first descended, Tom formed a line with some of the blocks. There was quite a bit of sculled up debris in the water from the fallen blocks, but they still had a good five to ten feet of visibility depending where they were standing. The rest of the group began lifting scattered blocks out of the sand and placing them behind the first row of blocks. Soon the piles of strewn blocks were moved and now resembled a flat wall resting on it's side. Tom turned and gave the "ok" signal to every one. They all signaled, "ok" back. Tom signaled to Gina for her to follow him and he waved goodbye to the others. The three men waved goodbye to Tom and Gina and off they swam. As they watched the three leave the visibility in the water began to improve and they could now see just how alone they were. There was sand in all directions with little else to see save a passing shrimp looking for a place to call home. Tom glanced down at his pressure gauge to check the remaining air supply in his dual tanks. He was good to go for another hour or so. He looked over at Gina's gauge as she was reading it herself, and saw that she was half way down on her air supply. Lifting the blocks had been hard work. He signaled "ok" then he motioned for them to swim towards the line attached to the float with the flag and the cluster of barrels. The line stretched out forty feet long in length and dragged on the sandy bottom a good twenty feet. Tom grabbed the line with his right hand and Gina grabbed it just behind Tom's hand with her left hand. Together they started swimming while holding on to the line.

On the way back towards shore he pointed out a flounder sitting on the sand, crabs buried in the sand, and thousands of little nudibranchs hanging on to the blades of sea grass. Gina appeared to be smiling the entire dive so Tom showed her everything he could think of. When she was down to six hundred pounds of air he found a moon snail plowing through the sand in search of clams. Tom picked it up and carried it several yards before finding a clam laying on the surface of the sand. He told Gina to stop while he set the large fleshy snail next to the clam. He had a little trick he wanted to show her.

Moon snails are the largest snails on the west coast, and adults may produce a shell larger than the size of your clenched fist, but the fleshy body that hangs out of their shell may make them appear twice their actual shell size. Chemicals in the skin coupled with their ability to burrow through the sand like a mole keep fish from nibbling on their exposed flesh. They congregate in spring and lay eggs in almost complete circular collars. The grayish collars look like neck seals from discarded dry suits and accumulate on beaches and in shallow waters by the thousands. Each collar of eggs contains thousands of eggs bonded to granules of sand, which prevent the eggs from being eaten by predators. Moon snails survive by sheer volume of eggs layed and hatched. They are not the swiftest or the smartest of the shelled hunters and neither are their prey. If a clam fails to sense the presence of a moon snail, a clam will just sit there like a rock and to make things more complicated, if you set a moon snail right next to a clam and if it fails to catch the clam's scent, the moon snail will crawl right over the clam and keep moving on. It's makes you wonder how many clams a moon snail will actually pass over before it can distinguish the difference between a bivalve shaped rock and a rock shaped clam buffet. If not for the sheer numbers and varieties of clams, moon snails might never have survived so many millions of years on this planet.

Today, however, Tom and Gina got lucky. Within seconds, this particular clam opened its shell and a long foot muscle came out of the shell and extended down to the sand. With a pull vault maneuver of the foot muscle, the clam leapt away from the near vicinity of the moon snail. Tom looked over to Gina's air gauge and saw that she was down to four hundred pounds. He gave her the signal to go up and they surfaced in seven feet of water.

"That was sweet." She exclaimed. At the same moment she lifted her mask up to her forehead and rotated it so that the viewing portion was now on the back of her head and the head strap was now across her forehead. "I've never seen that interaction before."

"I'm glad you liked it." Tom responded. He was also relieved to see she wasn't one of those that left the glass faceplate of her mask resting on her forehead. The way she now placed her mask made her look like a deep technical diver. Mask placement used to be one of his pet peeves as an instructor. He brought his mask down off his face and let it hang around his neck. It didn't look as cool around the neck, but the movement only required minimal effort and one free hand.

"Are you going out tomorrow?" she asked.

"Yeah, every Saturday and Sunday."

"I'll be there," she said with a big smile on her face. They started swimming towards shore with the barrels in tow behind them.

"This looks like a good spot." Tom spoke up as he then stood up in the waist deep water and began leaning over and taking off his fins. Gina in turn followed his lead. With fins in hand they began wading through the water towards the beach.

"So would you like to go get some lunch?" Tom asked.

"No, I can't." Tom felt immediately disappointed and she could sense it. "I've got some things to do, but if you want to come over later I'll make you dinner. Say about eight?"

"That works for me," he responded.

"I'll help you carry the gear back to your truck, then I better be going." She said.

"No, don't bother. If those guys don't get a good workout they'll think I don't like them anymore."

"Whatever. I'll let you handle the gear." She leaned closer to him and he thought she might kiss him. "And thanks for not mentioning anything about last light to your friends," she whispered. She was beginning to think this relationship just might work. She looked him in the eye for a moment then she started to turn away.

"My pleasure. Definitely my pleasure," He quickly responded. She started to walk away towards the showers. Tom went back into the water and pulled the barrels closer to shore. He had his mind on her the entire time he hauled the barrels and cargo up to the high tide line. Gina was a diver, she came out and worked on the park, and in bed she was almost insatiable. He thought he'd died and gone to heaven. One might have thought it would take a strong wind to knock him off his cloud and bring him back to earth, but as he began to unhook the cargo net from the barrels his attention turned to the ominous signs of cuts in the net. The cuts were deep, they were applied to each of the four corners of the net, and they were definitely done on purpose. Had someone been under the net at the time the net gave way, someone could have been severely injured or killed. He wondered why anyone would do such a thing? More importantly, who would do such a thing?

Return to the Dive Shop

Tom pulled into the adjacent public parking lot next to the dive shop. He had folded up the cargo net and placed it in the back of his truck before John, Vic, and Paul could see the damage done. He placed the barrels on top of the net to cover the view from any prying eyes. There had already been one tragic accident in the park over the last weekend and there was no need to leak it out to the general public that a second accident was so nearly avoided.

Tom got out of his truck and hauled his twin tanks out of the back end. He carried the scuba tanks towards the front of the shop and fortunately, he was stopped by someone who was just coming out of the shop. A young guy wearing a dive hat held the door open for Tom as he carried his tanks into the shop.

"Thanks," Tom said as he passed by the guy.

"Don't mention it." The guy answered as he looked at the twin tanks. The young man thought that the tanks looked too heavy to carry and there was no way you'd ever catch him dragging around more than one tank at a time. The young guy shook his head and let go of the door once Tom passed by.

Inside Tom brought his tanks over to the air fill station. There were no tanks connected to the high-pressure air hose lines so he hooked up his tanks and began to slowly fill them. Tom occasionally taught a naturalist course for the dive shop so they considered him part of the extended family of in-house instructors, which meant, he was left alone to fill his own tanks, repair his own equipment with the shops tools, and be ignored if any paying customers happened to be loitering in the shop. Right now a man wearing a John Deer hat with an extended belly that rolled over his belt line and flopped over on his blue jeans was commanding Steve's full attention.

"You don't sell used gear here?" The man asked Steve.

"No, the only place that takes used gear is a store in Seattle." Steve replied. Tom had heard this dialogue a million times.

"Why not?"

"We only sell new gear here. That's the way the owners want it." Steve politely told him.

There wasn't much profit in used gear he wanted to say, but didn't. "You might try selling it in the newspapers," Steve added.

He tried to look sympathetic to the man's needs. Negative word of mouth comments were something he didn't even want a cheapskate to pass on to others.

"I might do that'" the man said. "Thanks for the advice.

"You're welcome," Steve replied as warmly as he could muster. The man seemed satisfied and was just starting to turn for the door when he turned back towards Steve.

"Oh just one more thing. Do you guys sell parts to regulators?" Steve's shoulders sank from the sudden weight he felt, but managed to keep a smile on his face. Tom opened up his valves to start filling his tank as he tried to keep from laughing. He had heard this one plenty of times over the last few years.

"We don't sell regulator parts," Steve conceded.

"Can you get the parts?"

"We get them in the service department."

"Can I buy them from the service department?"

"Sorry, but only our technicians have access to the parts."

"I'm a technician," the guy exclaimed.

"Oh," Steve smiled and said. "Then you can call the manufacturer and order direct." The guy's face dropped into a sullen poise.

"I did call, and they told me the only ones they shipped parts to were dive stores. I've been all over this town asking every dive store the same thing." They guy appeared half sad and mad at the same time.

"Every store?" Steve repeated. "That is unfortunate, but I can see why they are doing it," Steve added.

"I know," said the guy. "It's all about liability."

"Unfortunately that's true." Steve replied.

"What if I worked in your shop?"

"You'd get a discount on labor, but we'd still have to charge you for parts."

"Couldn't you just cut the labor and sell me the parts,' the guy persisted.

"Well see, then we'd be liable." Steve folded his arms. It was a sure sign he was getting tired of the conversation.

"Look at it this way," the guy continued. "Are car part stores liable when I incorrectly install new brake parts in my car?"

"We don't sell car parts," Steve countered. "We're a small industry just trying to keep the government out before they come in with a lot of new rules. Steve's smile had left his face, but he didn't appear mad yet. Tom looked on and wondered in admiration how Steve could day after day deal with all the customer interactions.

"So what you are saying is because of the government I'm screwed."

"How long did you work as a technician," Steve asked trying to change the subject.

"Three years in Southern California."

"Are you looking for a job?" Steve asked. He already knew the answer.

"No thanks," the guy responded as he shook his head and then smiled. "I make a lot more pay then I did then."

"Well, do you want to give our technicians some work and send you reg in for service?" The guy stopped and thought for a moment.

"You know, I might as well," he finally conceded. "I can't seem to do it by myself." Steve wanted to smile, but reframed.

"Sorry about that," Steve said. "But they will do a good job." Steve pulled out a maintenance slip and pen and placed them next to the man's regulator assembly sitting on the counter. The guy took the pen and absentmindedly started filling out the form.

Tom turned back to his tank and noticed that the pressure in the tank had equalized with the pressure in the lines. He hit the button for the boost pump and the air pressure in his tanks slowly began to rise. When he reached maximum tank pressure he turned off the switch. He unhooked his tank and left it standing there to cool down. He then turned around and found that the guy who needed the regulator repaired had already left the shop. Steve was putting a bag around the regulator assembly in question, and tying a slip of paper to it. Steve was smiling at Tom but he didn't know if it was his real smile or the one he used when he was irritated.

Steve was a real good salesman. He just hoped that after dealing with that last customer, Steve was still in a good mood. Steve casually looked over at Tom and could tell Tom wanted something.

"How can I help you Tom?" Tom left his tank by the fill station and approached Steve.

"Do you have a second?" Tom asked.

"Sure Tom." Steve turned to the rental room. "Hey Eric?"

"Yeah?" a muffled voice called back. A second later a nineteen year old kid with short brown hair walked out of the rental room wearing a smudged tee-shirt and jeans.

"Could you watch the front for a second?"

"Sure," said the kid. Eric strolled over to the cash register and picked up a copy of a well-thumbed dive magazine. It was slow at the moment because most people were still over at the park completing their first or second dive. Steve and Tom headed back to the classroom. Tom entered the room and Steve shut the door behind them.

"What can I do for you?" Steve asked as they both sat down.

"Someone deliberately cut my cargo net." Steve leaned back in his chair and was quiet for a moment. He wasn't sure how to read Tom sometimes.

"Are you sure?"

"Yep," Tom replied. "All four corners were sliced just enough to hold until we loaded it. One corner snapped on the way out to the new boat."

"Was anybody hurt?" Steve sat up and asked.

"Paul got a bruise on his cheek. I dropped the load before anyone else got hurt."

"Well, I'm glad for that. We can't afford another accident after what happened to Carl the other night." Steve began to rub his forehead. He had a headache from all the questions divers were asking him about the accident.

"I understand." Tom said as he fidgeted in his chair. He should have checked the net before they got in the water he thought to himself.

"So you think someone did it on purpose?" It was a rhetorical remark and didn't need answering by Tom.

"The question is who and why?"

"Any thoughts?" Steve asked. Tom looked at him searching for an answer.

"Maybe someone is jealous." Tom thought out loud. "Maybe someone doesn't like us, or maybe they don't like all the enhancements we've made to the park."

"Or maybe they don't like the entire park," Steve added. "The retired people don't mind the park. They just want to keep this town quiet as possible, but they can't even cut their own steak let alone your net. So I guess that let's them off the hook. You think you might be able to narrow it down just a bit."

"Believe me Steve, I've been thinking about it all day," Tom said.

"Well I know one thing," Steve began. "You'll have to change procedures until you figure this out."

"Such as?" Tom asked getting mad at Steve's intonation.

"Inspect everything before you use it, and don't let anyone near your gear you don't know." Tom sighed in dismay.

"The people who work on the park are all volunteers. Some come and some go. If I don't let anyone new work on the park, we'll soon be out of volunteers."

"Well Tom, from what you've told me you almost lost one today." Tom held his hands up in a gesture of surrender.

"I give up Steve you win."

"It's not me. It's about the park. We regulate ourselves or the city will come in and regulate us out of business."

"I understand." Tom stood up and moved towards the door. Tom didn't look as concerned about the situation as Steve would have liked.

"So what are you going to do about it?" Steve demanded. Tom stopped by the door. He gave a little sigh and turned to look at Steve.

"First, I'm going to double check everything before every dive. Second, I'm going to find out who did it." Steve nodded that he was satisfied and then stood up.

"Be careful Tom. Who ever did this couldn't care less if you were hurt or killed. In fact, that may have been their goal."

"Thanks Steve." Tom left the classroom feeling very somber. Steve left the classroom just a few steps behind him. A large man over six feet tall immediately approached Steve. Steve saw him coming and said his standard, "Hello".

"There you are. You remember me? I called two weeks ago about getting an extra large ranger BC."

"Oh yes," Steve answered with a smile. In reality, he had probably answered a hundred calls the last two weeks concerning buoyancy control devices. Tom left the shop before he heard anymore of the conversation. He needed to figure out who had cut his net and he needed to figure it out soon before any other accidents cropped up. He decided to drive back to the park and take a nice long walk along the beach to give himself some time to think about who might a have done it and why? But just as he reached his beat up old truck, Ian came towards him with a slight noticeable limp in his step. He wore a big smile, which always directed Tom's attention to the fact that Ian was missing his two front upper teeth.

"Good afternoon Tom," Ian said.

"Hi Ian. Lunch break?" He knew that every day on his lunch break Ian would stroll down from the marina to the underwater park. He did it part for exercise, and partly to talk to all the divers down at the park. After a while, from just talking to everyone, he knew the water conditions and dive sites better than some of the divers that actually dove in the park.

"Yep." Ian said. "Thought I better get out and work my legs. They seem to be doing better than last year. If they keep improving, I might finally get a chance to take that scuba course at the shop." Tom had heard a rumor that the leg problem was due to diabetes, but he didn't want to come right out and ask Ian what was the real problem. That would be a little too personal and maybe a little too upsetting to deal with. Ian had had the leg problem to contend with for the past several years.

"That's good Ian. I'd be glad to show you around the park."

"Yeah, that would be good." Ian paused while Tom set his tanks in the back of his truck. "Have you seen your brother's new boat yet?" Tom stood there in shock. Last night he remembered Kevin was borrowing fifty bucks from his mother.

"What boat?" Tom asked.

"He bought a used twenty-six foot Bayliner boat at the marina. It was advertised for twenty thousand, but your brother told me he bought it for fifteen. It needs some work on the engines and new shaft seals, but it runs ok close to shore."

"I wonder where he got the money?" Tom said more than asked.

"I heard he paid cash. I put the boat in the water myself otherwise I wouldn't have believed it."

"Well thanks Ian. I'll have to go see it. Any idea where he took it?"

"I think he went up to Everett."

"I know the place." Tom said. His brother had berthed a boat up there years ago before his last boat got confiscated up in Alaska. "Well thanks Ian. I'll definitely go take a look at it." There was only one way his brother could get that kind of money that quickly, and it had to be under the table and probably illegal as well.

" Well, I better be going?" Ian said. He started to walk off before Tom had a chance to reply."

"Bye Ian." Tom got in his truck and decided before he did anything else, he would go north and pay his brother a visit.

Everett Marina

Tom pulled into a large parking lot with boats in different points and processes of repair. Some were still on their trailers, while other boats were suspended in the air by wooden blocks and other handy stackable items. Some of the boats looked like they hadn't been in the water for years, while others were ready to go just as soon as they got one last coat of paint. At the far end of the parking lot was a maintenance building and town meeting hall for local yacht skippers. Everett had a few marinas to choose from, but this is the one Tom remembered. This is where his brother hung out before his fateful trip to Alaska. Tom drove slowly passed the boats and parked cars. He was looking for his brother or where his truck was parked. He spotted the big dodge ram truck half way down the lot. There was a canopy on the back end and it served as Kevin's living quarters when he was between jobs. Tom pulled up next to the dodge but he didn't see any sign of Kevin. Tom got out of his truck and looked around. He figured Kevin would be close by because Kevin didn't like to walk. Kevin would drive around a parking lot three times just to get a spot close to the entrance of a grocery store. He would rather empty his gas tank before taking twenty more steps. He had been that way all his life. But on the other hand, if he was out at sea, Kevin would work a twenty-one hour day, get three hours of sleep, and be back at work and ready to go for another shift. He could work this way for a week straight if the fishing was good. On land he could just care less.

Tom marched over towards the closest boat ramp. He stepped through the open door way and descended down the wooden ramp. The place looked deserted except for a lone seagull flying overhead. He started walking down the floating cement dock. After passing by several moored boats of various types and sizes, he heard a tool drop. The sound came from a small twenty-six foot boat only a couple of boats away from where he was standing. He figured it was either his brother or at least he could ask who ever it was if they had seen his brother. He approached the boat but couldn't see anyone on deck.

"Hello," he called out as he tried to look inside the curtained windows. He heard the thump of more tools being set down followed by heavy footsteps coming his way. His brother came out of the cabin with a grease-laden rag in his hand.

"What the hell are you doing here?" Kevin asked him. He wasn't smiling, nor did he seem mad.

"I heard you got a new boat." Tom replied. "I thought I'd come by and see it." Kevin wiped his hands with a rag, and then placed the rag in his back pocket.

"Who told you?" Kevin asked.

"Ian. He said he put it in the water for you."

"I wish he could keep his mouth shut once in a while." Kevin stated. Kevin stood there as if blocking the entrance to the boat. Tom looked around and noticed the state of disarray. Tools lay strewn on the aft deck with the cover to the motors held open by the broken end of a red wooden paddle. A small rowboat with a five horsepower engine was tied up to the stern of the boat.

"Well aren't you going to show your brother aboard?" Tom asked.

"I would, but I've got parts of the engine sitting on the cabin floor. I need to get her fixed up. I'm going salmon fishing in May."

"Copper River?" Tom asked.

"Yep. I could make over forty grand in a few days, and that would get me back on my feet again."

"So where did you get the money for this?" Tom had patiently waited for a good moment to ask. Kevin frowned then looked away from Tom.

"Got some work here and there that finally paid off."

"I see," said Tom. He knew he wouldn't get much more information out of his brother. He looked over and saw his father's old salmon fishing pole resting on a side rail. Tom noticed a green glow in the dark minnow lure tied on the end of the line.

"You catch the ling with dad's old pole?"

"Yeah, still works good, but that's my last lure. Lots of snags out there." Tom tried to think of something in response, but couldn't. His brother was doing his own thing and didn't want Tom intruding in his life.

"Well Kevin, I better go and let you get back to work."

"Yeah, I got lots to do." Kevin replied. Tom turned and left the dock in exasperation. There were only a few ways his brother could have gotten the money to pay cash for a boat this big and none of them seemed too legal. Tom was determined to find out how Kevin did it."

Dinner with Gina

Tom made it back home with just enough time to shave and shower."

"I see you got another hot date tonight," his mother stated more than asked. Tom was in the middle of putting on his shoes by the front door.

"Sorry mom. I'm late."

"Well it's about time!" she scolded him. "You should have been out there years ago." He got his shoes on, opened the door, and then leaned back and blew her a kiss. She pretended to ignore the gesture.

"Don't come back unless you bring grandchildren." On second thought she added.

"Love you mom. Have a good evening." He shut the door and flew down the stairs. She watched him drive off from the window. She smiled and waved goodbye as he sped away.

Tom arrived at Gina's house with six minutes to spare.

"You're early," she exclaimed as she opened the door. "Come on in." Tom started to enter inside but suddenly stopped in mid-stride.

"I forgot the wine I was going to bring."

"That's ok," She said. I've got a complete wine cellar comprised strictly from left over office parties."

"I see," he said as she ushered him inside her house. "Do you host a lot of office parties?"

"Not really. But when we do, we always order too much." She shut the door behind him and before he could utter another word she had wrapped her arms around him and planted a deep long kiss upon his lips. They stood and kissed for several minutes before they broke apart to get some well deserved air.

"Would you like some wine? I have steaks in the oven, red potatoes in butter and garlic, and a nice salad on the table." Her mind was racing a mile a minute.

"Uh, the wine sounds good." He stammered. "In fact, the whole meal sounds good."

"Your mother told me it was your favorite meal." She said as she headed for the kitchen. He followed after her.

"You talked to my mother?" He couldn't believe his ears. She looked at him like he was silly.

"No, my mother talked to your mother then she told me. You're mother and mine are friends down at the senior citizen center." She poured two glasses of red wine then handed him one of the glasses. "I heard Shiraz is one of your favorites." Tom took the glass, but he wasn't feeling very comfortable about the present situation.

"What else did she tell your mom to tell you?" She took a sip then smiled.

"Everything. Except for your brother Kevin. She didn't say much about him." Tom took a sip. It was a very good Shiraz. One of the best he had ever tasted.

'That is a good wine."

"So what's the story with your brother?" He shook his head then took another sip.

"My brother and I are sort of opposites. I build marine reserves, while he shoots endangered species.

"You're kidding me?" she said as she pulled the steaks out of the oven.

"I wish I was, but unfortunately it's the truth. Two years ago he was caught shooting seals up Alaska. He spent six months in jail, they confiscated his boat, took away his catch of salmon, and I believe he's still on probation."

"You're kidding me?" She dished up the steaks and potatoes and placed them on a set table. "Have a seat."

"Yeah, it's not the best thing to talk about right before dinner." They both sat down.

"How many did he kill?" She asked in dismay.

"I'm not sure, he admitted to killing four, but there may have been more. He was up there for quite a few years, only that last fishing season was bad, and he blamed the seals for the poor salmon run."

"He's lucky he didn't get a longer jail sentence," she said as she placed a napkin across her lap. Tom copied her gesture.

"Not the way he sees it. Kevin knows that the Japanese kill hundreds of whales each year in the name of scientific research and then sell the meat back home." Tom cut into his steak and took a bite.

"Hey, this is really good."

"Thank you," she said. "Does your brother think he should be treated on the same level as the Japanese government?"

"It's not just the Japanese. He also objects to our own navy killing whales with their new LFA sonar system. A couple of pings from their test system and hundreds of marine animals from miles around have instantaneous brain hemorrhages. Kevin thinks you might as well hold a gun to a whale's head and play Russian roulette and on this occasion, I think he has a point."

"That may be," Gina said between bites, "but just because a government can cover it up doesn't mean he can do it. He should know two wrongs never make a right."

"And I agree with you there. And that's why I have such a terrible time dealing with my brother."

"What's he doing now for a living?"

"To be honest with you I haven't a clue. All I know is that he borrowed fifty dollars from Mom last night, and bought a used boat today."

"Chances are, he already had the money," she said. "I bet he took the money from you mom just to make her happy." Tom was stunned and looked at her quizzically.

"What do you mean?" he finally asked.

"I think she offered him the money and he took it just to make her feel good. Moms do like to help their offspring."

"You know, I think you're right," Tom admitted. "I guess I've been a little too hard on Kevin lately."

They both took a sip of wine then suddenly she looked at him.

"Do you think he cut the net?" she asked. Tom set his glass down.

"I saw the cuts when you were checking the net."

"I really don't know, but why do you ask?"

"Well," she began. "Perhaps he's jealous or maybe he's perceived you incorrectly too.

"It's a thought," he admitted. "But I hope it's not true."

Geoducks

Kevin couldn't work after the confrontation with his brother. He knew Tom was wondering where he got the money to buy a boat, but there was no way he could tell Tom. Tom might squeal to the probation officer and that would be the end of Kevin's future plans. Oh sure, his brother meant well, but he could be a real pain in the butt sometimes. Kevin tossed his tools inside the cabin and locked the cabin door. He had a long drive ahead of him tonight and he wanted to get started.

He drove down to Edmonds and caught the ferry over to Kingston. Sunday night was usually an easy night to get to Kingston. Most of the people were trying to get back from Kingston and from their weekend retreats. Kevin's truck was one of thirty vehicles that made the trip across the water. As they neared Kingston, he could see that the Kingston ferry dock was full of cars in the lot, cars waiting at the tollbooths, and cars snaking up the nearby hill. The return ferry would be full for at least the next three trips.

Kevin drove past the weekend sightseers and headed down highway 101 towards a place called Hamma Hamma. It took him well over two hours to get there. He pulled down an unmarked driveway paved with oyster shells and parked his truck between several hillocks of piled high oyster shells. He got out of his truck and did a visual sweep of the spit of land. There was no one around. He went to the back of his truck and started to unload his scuba gear. He pulled twin one hundred and twenty cubic foot high pressure steel tanks from the back of his truck and set them standing up. The tanks each bore a bright yellow and green nitrox sticker, but Kevin concealed the stickers with black thin neoprene covers. The tanks were filled with 36% oxygen, which gave him seventy-five minutes of bottom time down to a depth of seventy feet. He next took out a yellow aluminum forty cubic foot low-pressure pony bottle filled with fifty percent oxygen rigged for tech-diving which also had a neoprene cover over it, and a big Kevlar type bag filled with all his other dive gear paraphernalia. As he set the bag on the ground, he heard the sound of a boat's engines.

"Right on time." He said to himself. He took out his hand truck and wheeled all his gear down a boat ramp made of crushed shells. He set the gear next to the waters edge and tossed the rusted hand truck to the side of the ramp. A twenty-six foot aluminum skiff was heading straight at him. Kevin waited for the operator to cut back on the engine, but instead, the operator kept coming at him and at the last second put the engines in reverse. The skiff slowed down abruptly as the bow dug into several layers of crushed shell. The skiff came up the shore and Kevin jumped back to get out of the way from the on coming craft. The skiff came to rest inches from Kevin's scuba tanks.

"Jeeesh!" Kevin exclaimed. He was shook up from the incident and then mad when he thought about it.

"No, just me," the man sporting a thick black beard stated matter-of-factly. "Are you Kevin?" He asked. He was wearing a faded Mariner's baseball cap, an old red and black logging shirt, worn and torn blue jeans, and what use to be considered white tennis shoes before they became stained with hydraulic fluid.

"Yeah," Kevin answered. "You almost killed me. You crazy black bearded bastard." Kevin was still trying to recover from the shock.

"Hey I like that," the man replied. "I think Blackbeard will be my new nick name." He gave Kevin a big grin as he pulled the beard away from his face and spit over the side of the boat. The fake beard then snapped back in place over a clean-shaven face. Kevin had no idea why the man needed a disguise.

"Besides, if I had wanted to hit you," Blackbeard continued. "You'ld already be dead. So as soon as you're through complaining, hop aboard." Kevin hesitated for a moment, and then started to put his gear on board.

"Do you need all that crap?" Blackbeard asked indignantly.

"Yes I do," Kevin replied. "Have you been drinking?" He could smell the alcohol on his breath.

"No," Blackbeard answered. It was a lie, but he didn't care. Kevin stowed his gear and then helped push the skiff away from the shore. Within minutes they were speeding at full throttle across the canal. After twenty minutes, Blackbeard idled back and came to rest next to a forty foot working platform boat. It was already getting dark and the boat was hard to make out until they got close to the boat. Most of the lights were turned off and the boat was anchored. The boat looked deserted except for noise coming from a compressor. Kevin suspected the compressor was located somewhere below deck. An air hose and a water pump hose ran down the port or right side of the boat and into the water. Blackbeard tied up the boat on the starboard or left side of the boat. The captain, a stocky man with gray hair and a large belly, came stalking out of the cabin holding a wrench. He looked more like Santa Claus wearing heavy-duty boaters garments than a deadly poacher. He took one look at Kevin and sized him up.

"So this is the best you could do for a replacement?" The captain said in disgust with a slight southern accent.

"Replacement?" Kevin asked. The captain ignored the question.

"Well, get your stuff on," the captain began. "The other diver's already down there." He turned and went back to check on the compressor. Kevin turned to Blackbeard.

"What happened to the other diver?" Kevin asked. Blackbeard shrugged his shoulders.

"He got the bends or something." Blackbeard vaguely responded.

"Well, that's good news," Kevin said.

"Don't worry, this spot is only thirty feet deep. You could stay down there for hours," Blackbeard explained. Kevin didn't reply. He'd check the depth out for himself when he got down there. He put on his dry suit, and the rest of his gear. The moment he was ready to go into the water Blackbeard handed him two goody bags. Kevin clipped these to his sides.

"We have two large collection baskets under the ship. When your bags get full, empty them into one of the baskets." Blackbeard stated. He next handed Kevin a hookah setup. It was nothing more than a second stage regulator connected to a long hose and attached on the other end to the air compressor. Kevin put it in his mouth and breathed off of it. The system didn't breath as effort free as Kevin's own regulators, but the system would work. Blackbeard last held up the water pressure hose. There was an underwater flash light attached two feet behind the end nozzle. A small wire ran out the back end of the flashlight and along the length of the water hose. The wire was clipped onto the length of the hose with plastic tie clips.

"Turn this red handle and water sprays out. Turn it back to turn it off. You can turn on the light once you get under water." Blackbeard explained.

"I know how it works," Kevin replied. Kevin got up from his resting bench while holding on to the hookah set up and the pump hose. Because he already had his fins on and his mask in place, he took his time and carefully walked over to the side of the boat. The main deck was only a foot and a half above the water line. The water was calm. He checked to make sure there was enough slack in both the air hose line and the water hose line. He put the hookah regulator in his mouth, took a breath to see if it breathed decently enough, and then he jumped over the side of the boat. He hit the water with a light splash, then immediately went under. The visibility was good next to the surface, but dropped to nothing as he drifted slowly towards the bottom. As his fins met the soft muddy floor, he held his depth gauge up to his face. The depth was thirty-one feet. He looked around and saw a light moving some twenty feet away. A plume of silt was billowing around the other diver's light. Kevin turned his own light on and looked down at a sea floor strewn with tube holes. Time to go to work he thought. He turned on the water hose and aimed it down on the nearest hole. The water tore at the muddy sediment sending plumes of silt around him. The water bored a hole over three inches in diameter and three feet deep in a matter of seconds. Kevin reached his arm down the hole and his gloved hand came in contact with a geoduck. Its siphon, or neck, was over a foot long even though the neck had already partially retracted. Kevin grabbed hold of the geoduck and extracted it from the hole where it lived for the past eighty plus years.

A larval geoduck typically drifted along with the currents for approximately three to four weeks before transforming and settling to the bottom. Once on the sea floor, juvenile geoducks dig down through the sediment at about the rate of one foot per year. After reaching three foot below the substrate, they stop digging and will remain in that location for the rest of their lives. It took Kevin just a few seconds to wipe out that home. He put the geoduck inside one of his mesh bags, and then moved on to the next siphon hole, which he already had in sight. This area had holes everywhere he turned to look. This area was rich in geoducks.

It didn't take long to fill both mesh bags and then he was forced to sift through the stirred up silt to find one of the collection baskets the vessel had lowered for the retrieval. The collection basket had a green neon glow stick strung on it to help him find it easier. He emptied his two mesh bags into the big collection basket, which he found to be nothing more fancy than a heavy-duty double ring crab pot. The operation was completely low budget he thought to himself. If this had been a legal operation, he would have been wearing an AUGA mask with two-way communication to and from the surface instead of his hookah regulator that might malfunction and shut down any minute at which time he would have to switch to his own backup scuba system. The surface team would also have had extra deck hands for safety purposes, and most of all, with a legit operation he would be working in daylight instead of groping around in the dark. At the moment it was so dark and the water so silted that he could have bumped into a killer whale and never known what he rubbed up against. Right now, his greatest fear was just getting tangled up in one of his own hoses. He could drift around for years entangled in a hose before anyone found him. If he drowned, got bent, got eaten by something big, or became entangled they would just replace him with another diver. No one would help him, no one would look for him, none of the crew would ever mention his name again, not that they knew his name to begin with, and that's why this job paid so well.

Kevin continued working until he filled the collection basket a couple of times. He checked his watch from time to time and until he determined it was time to quit. He ascended to twenty feet and turned on his stage bottle filled with fifty percent Oxygen. He would need to breath off of this bottle for a few minutes just to get rid of some of the excess nitrogen. After three minutes of remaining neutrally buoyant he ascended to the bottom of the boat. He quickly worked his way back to the keel, and then ascended to the surface next to the ladder.

The captain watched as Kevin's head cleared the surface. The captain had timed Kevin's safety stop too. A risk-taking diver could get the bends and possibly lead the authorities back to their illegal operation if an investigation were initiated.

Blackbeard began to reel in the air hose and the water hose. Not a word was spoken as not to give away their clandestine activities. The sound of a faint voice could carry a great distance across the water at this time of night. Kevin took off his fins and hung them by their straps on his left arm. He then climbed up the ladder. The captain eyed him with suspicion as Kevin walked over to the spot where he originally geared up. Kevin had to walk past another diver waiting to take his place underwater. The diver had his mask on, so Kevin couldn't make out his facial features. Kevin sat down on the bench a few feet away from the other diver. Meanwhile, Blackbeard lifted the collection basket for the last time on Kevin's shift. The captain raised the ladder and then turned to see how full was the metal basket. The captain picked up one of the geoducks, examined it, then put it back in the basket and walked away. Blackbeard smiled at Kevin. The captain was never pleased, but you could definitely tell when he was angry. Blackbeard thought bringing Kevin aboard was the best thing he'd recently thought of. Kevin worked well, and best of all, as a convicted felon, he was not about to make a mistake and tell the world what they were doing out here. Now with another diver this operation would be more profitable. Kevin and Blackbeard watched as the other diver jumped into the water. He wore an aluminum eight tank on his back as his emergency backup system. That was the only thing Kevin could tell about the diver in the moonlight. A hose went over the other side of the ship so he had to assume there was another diver down on that side as well. As he began to remove his scuba gear, Kevin wondered how many men actually took part in this operation and how many boats in all made up the poaching fleet.

Blackbeard packed the geoducks on wet paper towels in short crates and then stacked the plastic crates on top of each other. After he had them about four crates high, he covered them with a dark green tarp. A geoduck could close its siphon and last a few days out of seawater. In some severe tidal areas they had to stave off dehydration on a daily or monthly basis. By tomorrow morning these geoducks would somehow find their way to Japan or Hong Kong and be transformed into somebody's sushi a few hours later.

When Kevin was dressed down to his fleece undergarment, he made his way towards an open hatch that he assumed was the doorway to the galley. He poked his head through the doorway and saw a fellow diver dressed in fleece sitting at a small table resting his head against the wall behind him. He held on to a dirty mug filled with hot coffee by his index finger. He looked exhausted.

"Hi," Kevin whispered, "I'm the new guy." The diver looked at him, but said nothing. Kevin grabbed a cup off a rack and poured himself a cup of the oil black liquid. He sat down across from the other diver.

"It's a good field out here. Too bad about the Shellfish alert though." Kevin said. The guy took another sip and cleared his throat.

"Don't believe all that crap about red tides, I eat the shellfish around here all the time and I've never been sick. They just say that so you won't harvest." Kevin didn't say a word. He took a sip of coffee and sat back on the bench.

Tom told Kevin all about red tides. Although several plankton species produced red tides, only one species produced toxins that could kill a human. *Alexandrium catenella* is the cause of Paralytic shellfish poisoning. Shellfish filter in this species of dinoflagellates and collect the poison inside their tissues. Some shellfish don't tolerate the toxins too well and will reduce feeding when *A. catenella* is present in large amounts. Butter clams are the kings at accumulating toxins and can turn their bodies into poison storage facilities for more than a year at a time. Anyone who eats shellfish with high toxin levels may feel a tingling sensation in their lips, fingers or toes, followed by loss of leg and arm movement, and finally death by paralysis by the inability expand and contract the chest "to breath". Removing the toxic shellfish from the digestive tract and induced vomiting may not be enough to save a patient; hours of artificial respiration may also be required.

So Kevin knew all about the cause of the shellfish poisoning. But what he also knew was that this particular diver didn't know anything about red tides. Lots of species of plankton in bloom formed red tides. Some species form purple and dark red patterns in the water. Others show signs of bioluminescence. *A. catenella* turns the water tea to rusty red colored, but is seldom seen as a red tide. *A. catenella* doesn't even have to form a red tide to be dangerous. You might never see a tide at all, but a sample of water or substrate would tell you all you needed to know to avoid a specific area. Just higher than normal amounts of some species floating in the water layers could be enough to close beaches or kill people eating the local shellfish. Kevin just hoped the levels of toxin in the geoducks they caught tonight would be low enough for human consumption. Poaching was a big gamble for everyone involved.

"So how long have you been working out here?" Kevin asked.

"As long as they tell me. It's best not to ask questions." The man replied.

Kevin sat and sipped on coffee for the next two hours in silence. The other diver fell asleep and began to snore. It was the snoring that kept Kevin awake or he would have been sound asleep too. Blackbeard came in and got a cup of coffee from time to time, then went out again to hoist up baskets, pack the geoducks in crates, and do whatever else was required. The captain stayed on the bridge and maintained a lookout. As soon as the other two divers had completed their shift Blackbeard loaded the divers up in the skiff along with all their gear and dropped them off along the far shoreline. They all parked in different locations. Kevin was parked the furthest away so he was the last to be discarded. Blackbeard handed him a wad of money as Kevin disembarked the skiff.

"Thanks," he said as he stuffed the money into his pocket.

"Captain wants you back. Meet here at eight tonight." Kevin checked his watch. It was four in the morning.

"I'll be here," Kevin replied. He helped push the skiff back into the water. Then he then put all his gear on his hand truck and dragged it up to his truck; he unlocked up the canopy window and opened the tailgate. He crawled inside the bed of his truck; he laid out his sleeping bag and fell face down. He was just about ready to fall asleep when he heard a knock on the side of his truck. He opened an eye and stared at a figure looking in his canopy's side window. The figure held a badge against the glass.

Tribal Fishing

A small fishing boat appeared out of the fog. It was carrying three men who were all members of the local Skykomish Indian tribe. The boat neared a buoy that marked the location of their last net to retrieve for the evening. Big Jimmy, a skinny little man twice the age of the other two men with a long braided silver pony tail who suffered from arthritis in both legs and arms, slowly brought the motor down to idle then shifted into neutral. One of the younger men with lighter skin named Ken, who kept his hair shaved close to his head, caught the buoy with the hook on the end of a pole and secured it to the side of the boat

"Ok Johnny," Big Jimmy said in hoarse voice. "Your turn to untie from shore." Without a word, Johnny a stocky built twenty two year old with a short braid of black hair and darker skinned than the other two, made his way to a small dingy tied to the back of the boat. He gently set his weight inside small aluminum structure so it wouldn't rock him overboard. He untied from the workboat and pushed off as he sat down on the bench. He grabbed the wooden oars and then started leisurely paddling the small craft towards the not too distant shore.

"It's going to be midnight before you get there if you row like that," Big Jimmy yelled at him. Johnny was full blood Indian plus he was his nephew and therefore Big Jimmy thought Johnny should be held to a higher standard, but he also knew Johnny was lazy and race had nothing to do with that. Johnny's dad was lazy too, Jimmy remembered. Johnny shrugged his shoulders and continued on his leisurely pace. Big Jimmy could have parked the boat right next to shore, but he wouldn't because he was afraid he'd hit something underwater or get caught in the net. So if Jimmy was going to play chicken little and make him row half across the ocean, then he was going to do it as slow as humanly possible. Big Jimmy would either see it his way, or he could send Ken out to disconnect the nets.

Johnny rowed as close to the net strand as he could without getting his oars wrapped in the net. He could see a few chum salmon stuck with their gills wedged between the strands of netting. It looked like they would make some money off the fish tonight. He rowed past the dead and dying fish and stopped

143

rowing only when the gravel scrapped against the bottom of the boat. He set the oars down and looked around. A streetlight barely visible behind a tree let just enough light cast down on the beach to let him see without aid of a flashlight. He carefully crawled off of the bow of the boat, stood up, and looked around. A creepy feeling overcame him and he felt like someone was watching him. He looked around but didn't see anyone. An apparently abandoned kayak was beached not too far away. He thought that was strange. He knew that when high tide rolled in, this part of the coastline would be submerged and the kayak would float away. He was halfway tempted to tie it up to the back of his boat and take it back with him, but he knew Big Jimmy would give hive grief over it so he immediately put it out of his mind. He walked some twenty feet over to the embankment and then reached up to where the end of the net was fastened to a loop of steel cable that was embedded into the side of the steep embankment. He heard a car go by on the road some fifteen feet above his head. He unfastened the net from the cable as he heard another car pass by. He heard a noise by the boat and turned around to see what happened. His boat was still resting in the gravel although a wave did make it rock up and down. With the net unfastened, he headed back to his boat. He looked over at the kayak one last time then carefully stepped back inside his boat with one rubber boot and pushed off the gravel with his other boot. The boat rocked back and forth as he sat down and grabbed the oars. Barely ten feet away from shore he stopped rowing for a moment as he noticed that water was seeping in the boat. A small pool of water was forming around his boots. He must have put a hole in the bottom of the boat when he hit the beach, because he was sure it wasn't leaking on his way to shore. For a brief instant, he thought he might be able to row back to the main boat without too much bother, but he changed his mind as he watched the water streaming into the boat. Great, he thought. Now he was going to have to stand on shore and yell like a mad man for Big Jimmy to come and get him. Big Jimmy was going to be pissed when he found out about the rowboat. Johnny slapped the oars against the water and pulled towards shore. The boat should have moved a few feet with each stroke of the paddles, but for some reason the boat only moved a few inches before coming to a complete stop. Johnny dropped the oars and looked down at the water in the boat. It was a good four inches deep around his boots. He looked over the side of the boat and saw the net nestled up against the side of the boat. Some how the boat had become stuck in the net. He couldn't figure out how, but he knew that in another minute or two the boat would take on too much water and capsize. He looked over at the shore just a mere ten feet away then turned back at the fishing boat. He could see Ken on deck looking in his direction.

"Hey Ken," he shouted.

"Yeah?" Ken could see Johnny sitting in the rowboat.

"The boats stuck in the net and taking on water."

"So? Row it on back." The boat looked a little low in the water from where Ken was standing, but not too bad.

"I'm going to swim for shore. Tell Big Jimmy to come pick me up." Ken heard the words but couldn't believe it. Big Jimmy was going to fire Johnny for pulling such a stupid stunt. Jimmy could see Ken walking quickly over to the cabin and mutter something to Big Jimmy. He could see Big Jimmy's hands flail in the air, but Johnny's attention was diverted, as he felt cold water trickle down inside his boot. He could have taken the boots off to help him swim easier to shore, but with only such a short distance to go, he figured his boots would do him more good on shore then out in a sunken rowboat. He heard the fishing boat rev up its engine. Then he saw the last rush of water sweep over the stern of the boat. He gasped for air as the cold water hit his body. He tried to push away from the rowboat so he wouldn't get sucked down with the boat. His arms were strong and he easily moved a few feet towards shore, then suddenly he felt something grab on to his left boot. It had to be the net he thought. He tried to kick free of it, but it held on like a clamped vise. His head went under water and he started to choke on the salty solution. He choked and coughed as he fought to keep his head above the surface. He was strong, but the cold water began to quickly take away his strength. He realized he was going to die if he didn't get his foot free. He kicked as hard as he could, but the water worked against his best efforts. Then he felt his boot being pulled on by some incomprehensible force. He slipped below the surface knowing his last breath of air was almost used up and with his next inhalation his lungs would fill with salt water. He never imagined this would be the way his life would end. He starred up at the surface until his eyes clouded over.

Ken saw Johnny go down with the rowboat. He saw Johnny surface briefly and then he watched with horror as Johnny went back down. It was an impossible sight. Johnny was too good a swimmer. The fishing vessel neared the spot where Johnny went down. Ken took his boots off and jumped over the side of the boat. The water was ice cold, but he didn't have time to think of anything else. He blocked the cold out of his mind and swam to the spot where he last saw Johnny. The shore was less than twelve feet away. There was no way it could be more than eight feet deep here. If he found Johnny soon enough, there was still time to resuscitate him. He took a deep breath and dove under water. His head immediately felt an ice cream headache coming on. He barely swam a few feet when he saw in front of him the dark outline of Johnny's lifeless body. He grabbed hold of Johnny's left arm. With his chest burning for air and his head screaming with pain from the cold, he used his free arm and pushed up towards the surface. He moved more than an arms length, then suddenly he felt a vice like grip on his right ankle and his decent was abruptly halted. For a split second he thought he got stuck in the net, but his ankle hurt too much to be mere pressure from the netting material. Perhaps a shark was attacking him, but he didn't feel teeth or any back and forth chewing motion. He felt nothing but the strong grip around his ankle. He was almost out of air as he looked down below him. In the faint moonlight all he could see was a large dark outline. It scarred him. What ever it was, it had a hold of his ankle and had no intentions of letting go. His lungs were on fire. He needed to breath or he was going to drown. He kicked with all his might, but the density of the water reduced his power and diminished his desperate efforts to free himself. Time seemed to slow down around him. He wondered if this is how Johnny went. He let go of Johnny and took a breath. The salt water initiated his gag reflex as it entered his mouth. The cold liquid filled his lungs quickly.

Big Jimmy cut back on the power, reversed thrust for a brief moment then stopped the engines dead. He caught a glimpse of Ken diving down below the surface. He hoped Ken would reach Johnny in time. He limped out of the cabin and across the deck of the boat. He thought he could help pull Johnny back on the boat. By the time he reached the side of the boat, he couldn't see either one of them. My god he thought to himself. This could not be happening. Then a hand extended above the surface. He ignored the pain and bent over the side of the boat and reached out towards the hand. He made contact with the hand and held it firmly in his hand. Suddenly a blue glove reached out of the water and grabbed hold of his wrist. Before Big Jimmy could figure out what to do next. He felt his body being pulled over the side of the boat. He came down into the water followed by a big splash. The blue glove held onto him tight as it pulled him away from the boat and down underwater. He ignored the cold numbing water. He jerked, twisted, and tried to pull back from the blue glove with all his might. Someone wearing blue gloves was trying to kill him. Why would anyone want to do this to him? He became still as the last air bubbles trickled out from his mouth.

Monday Morning

Steve pulled into the public parking lot adjacent to the dive shop. He saw an Edmonds police car sitting in the front of the store. He wondered what the police were doing down at the shop so early. The last time they were there so early, the front window had been broken and four dry suits, several computers, and a few regulators had been stolen from the shop. The thieves had previously cased the store and knew exactly what they were looking for. They were in and out of the store in less than two minutes. The store alarm had gone off, and the police had arrived within minutes, but by then the thieves were long gone. Metal racks to hold merchandise were installed on all the windows soon after that burglary along with a new alarm system and other unmentionable security enhancements.

Steve pulled into his parking spot behind the dive shop and came around to the front of the building. He recognized the officer in the car. It was Sergeant David Johnson. David had trimmed black hair and mustache. He was a stocky short man with well-developed upper body muscles from years of working on his side business. David was a commercial diver on his days off. He cleaned the undersides of boats sitting in the marinas; he changed heavy propellers, installed zinc blocks, and did all kinds of preventive maintenance to boats while they remained still in their berths. He had a thriving business, but because of his business, he seldom dove for fun, or rarely had a chance to descend more than ten feet under water.

David was currently talking on the police radio as Steve approached the front door to the shop. Steve did a quick cursory inspection and noted that all the windows were still intact. He waved hello at David, and David waved back. Steve unlocked the front door to the shop, stepped in and went to the back room to turn off the alarm system. He then got the change fund and brought it out and set in inside the open till drawer. He turned on the radio, the overhead lights, and set yesterdays receipts on the counter next to the cash machine. The radio was tuned to the sports channel. He started to thumb through the receipts as he listened in on how the Mariners baseball team did over the weekend. They had won the last five out of six games. The

Mariners were typically at the top of the rankings until September. Next Sunday he had tickets to the afternoon game. Beer and hot dogs was his favorite way to spend a day.

David set the radio microphone back down in its cradle. He got out of his car, adjusted his vest, then opened the door and went inside the dive shop.

"Good morning Steve."

"Good morning David. How are you doing today?"

"Oh just fine." David began. "You still going to the game next weekend?"

"I sure am," Steve smiled and replied.

"You know the Yankees are going to beat them." David had to add.

"You know, even if the Yankees spend three times as much money as we do on players, we still beat them close to half the time."

"You've got a good point." David had to admit. He shook his head and looked at Steve. "I wonder how we do it?"

"I'm not too sure either," Steve responded. "But I guess it doesn't really matter as long as they don't run out of beer and hot dogs."

"That's true too." David agreed.

"So what brings you in so early today?" Steve finally asked as he set the receipts aside for the moment.

"It's about Carl," David solemnly replied.

"Oh?" Steve said.

"The coroner says the cause of death was drowning."

"Did he run out of air?" Steve asked.

"No his tank was half full. We checked. We think he drowned while he was unconscious."

"What could have caused that?" Steve asked.

"The coroner said part of his skull was fractured by a large flat surfaced object." David answered.

"You mean like a hammer?" Steve wondered.

"No, more like something flat and wide like my hand." David held up his hand with his fingers spread out wide.

"So you think it was an accident?" Steve was really unsure of where this conversation was heading. He shut the register and stood there waiting to hear what David would say next.

149

"Carl was hit by something with a lot of force while out in the park; the kind of speed and force you just can't deliver underwater. A large baseball bat could have done that degree of damage on land, but underwater you can't swing a bat that hard. The water would slow your swing down to a crawl. You could have something fall on you and crush your head underwater, but how do you crush just the right upper side of your head and not sustain an injury to the other side of the skull?" David said this more to himself than to Steve.

"I have no idea." Steve answered. The two men looked around the shop as if the answer could be found on some portion of a wall. "Do you think he could have been hit head on by a lingcod?" Steve finally broke the silence and asked.

"I doubt it." David stated. The amount of force used almost rules that idea out." Steve cued in on the word "almost". That's all he needed, a fish murdering divers in the park. Business was bad enough when the movie *Jaws* came out. He could close the door and take a long vacation if a rumor spread that some giant lingcod killed a diver.

"So what are we going to do?" Steve asked concerned for the health of the dive shop.

"The department has ruled it a homicide. We've talked to Terry but he doesn't have a motive. He barely knew Carl. He didn't know how big an ass Carl was until that dive, and he still dumped his own gear trying to bring Carl back to shore and save him."

"I heard he did mouth to mouth on the way in." Steve said.

"Mouth to mouth as he took off his gear and brought him to shore and CPR until the ambulance arrived." David added.

"Wow, he sounds like he did a good job." Steve said.

"Not according to him. He thinks he could have saved Carl if he had just gotten to him a little sooner.

"That's too bad," Steve replied.

"I think so too. But now we need all the clues we can get to solve this case." David stated.

"How can I help?" Steve asked.

"We found all the gear except for Carl's mask. The impression on his forehead leads us to believe that the mask may have taken part of the blow. If we can find that mask, we may find another clue to what happened out there."

"I'll keep my eyes and ears open," Steve replied.

"Thanks," David said. "I think I'll go down to the beach and see if I can find anything."

"Thanks David, good luck." Steve really meant it too. The sooner this case was solved, the sooner the rumors would stop and business would get back to normal. David left the shop and got in his car. He turned the motor on and headed down to the park.

The Fishing Net

Dennis pulled over on the side of the road. The sky was overcast and it looked like it would rain any minute. Deputy sheriff Willey stood by his car bundled up in his patrol jacket and holding a cup of coffee that he just poured from his thermos.

"Good morning Willey," Dennis said as he got out of his car. He gave a good cough, and then lit up a cigarette.

"Morning chief."

"Who called it in?" Dennis took a big puff then stepped over to the edge of the embankment and peered down into the water. He could barely make out the white outline of the boat some two feet underwater. The tide moved in and the gravel-laden beach lay underwater also. A radio antenna stuck out above the surface a few feet. He exhaled as he watched a trail of diesel fuel coming up to the surface and drift slowly southward.

"Kevin Greely. He was out on his Kayak when he spotted the slick of diesel fuel. He paddled north to investigate and found the boat."

"Any boats missing?"

"Yeah," Willey said then took a sip of coffee to clear his throat. "Dandy Salmon, didn't show up at the harbor last night. Three tribe members are missing."

"Who are they?" Dennis asked.

"Jim Thorton."

"Big Jimmy?" Dennis asked in surprise.

"I'm afraid so."

"So I bet the other two were Ken Jenson and Johnny Smith."

"You guessed it Chief."

"All three of them were good swimmers. How far out from shore do you think that boat is?"

"I'd say about thirty five feet chief."

"And on a low tide?"

"About fifteen feet chief."

"So we got three able bodied swimmers less than fifteen feet from shore and no sign that they made it to shore."

"That about sums it up chief." Dennis took another long puff then let out a billowing sigh of disappointment.

"Call out the divers, and tell them to expect to find some bodies."

"Got it." Willey went to his patrol car and grabbed his radio mike.

A half hour passed before two trucks pulled up behind them. Hunter Kelso a robust welder and chief diver with biceps bigger than most people's leg muscles got out of one truck and Brian Kirkland a tall volunteer off duty state trooper got out of the other truck.

"What's up Chief?" Hunter asked Dennis. Dennis pointed down at the sunken boat.

"We got a boat right next to shore with possible occupants." Hunter looked down at the boat.

"If we wait a few hours for the tide to go out, we might be able to walk straight out to it," Hunter said.

"Along with any evidence or bodies," Brian added.

"That's what I was thinking." Dennis said.

"Well, let's get going Brian." Hunter turned back towards his truck. In just a short time Hunter and Brian had suited up in their dry suits, strapped a tank and buoyancy compensator on their backs and were walking down a set of rickety old wooden stairs to the water. Willey saw the large knives on their legs and couldn't help comment to Dennis.

"What are those big knives for? Fighting sharks?"

"More like cutting rope." Dennis replied.

"How come you know so much about diving Chief?"

"I used to dive. Cutting a shark puts blood in the water, and that's the last thing you want to happen around sharks."

"I see your point. How come you don't dive anymore?"

"Can't smoke underwater." With that Dennis flicked his cigarette out into the water.

At the edge of the water and while holding on to the bottom of the wooden stairway they talked about how they wanted the dive to go, then each put on their mask and fins. They walked out a good ten feet before the water was up to their waists. They inflated their Buoyancy compensator devices known locally as (BC's), and swam out until they were directly over the boat. The two of them then signaled to one another, deflated their BC's, and slowly descended side by side underwater. As they drifted down below the surface they found they had less than ten feet of visibility. They could see the boat better than they expected. Hunter turned on his dive light and took the lead. Brian switched his light on and trailed right behind him. With a quick glance to the stern of the boat, and a quick look towards the bow, they ruled out the possibility of any deck hands still remaining on the outer deck area. If there was anyone on board, they were either inside the cabin or swept away with the currents. Hunter shined his light inside a forward window of the cabin. Through another window Brian lit up the aft end of the cabin. There were no signs of victims. Hunter tapped Brian on the shoulder and signaled for him to follow. Hunter swam off the deck and went towards the back of the boat. He could see the beam from Brian's light following right behind him. At the stern of the boat he encountered a two foot long Lingcod. Already the local fish were moving in and claiming new territory. The Lingcod was perched on the bulwark cap. Below the long slender brown and black spotted fish, light blue letters spelled out the name of the boat "Dandy Salmon". Hunter turned to go over the fish and the railing and into the cabin when a thin tag line rope he saw out of the corner of his eye half covered with fresh silt caught his attention. The rope trailed on the silt-laden substrate from the other side of the boat then down the sloping landscape back behind the boat. He pointed the rope out to Brian. It was the type of rope you expected to see on a dive reel. Not hanging off the back of a boat. The two divers followed the rope down the contoured slope. They cleared their ears several times as they swam along. At eighty feet below the surface they stopped. The rope kept on going downward. By the dim light of their flashlights they signaled "OK" to proceed and they continued diving down to ninety feet. Hunter's knees began to hurt and then suddenly they popped and the pain was gone. It always happened to him around a hundred feet and he never could get a doctor to tell him why it happened. They always told him that as long as it didn't hurt, he was just going to have to live with it. They checked their depth and air gauges. One hundred and five feet and two thousand pounds of air left in their tanks. The water was pitch black around them. They moved on a few more feet guided by their lights. The reel line came to an end. The line was tied securely to a corner of fishing net. The divers shined their light on the net and both of them froze with eyes wide open and hearts pumping like racehorses about to cross the finish line. There in front of them, balled up in the net, were three bodies with terrified looking expressions permanently etched on their faces. The divers waved their lights over the bodies for a brief second then looked back at his air gauges. Hunter was down to a thousand pounds of air. Brian was down to twelve hundred pounds of air. They signaled to each other to ascend straight up to their first decompression stop at thirty feet. If they had enough air left over when they reached their second decompression stop at fifteen feet they would follow their compass headings back to their original entry point.

When the divers first went underwater Dennis and Wiley could easily see their bubbles on the surface. However, the deeper the divers went the more difficult it was to discern their bubbles from the splash and spray made by the undercurrents and surface ripples.

"Where did they go?" Willey asked. "The boat is right next to shore."

"I don't know. They must have found something worth checking out." Dennis surmised. It was odd for the divers to take off like that.

Around the wreck there were no signs of bubbles, but a loose collection of bubbles a ways out from shore finally caught Dennis's attention.

"I think they're out there." He pointed to the spot. Willey looked out at the general area.

"What are they doing way out there?" Willey asked.

"I'm not sure, but they seem to be coming towards us." They tracked the bubbles until the divers broke the surface. Hunter and Brian inflated their BC's then signaled to shore that they were both "OK". The two of them rolled over on to their backs, put their hands to their sides, and while laying back on the surface they began kicking with their fins and propelling themselves backwards towards shore. Every so often they turned their heads and looked behind them to make sure they were still on course.

Dennis and Wiley went down and waited at the bottom of the wooden steps for Hunter and Brian. As soon as it was shallow enough to stand up the two divers removed their fins and took off their masks. Both divers were quieter than Dennis ever recalled.

"Well?" Dennis prompted.

"We found them. Brian and I will change out tanks and go back and take some pictures. All three of them are set in a net at just over a hundred feet."

"What do you mean set?" Dennis asked as the two divers walked towards them.

"That's the best I can describe them. Most likely they were placed in the net after they died."

"You're saying they were murdered?" Hunter stopped in front of Dennis dripping wet and looked him in the eyes.

"You've got one sick bastard on your hands. I can guarantee it." Dennis and Willey moved aside and let Hunter and Brian step past them on the stairs.

"You think it's related to the "Misty Fog"? Willey said in a hushed tone. Dennis leaned against the rail and looked out into the water.

"I don't know. The men weren't poachers they were Tribal fisherman."

"I know a lot of people that don't like Indian fishing rights."

"That maybe true Willey, but it's never led to murder." Dennis pulled out another cigarette and lit up.

"Chief, you mind if I go get something to eat?"

"Go ahead Willey. I bet it'll be another hour before those two are ready to get back in the water. Oh . . . and give Gordon's office a call."

"Will do Chief." Willey ran up the steps as if he hadn't either eaten all week or he was just making sure Dennis couldn't change his mind and leave him stuck guarding the crime scene all day without anything to eat like he had to the day before. Dennis shook his head in disbelief as he watched Willey practically run to his patrol car. Where was the fire he thought? Willey's patrol car sent gravel in every direction; he drove off in such a hurry. Dennis turned back and gazed out at the water. The saltwater setting was so picturesque and so peaceful that he momentarily forgot it was also the site of a violent crime scene.

The Paper Chase

Dennis sat in his office chair looking through a stack of paperwork that never quite dwindled to nothing before it self-replicated and stacked up again in an uneven pile. From the next room he could hear Mary typing away behind the reception counter. He could also hear Willey's voice crackle on the radio.

"Mary. This is Willey. Over." The staccato noise on the keyboard abruptly stopped.

"Go ahead Willey."

"Gordon's here."

"Roger that Willey." Mary pushed back from her keyboard and started to get up, but stopped when she saw Dennis coming out of his office. He already had his jacket on and was just finishing putting on his hat in place.

"I heard." Dennis replied as he quickly headed down the hall. He reached for a cigarette and placed it between his lips as he exited the back door.

Pulling up on the shoulder of the road he lit another cigarette as he left his car. Willey had put crime scene tape all over the staircase that led down to the water. Gordon's Van was parked next to the stairway. Dennis cringed as he tried to take another puff. The scene looked like an entrance to a circus for news reporters. He took a few puffs off the cigarette to calm himself down before he crossed the street to the big taped off entrance.

"Hi Chief," Willey said as he came marching up the stairs. He was holding a big roll of yellow crime scene tape in his hands. Dennis looked down at Willey's pants. The bottom part of Willey's left leg was soaking wet. Willey suddenly felt embarrassed.

"I fell in."

"Did you tape around the boat too?"

"Chief, the boat's underwater."

"So what stopped you?" Willey just looked at Dennis. He didn't catch the tone of sarcasm in his voice.

"Mind if I go change?"

"Go ahead Willey. I'll see you back at the office."

"Hello Dennis," Gordon said as he came up the stairs.

Willey stepped past Dennis and headed for the back of his patrol car. Dennis met Gordon on the steps and shook his hand.

"You we're quick." Dennis said.

"I thought it best. Two major crime scenes in less than a few days, that's not a good sign."

"I feel the same way." Just then a diver surfaced. It looked like Hunter with his face squished together tightly by his wetsuit hood. This time however, he was wearing dual one hundred cubic foot tanks on his back. He was holding a corner of a fishing net in his hands. Brian surfaced ten feet to Hunters right. He was also holding on to a piece of net. Some ten feet behind them he could see the outlines of three bodies entwined in the net. The divers took off their fins and then their masks.

"I thought I told you to bring them up one at a time," Gordon yelled down to the divers,

"We couldn't," Hunter exclaimed. "Unless you wanted us to wait til tomorrow."

"What do you mean?" Gordon went back down to the bottom step. The gravel beach was covered by just a few inches of water at this point in the tides change.

"Whoever put them in the net put them in securely. We could have cut them out if we had the time and we weren't already saturated with nitrogen. But even then, diving around hundreds of feet of netting at any depth is a dangerous proposition."

"I see your point." Gordon replied. Hunter and Brian waded thru the shallow water until the net began to drag against the bottom. They both then dropped the net and waded towards shore.

"We'll take off our gear then bring up the bodies," Hunter said to Brian. The divers stepped towards the stairs sopping wet and dripping saltwater. Gordon and Dennis moved up the stairs and out of the way.

Hunter and Brian sat down at the back end of their vehicles and unfastened their twin tanks from their backs.

"Now that feels better," Brian finally spoke up. Hunter grinned at him.

"I was wondering why you were so quiet."

"It's the work. Seeing dead bodies always freaks me out." Brian grabbed a bottle of water and sucked it straight down. It freaked Hunter out too, but he was able to put on a better poker face and keep it to himself. He grabbed a water bottle as well, but forced himself to sip on it. He then sat with his eyes closed for a moment trying to relax and clear his mind of any thoughts.

Dennis kept an eye on the bodies while he lit another cigarette. The tide was starting to go out ever so slowly. Gordon went back up the stairs and from the back of the van he pulled out three black body bags. He carried them down the stairs and sat them down next to where Dennis was standing. Hunter and Brian heard Gordon rummage around in the back of his van and then watched him take the body bags down the stairs. They stood up still dressed in their dry suits and stretched, then headed after Gordon. Brian and Hunter passed Dennis and Gordon on the stairs, stepped past them, and sloshed thru the water towards the net. Hunter had a big pair of stainless steel scissors in his right hand. Brian held the net still as Hunter cut the strands of net around the first body. It was like cutting a paper doll outfit. He cut an outline around the body in the net, and when he was finished. The body floated free of the cut out opening. Hunter and Brian lifted the body and placed it in the body bag over on the stairs.

"That would be Johnny Smith," Dennis said solemnly. Johnny had a look of fear frozen on his face.

Gordon zipped the bag up and along with Dennis's help, carried the body bag to the back of the van while Hunter and Brian returned to the task of extracting another victim.

"I'm getting too old for this type of work," Gordon said as they finished loading the body in the van. He notice Dennis looked a little out of breath too.

"If you want I can call Willey back?"

"No don't bother Dennis. It's just my body is giving out on me."

"When are you going to retire Gordon?"

"Never. As long as they can use the help, I'll come. I don't want to retire and then die a few days later. Those statistics people, love that kind of data."

Dennis looked down the side of the embankment. They were just freeing Ken Jensen's body from the net. He could see from here that as death took him, Ken wore a look of panic.

Gordon and Dennis made their way down the stairs as

Hunter and Brian set Ken in the body bag. Gordon did the honors of zipping up the bag. Behind the divers, Dennis could see Jim Thorton floating on the surface. He stared out at nothing in particular with glassy eyes and a look of disbelief etched into his last moments of life. Gordon looked over and pointed.

"If it's ok with Dennis, you guys can zip and bring him up if you would."

"That's fine by me," Dennis quickly seconded. Gordon and Dennis lifted the bag and proceeded to carry it up the steps.

Hunter and Brian brought up the last body bag moments later. Gordon was sitting in the van filling out paper work as Jim's body was placed in the back of the van. Dennis leaned against his patrol car and was lost in thoughts as he smoked another cigarette.

"You know those things will kill you," Hunter came up to Dennis and said after they had put the last of the bodies in the back of the van.

"That's the sad truth," Dennis replied.

"Then why don't you stop?"

"Too late. Hunter." The look in Dennis's eyes told Hunter the rest of the story. Hunter realized he was the first to be let in on a deadly secret. Dennis was dying from cancer. Hunter stood still, stunned by the revelation. There were so many questions to ask, but he knew Dennis didn't want to talk about it. Hunter had a good friend that passed away from cancer. Everyday of his remaining life he spent answering peoples questions about how he felt, explaining what type of cancer he had, and how long the doctors gave him to live. The last thing Dennis wanted to hear was "how do you feel?" every time he bumped into someone.

"Sorry Dennis, but I understand."

"Thanks," Dennis almost whispered.

"No problem. Say, you want to come over to the house tonight? I'm grilling and I only make enough for an army," Hunter added.

"Sounds good."

"Be there around six and tell Willey and Mary too." Hunter didn't include Gordon, because he already knew that Gordon would be back in Olympia in his lab hours before the first burger ever hit the grill.

"Will do," Dennis replied. Hunter started unzipping his

drysuit as he walked over towards his truck. Dennis took two last puffs off of his cigarette then walked over towards Gordon who was just finishing off his paperwork.

"You want to sign some paperwork Sheriff?" Gordon asked as he passed a clipboard out the window.

"Sure," Dennis acknowledged.   Gordon put the keys in the transmission and started the van.

"You leaving already?" Dennis handed back the signed forms as Gordon nodded his head.

"Evidence soaked in saltwater waits for no one."

"You think they might be tied in with the other case?"

"I hope for your sake they're not,' Gordon solemnly replied. "Other wise you've got a cereal killer on your hands and chances are he'll strike again soon."

Stake Out

Back at the office Dennis told Mary about Hunter's invitation then he went to his locker and pulled out some well-worn thirty-year-old hiking boots. Mary stopped and looked at him. She couldn't remember the last time he wore those old things. It had to have been last year when they arrested the elk poacher. Craig Swenson had been shooting elk out of season, smoking the meat, and then selling it along the roadside to passing tourists all right out of the back of his 65 ford truck. Not much overhead, just a cardboard sign "Smoked Buffalo", a plastic bag vacuum sealer, a few labels, and the rest was pure profit . . .that is until they caught him in the act. The locals know the local elk herds. Some of them think of them as pets, and know when they're arbitrarily being thinned out.

"Where are you going?" she asked.

"Up a trail I haven't been on since I was a kid behind the Richter's house."

"Will you be back in time for Hunter's Barbecue?

"I plan to, but I'll be out of contact most of the afternoon." Dennis left with the jacket draped over his shoulder.

A few hundred yards up on a gravel side road he parked the patrol car. Wearing the long coat over his uniform and a large pair of binoculars he headed up the hill and straight through a patch of blackberry bushes. Farther up the hill he made his way through a group of Douglas fir trees some forty feet in height. Thirty years ago this area had all been logged and the most of the former stumps had decayed or were grown over. They didn't leave any old growth trees standing in those days. Everything was cut and everything now growing looked to be the same height. The lack of old natural trees falling over and resting on the forest floor made it easy to hike up and over to the next hill which was really his main goal. Two hours later he had reached the spot he had in mind. He laid his coat down on the ground next to an overhang. On his belly and next to the edge of the cliff that he dared, he took the binoculars out and peered down at the valley. He could make out the Richter house as well as a few other houses down below. A few houses had tendrils of smoke rising out of their chimneys, but the Richter house looked void of life. On the other side of the Richter house and not too far up the shorter far side ridgeline Dennis could just make out a few wisps of smoke; the kind made by a small campfire. Bingo, he thought to himself. If he hurried, he could make it down to the site in no time, but this task at hand required the skills needed to stalk a skittish deer and he had learned to do that growing up in these woods, and this skill took as much time as the landscape dictated. He moved slow and softly a good two hours.

Sheriff Down

The tall figure walked into the clearing carrying a bundle of firewood he had gathered up in the next ravine.

"Sheriff. Don't move or I'll shoot," Dennis called out. The man stood still and looked around for the best direction to run. "Three steps and your legs will give out. It's the bullets, not the gun that hurts people." Dennis said as he stepped out from behind a nearby tree with his gun drawn. "Why don't you just drop that wood and take a rest."

"I see you still have the same sense of humor, Dennis." Dennis recognized the voice right away.

"So it's you Claus?" Dennis sat down on a stump about twenty feet away with the gun still trained on Claus.

"Yeah, I've come back from the dead. Sort of."

"To do a little murder of your own. Sort of."

"I can explain Dennis."

"I'm sure you can . . . If I got this right, you killed Frankie for hitting on your wife."

"No, he was using my boat."

"But you we're dead."

"And so is he." Carl sat back, stretched out his legs, and leaned back on his elbows. Dennis rested the gun on his leg but still kept his finger on the trigger.

"And Big Jimmy, Johnny, & Ken?"

"Big Jimmy recognized me the other day. Simple as that."

"So who is next on your list?" Dennis had to ask.

"No one in particular. As long as I can make some money under the table, I plan on reforming and becoming a peaceful law abiding citizen."

"And no more killing Nancy's boyfriends or locals that recognize you?"

"Something like that." Claus said as he lay down and looked up at the overcast sky. Dennis finally stood up and stretched.

"You mind turning over so I can handcuff you? I have to take you in even if you are a changed man." Claus did as instructed. Dennis put his gun back in its holster. He put the cuffs on Claus and then helped him up to his feet. Claus noticed a weird expression on Dennis's face, like the kind you get just before your going to kill someone.

"Something bothering you Dennis?" Dennis nodded.

"Yeah, something's bothering me. I thought the killings were leading up to something. Like in those mystery books. Like first it was the geoduck collectors, next the native salmon fishermen, and next perhaps the Makah tribe whale hunters. You know like a progressive racially over toned environmental stakes challenge."

"Sorry to disappoint you Dennis."

"It's not you fault. It's just that you've got the perfect cover, being dead already and all. You could be the perfect assassin for all the gluttonous CEOs."

"All the CEOs?" Claus asked.

"No, I guess not."

"I'm not sure I follow you." Claus moved his wrists so the cuffs wouldn't fee so tight. Dennis motioned for them to start walking down a well-worn trail as he continued.

" Just the new wave CEOs. The ones that come join an already existing company, reduce the employee's wages or lay them off, then steal money from the company legally by calling it a bonus. They ruin thousands of lives, but nobody takes them out because all the worker bees have families and can't afford the jail time."

"So who should take them out?"

Dennis suddenly stopped and looked at Claus. Claus stopped too.

"Someone like you Claus. You're dead as far as records go, you have no immediate family, and you've already shown a skill, if not passion, for killing people. There's even a chance certain people or unions would pay to get rid of those CEO's. You could become a sort of covert CEO market regulator."

"Doesn't sound like me." Claus stated

"And that's why I have to drag you in; just another case of good talent going to waste. You didn't even take out one filthy rich oil exec, just some guys barely making ends meet." Dennis motioned for Claus to begin moving along again.

"Sorry Dennis."

"That's O. . . The "k" never left his lips. Claus head butted him so hard that they both fell over on the trail. Dennis was knocked unconscious. Although dizzy, Claus found the keys to the handcuffs and set himself free.

As Dennis woke up, he felt a pain surging inside his head. He saw his handcuffs lying on the ground with the keys next to them. Taking a quick survey, he found his gun still in his holster. Claus had hit him and took off, and from the looks of the setting sun, Claus had a few hours head start on him. Dennis reached inside his coat pocket and found it was empty. Great, he thought, not only did he loose a suspect already in handcuffs, but he received a concussion, missed the grill party, and had his cigarettes and lighter stolen as well. But what puzzled him the most was why Claus had spared his life?

Poachers

FBI agents had surrounded Kevin's truck and they were firing at will. Bullets whizzed by his face, tore through metal, and broken glass rained down on top of his sleeping bag. Kevin bolted strait up to a sitting position and opened his eyes. He immediately focused on the small paper bag left by the foot of his sleeping bag. He ignored the paper bag on purpose, but he was very aware that all was quiet around him. He was breathing heavily from the dream and it took a moment for Kevin to calm himself down. He had had this dream or one with a similar theme for the past two weeks. He yawned then looked at his watch. It was five PM and time to get something to eat. He got out of his sleeping bag. He was still wearing the clothes that he had on the night before. He smiled when a thought crossed his mind. It occurred to him that the only difference between him and the homeless was that he had the privilege of sleeping in the back of a truck instead of under a bench or behind a bush. It wouldn't be long until all this changed he thought to himself.

He found a packet of beef jerky in the back seat and began chewing on a dried out chunk. He washed it down with a can of warm orange soda. Having eaten, he opened the paper bag and took out the contents. He held a small device in his hand. He took the device over to his dive gear and placed it in one of the side pockets of his BC. He then hauled his gear down to the water's edge, sat down on his tailgate, and waited.

About a half hour later, Blackbeard approached him in the skiff. He rode the skiff up to shore and it came to rest right next to Kevin's dive gear. If the skiff had touched Kevin or his gear, Kevin was ready to deck him.

"I'm late, so you've got second shift tonight. We're having trouble with the motor. Grab you're gear and hop in." This was definitely not what Kevin wanted to hear. He put his gear on board and climbed in.

"What's wrong with it?" Kevin asked. Blackbeard shrugged his shoulders.

"Don't know, otherwise I would have fixed it. I'll take a look at it while you guys are diving." With that said, he gunned the engine and off they went across the bay. Kevin looked back towards shore. He realized that he left the back end open on his truck. He didn't mean to do that and it especially was not a good night to be making any mistakes.

Halfway across the bay the motor began to sputter. Blackbeard throttled back on the engine and it seemed to help stabilize the sound of the engine. But as they neared the workboat, even at reduced speed, the engine started to sputter.

"What's wrong with it?" the captain asked as the skiff came to rest against the side of the workboat.

"Not sure," Blackbeard replied. Kevin began placing his equipment on the workboat.

"Have it fixed soon," the captain ordered. He then walked away. He didn't even seem to notice Kevin's presence. It was better that way. The less any one knew about the operation, the better it was for all.

Kevin began to get his gear ready. Before he zipped up his dry suit, he took a quick leak over the side of the boat. It always felt good to Kevin to relieve himself as he viewed the last rays of light over the horizon. As he zipped his suit up, he glanced over towards the nearest shore and suddenly saw the white and gray spotted head of a harbor seal pop up above the surface. The harbor seal looked towards Kevin, and then went back underwater. Harbor seals can hold their breath for close to thirty minutes. They exhale right before they dive and they store oxygen in the blood and muscle tissues rather than in the lungs like humans do. Seals have a greater concentration of myoglobin in their blood, where oxygen is stored and they also have a greater blood volume than similar sized land mammals. They can drop their heart rate as they dive from 120 beats per minute down to 6 beats per minute. They shunt blood away from their extremities and their organs including their heart, their brain, and unlike humans, they can tolerate low levels of oxygen. By doing all this they can dive longer and dive deeper than any human ever thought possible. Some harbor seals have dove close to three hundred feet deep. They stay warm during all these events not by using their hair as a layer of protection like land restricted mammals, but by the insulation properties of their blubber that they retain under their skin which in the winter time can make up 30% of their body mass. Seals in general have a high metabolic rate in order to heat up their bodies. This means they need to eat more than a similar sized land mammal just to keep their fire stoked; to do this they eat anything that fits into their mouth, is fun to chew on, tastes good, looks colorful, looks like a fish, looks like a clam, moves like a crab, or sits still like a rock. They ultimately test and come to recognize the world around them by way of mouth.

Kevin owned a pair of green fins that had teeth marks all over the tips. The green neon color of his fins used to drive the harbor seals crazy. They would sneak up behind him while he dove and nip at his fins. When he turned around, they would swim off in a flash. When he moved on, they returned to nip again. He didn't mind harbor seals the same way he did stellar sea lions, because stellars concentrated on eating salmon and anything that competed directly against him for salmon was not fit to live. The only exception to this rule was killer whales. On the one hand, the resident populations of killer whales ate salmon, but the transient populations of killer whales ate seals and squids. A small pod of transient killer whales could clean out five hundred seals before moving on to another location. They, in effect, kept the seal populations in balance and therefore were good for salmon populations. Kevin had witnessed a killer whale chasing a seal up in Alaska. The sea lion jumped clear out of the water and into a nearby fishing boat. The sea lion slide across the deck and fell into a hold filled with salmon. The sea lion got so scared it went into shock and refused to budge. With teeth that could crush through human bones, the seal's state of panic was dealt with very carefully. Those fishermen lost half a day's pay by having to stop fishing while they figured out a way to get the eight hundred pound seal out of the hold. Kevin would have just shot it and dragged it over the side where the killer whale was patrolling.

Kevin saw the seal's head pop up again farther away from the boat. It appeared that their underwater operation was just too noisy for the creature and that was fine by Kevin. He turned his attention back to his gear and finished getting his equipment ready and set in place. Another diver came out of the cabin wearing an old orange and black rubberized Viking dry suit. It was the kind with the old inflation valve that was notorious for popping off in the middle of a dive. Kevin couldn't believe what else the guy was wearing. He had an old steel seventy-two cubic foot tank fixed to an old widow maker style harness and an old Tabata regulator. Kevin bet the regulator breathed like a pig. Having to work to get air out of a regulator was not his idea of a fun time. Tabata upgraded their equipment when the company changed names and became TUSA years ago. The guys steel seventy-two cubic foot tanks haven't been used much in the last fifteen years. Kevin figured that most of the guy's gear was over twenty years old. There was no way Kevin would ever dive using gear that old, that was just asking for trouble. Besides, where would the guy ever get spare parts or find someone still qualified to do repair work on such old equipment?

The diver noticed Kevin staring at his equipment, but his gear configuration had served him well for quite some time and by now he had become accustomed to the ribs and teases he got when divers first viewed his equipment. A car as old as his dive gear would have been considered a classic, but life support equipment old as his got little respect from fellow divers. He happened to look over at Kevin's dive gear and wanted to ask him about it, but he knew you were better off not talking to or getting close to anybody on this operation. Instead he turned toward the water and said in a hushed voice, "I sure could use a smoke right now". Kevin didn't answer. He didn't think about the fact that the flash of a match would make them stick out in the water like a lighthouse. What bothered him were divers who smoked. Divers who smoked were taking a heck of a risk underwater. The chemicals in cigarettes on the surface took years to destroy your body, but those same chemicals in your lungs at fewer than sixty feet of depth could take their toll much faster. At a hundred plus feet of depth the increased partial pressure of those chemicals could kill you. Perhaps smoking and depth wouldn't affect every addicted diver, but who wanted to go deep after a quick smoke only to find out that this time around depth and partial pressures of tobacco related chemicals proved to be lethal a combination?

Kevin and the other diver sat next to their gear and waited. There were two divers down already, and soon as they popped their heads out of the water, Kevin and the other diver would take their place. Blackbeard hoisted the collection baskets, dumped the contents on the deck, and lowered the baskets back in the water. Kevin and the other diver watched as Blackbeard placed the mostly six to ten pound geoducks on wet paper towels inside the plastic storage bins. Blackbeard had just finished placing the filled crates under the tarp, when the motor on the water pump shut off. Kevin immediately knew what that meant. Two divers below would be left on the bottom with no means of excavating the geoducks save for waving their gloved hands. Blackbeard dropped the tarp and ran. By the time he got to the water pump, the captain had already found the problem.

"The pump motor's frozen," the captain said. "I can't fix it. It'll have to be replaced."

"What do you want us to do?" Blackbeard asked.

"Pull up the hoses. We're done for tonight." The captain replied.

Blackbeard came on deck to deliver the bad news.

"You can put away your dive gear. The water pump's dead." Stunned by the news, Kevin just sat there and looked at him in disbelief.

"There goes our pay," the other diver complained. The other diver turned to disassemble his equipment. Blackbeard gave a subtle yank on each of the air hoses, and then waited for each hose to go slack. He reeled in both air hose lines and water hose lines while the two divers down did their safety stops. As he started to raise the collection baskets he noticed that Kevin hadn't moved. Kevin wasn't sure what to do at this point. He didn't see Blackbeard work much on the skiff, and now it was tied to the back of the workboat.

"What's the matter? Aren't you going to pack up?" Blackbeard asked.

"Did you get the skiff working?" Kevin asked.

"No, but what's that got to do with anything?" Blackbeard questioned.

"We're going to have a full boat of people towing a skiff in the middle of the night. If that doesn't catch the eye of the coast guard, then I don't know what will." Kevin fumed.

"So what? You going to sit there geared up till we reach shore?" Blackbeard asked. He began to hoist up one of the collection baskets.

"That's my plan. And if I see any boat approach us, I'm going over the side." Kevin answered. Blackbeard shook his head.

"You are more paranoid than the captain." Blackbeard said.

"I've got a record. I can't afford a second strike."
Blackbeard shook his head.

"Fine, suit yourself, but don't expect us to come look for you after you jump over board." Blackbeard stated.

"Not too worry, if I go overboard, no one will find me," Kevin replied. The captain came over to help haul up the other collection basket. He heard the last part of their conversational exchange. He shook his head too. Divers thought they were all superman he thought to himself. The sooner the other two divers surfaced and they were out of here the better for everyone concerned.

As soon as the other divers had returned to the boat they took off with the broken down skiff in tow behind them. All the divers save for Kevin went down below to sit around and drink coffee. Kevin stayed on deck and kept his eyes peeled for boat lights. The captain looked back once to check on Kevin and noticed that he had moved to the back of the boat next to the tarp covering the crates. Maybe he thought the view was better at the stern, the captain didn't really care. A small-unmarked boat passed by them but far enough away so the captain couldn't see any occupants looking their way.

"That's strange to see a small boat like that out here at this hour." The captain half muttered to himself. He peered at it with his binoculars. He still couldn't see anyone on deck. The boat passed on by. The captain then looked back and found that Kevin was nowhere in sight.

"Go back there and see where that idiot's gone to." The captain ordered Blackbeard.

"I'll find him," Blackbeard muttered. He was mad that he had to go check in the first place. Kevin was beginning to be a pain in his neck. Blackbeard stepped out of the bridge and went to the stern of the boat. He came back to the bridge in a hurry.

"He's gone." Blackbeard exclaimed.

"I'll be damned," said the captain. Then as an after thought, "Did he leave anything?"

"Nope, took all his gear and vanished." Blackbeard answered.

"All because of a little boat?" the captain asked.

"You know divers. They get spooked easily. He probably figured that since two things had gone wrong, a third was bound to happen," Blackbeard replied.

"Let's hope for his sake he isn't right." The captain muttered.

"Do you think he'll be all right out there?" Blackbeard asked.

"It's where he's most comfortable." The captain admitted. "Damn idiot probably thinks he's some kind of Navy seal."

Kevin rolled back and off the side of the boat as soon as he saw the small craft. He had been strategically seated and patiently waiting for such an excuse. He hit the water hard and was initially tugged back into the boats wake. He went under water just enough to make sure the trailing skiff wouldn't run him over, then he came back up to the surface after the sound of the boats engine subsided. He inflated his BC on the surface and spit out his regulator. He looked at his compass to get a fix on where he was, and then he started slowly kicking his fins. It was going to take the rest of the night to swim towards the far shore, but time was something he currently had plenty of to spare.

Earlier he had planted a small transponder in one of the crates near the stern of the boat between the wet paper towels that the geoducks rested on. His original plan was to hide the device, get back on the skiff at the end of his shift, and get away from the entire clandestine operation. He didn't know when the Feds were going to show up. He just knew that he didn't want to be there when they intervened. He had done what was expected of him, and after that, his participation in the operation was finished. He slowly kicked through the small choppy waves. Keeping a steady pace was the main thought on his mind now, once he got through the boating lanes he figured the water would flatten out and the rest of the distance could be covered more efficiently. The current seemed to be going his way at least for the time being. He looked up at the stars through his mask. He figured a couple of hours to swim across the gap of a few miles including drift, and then a short distance to hitch hike back to his truck. Who could resist picking up an unshaven guy dripping salt water, wearing a dry suit, and smelling like seaweed on the side of a dark road? With what he had going for him, he could afford to be picky. Maybe even let a few cars pass by until a blonde in a

Ferrari pulled over and gave him a lift. It could happen, provided she wasn't a serial killer. Without warning, he suddenly bumped against something hard. It just about made him jump out of his dry suit. All of a sudden he didn't feel quite so safe or brave. The waters up here were home to a very ancient line of shark called "six gills"; modern sharks only had five gills. Kevin had seen the ancient gray fifteen-foot long creatures scavenging for food at deeper depths. At a hundred and seventy five feet one even bumped into Kevin's dive light once just to check him out. He rarely saw them shallower than eighty feet deep. Six gills besides the obvious have blunt noses and the dorsal, or top fin, is located back closer to the tail than in the center of the top like you see in modern sharks. The dorsal fin is small too. So small, that you might not even see it on the surface passing between small waves. Their body plan allows them to eat from any angle or position including straight downward. They can point straight down and hover above a dead seal lying on the substrate and keep chewing away until their extended stomach can not accommodate any more food. Nothing goes to waste in these waters and six gills are great bottom feeders, cleaners, and recyclers.

What bothered Kevin was that fishermen using surface lines had caught six gills at night. They may come up at night to feed on squid or other fish, but the true story on their feeding habits was still open to investigation and interpretation. Kevin braced himself for another bump or bite. Another half hour of swimming passed by and suddenly he felt another bump. A rush of adrenaline went through his body as he quickly rolled over to find himself staring face to face with a menacing and jagged branch of a drift log. He shook his head and tried to calm himself back down to normal. That's all he needed he thought; unprovoked attacks from killer logs. Where's the theme music to the movie *Jaws* when you needed it?

The Barge

Ian placed the fifty-gallon barrel on the hand truck and carefully wheeled it down the ramp. Although it was only half full it still took all his strength just to keep it under control. If he lost his grip or the weight became too great, he would be left helplessly watching the barrel roll down the ramp and into the water. There was no way he would ever allow that to happen. He needed the barrels and their contents for a rather diabolical purpose he thought up all by himself.

He rolled the barrel down the ramp and then up a short plank onto a thirty-foot barge. The barge was old but it made a stable platform when working around other boats. He had it hauled down to the marina two days ago and the manager of the marina still hadn't appeared to notice or say anything about the derelict vessel. The spot where it was presently berthed belonged to a family and owners of a thirty-six foot sail boat. Every year they sailed away for the summer. They left in early June and they were back by late August. Their two teenage sons worked the boat while the parents no doubt enjoyed the scenery. The family usually went up as far as Sitka Alaska before turning around and retracing their wake created foam back down the Puget Sound. The sons told Ian all about the whales, eagles, and dolphins they saw along the way. The family had done this trip three years in a row, but on the last trip, they encountered some derelict logs that hit the boat during the middle of a small storm. The boat was struck mid cabin and in the stern. The outboard engine was crippled. They managed to limp back into port under sail and the boat's been in dry dock ever since. The cracks in the boat had been patched up, and the motor re-welded and refitted with a new stainless steel propeller, but the boat wouldn't be put back in water for another month or so according to the guys who worked on the boat. Ian let down the barrel on the deck. He had twenty-five barrels on the barge. He could put more onboard, but he wasn't sure if he had either the time or the energy. He would just have to make due with what he had gathered so far. The barrels contained old oil, toxic chemicals, and discarded paint. No one bothered to find out what he was doing, and when his plan came to fruition, he would deny the whole event. He looked over at the boat tied next to the barge. The boat was a Nordic tug over thirty-nine feet long. The Nordic tugs were built to handle just about any marine conditions and still keep on going.

The owner of the boat passed away from a heart attack two months ago. The widow hadn't stepped aboard the boat since her husband's death. Ian told her he would run the motor every so often if she wanted him to. She accepted the offer and thanked Ian profusely. Now he looked over at the Nordic tug as if it was his very own property. He even thought of legitimately buying it from the widow once he got her to bring down the asking price. With a little more time and a few more things going wrong on the boat, she might even ask him to take it off her hands for next to nothing. Things at the moment couldn't be going better he thought.

He moved the hand truck out of the way and then went down into the hull of the barge. There was a small room in the hull. A bottle of whiskey was sitting on a metal counter top. The only other item in the small room was a first aid kit on a top cabinet shelf. Ian figured that if he took out the first aid kit, then something tragic would happen to him. So he left it in the same place where it had sat for at least eleven to twelve years. Ian took the bottle of Jack Daniel's whiskey; he removed the lid, and took two good-sized gulps. He felt immediate warmth engulf his throat and stomach. That really hit the spot he thought to himself. Things were working out beautifully.

Wednesday At The Park

Jarred and Christie were both advanced and nitrox certified divers. Their jobs with a local software company provided them with more than enough money to spend on all the latest high tech scuba toys. They both wore brand new crushed neoprene dry suits, titanium regulators, shinny high-pressure steel tanks and the latest in streamlined BC's. They both carried halogen lights and computers that could read and calibrate two mixtures of gas besides the one in their tank, which currently was 36% oxygen. The way they looked at it, if plain ordinary air in their tanks was good, then 36% oxygen was even better. Enriched air fills didn't cost much more than a regular air fill. Cost conscious divers might have argued that enriched air cost more than double the price of a regular air fill, but the price of an air fill was so cheap that the doubling in price didn't really matter to them. To fill a scuba tank with air in Seattle cost about the same or less than an espresso coffee and they drank several espressos a day.

Once a diver got certified and put in a modest initial investment, a diver could get by with basic gear for years. A diver could frequent local dive spots, carry his own lunch, and a weekend of diving would cost no more than a few air fills and gas for the car. Diving realistically only got expensive when you wanted to dive around the world, spend a week on a live aboard vessel, or spend a few weeks in Guam, Truk, or Palau. A skier on the overhand, after making their initial investment in gear, had to pay for lift tickets every time they went to the mountains. Ski resorts are famous for higher priced food and lodging; not all, just most. Diving was also easier on your body than skiing. Money aside, another benefit was that once your knees gave out on the ski slopes, you could still discover the world underwater.

More importantly, sports like skiing were seasonal, where diving was all year round with the best visibility actually during the winter months. The main attraction with diving was discovering for one's self what was under seventy five percent of the earth's water coated surface. Being underwater is a humbling experience. While we may think we are the dominant life form on this planet, underwater we are just an oddity to be avoided, tolerated, used for shade, or scrutinized. We feel like empowered giants as we swim over the tiny shrimp, but looking right in the eye of a gray whale reminds us of our own limitations and insignificance in the grand scheme of things underwater. And most importantly once underwater, no longer do we worry about our jobs, bills, or possessions. Suddenly, all our attention is focused on a starfish slowly moving along on its tube feet trying to find a clam close to the top of the substrate. We pass by a Dungeness crab scurrying away from us but inadvertently heading in the same direction we are kicking with our fins. A few fish come into view and then we see a boat or two that were sunk years ago. Before you know it, you have been mesmerized for over the past hour and it's time to make your way back to the surface near shore. You feel energized after seeing nature's beauty, and you want to go down again, just as soon as you can get your hands on another tank of fresh air, find another dive buddy, or what ever it takes to get you back under as soon as possible. Diving on air is addicting, and watching creatures survive and even thrive in the cold waters off the pacific coast makes the diving even that much more spectacular.

Jarred and Christie couldn't wait to get back in the water. They helped each other put on their tanks and made sure all they had all their gear adjusted just the way they liked it. They talked about the dive plan since last night, so there wasn't much to cover before they made their way down to the water. They were going out to the Triumph. They would follow Jetty Way out west turn right on Northern lights, go north until they hit Cathedral Way, turn left and continue west again until they found a small trail running north. From there, they would swim a few kick strokes north, and turn on a trail that was made up of five or so red oblong cinder blocks. At the end of that short trail, they would run right into the back section of the Triumph.

Jarred and Christie followed their dive plan and ended up looking up and over the starboard side of the Triumph. Anemones hung to the east side of the wreck. Shrimp filled all the cracks and crevices, and smaller varieties of marine life spilled out of the recesses too small for the shrimp to occupy. The two divers compared air gauges then they swam northward towards the bow of the boat examining all the tons of life along the way. They stopped to look at colorful flat worms and starfish, but they mostly liked the colorful patches of sponges and bryozoans. If Picasso could have painted underwater, this is what his work would most likely resemble.

They turned the corner at the bow and were presented by a bleak port side or west side where the currents slammed into the side of the hull and made it impossible for all except the hardiest of creatures to claim as their home. On this side of the wreck boards were slowly pried and separated by the relentless pounding of the currents over the course of months from the main structure. Shrimp filled all these crevices and an assortment of fish swam close to where the shrimp gathered. If for a split second, a wave rocked a shrimp off of its perch, a fish was there to consume it in one split gulp. Even walking along in the sand shrimp were in danger. Translucent stubby nose squid, which as adults are no bigger than your thumb, would spring out of their hiding spots in the sand and ensnare the unlucky transgressors.

Shrimp didn't live long in the park, but they could reproduce faster than they could be eaten. Billions and billions of shrimp over millions and millions of years spoke well for their story of reproduction success. Shrimp had undergone hardly any physical changes since before the dinosaurs roamed also said something for their basic design success rate. A new species of shrimp might appear in the Puget Sound over the next couple of million years, but by then, mankind with all it's intellect and with less than a measly seven million years of trial and error may have already passed on with all the other species the shrimp had collectively out lasted or watched come and go.

On this side of the boat clown nudibranchs with white bodies and orange colored tips paired up to reproduce. These nudibranchs are hermaphroditic; each one has both male and female sexual organs. They circled each other, climbed over one another, and produced clusters of lattice linked white tiny eggs.

The sand next to the hull of the ship formed a small indentation where a large red rock crab patrolled and defended against the encroaching shrimp. Four years ago the Triumph tugboat wreck had a main cabin and a second floor bridge. Close to two years ago, the cabin caved in after a rough stormy night and only the forward wall of the bridge remained in tact. The wall standing some fifteen feet tall made a great background for silhouette pictures. The window frames had small pieces of seaweed hanging from all sides and fish swam through the window openings with the sun and surface making a natural background lighted spectacle. But all this ended last year when another storm tore down the last standing wall. Now the Triumph was battered down to the main hull and on the main deck, part of the cabin's floor had caved in and sunk inside the hull. Part of the cabin and bridge tumbled over the side and lay in the surrounding sand.

Jared and Christie were hovering over the cabin debris that still clung to the main body of the ship by half broken timbers and half lay in the sand. Christie suddenly spotted something that looked out of place. It looked like a little fish attached to a silver swivel. As she swam closer she could see a piece of clear line drifting behind the silver swivel. It was a fishing lure! She had found a fishing lure in a marine reserve. She suddenly clenched her jaw and shook her head. She tapped Jarred on the shoulder and pointed at what she had found. He looked at the lure and smiled. He quickly pulled out his knife and pried the three-prong hook out of the wood. He held it up for both of them to examine it. The lure was brand new and didn't have any rust on it. He thought it was a great find and he gave Christie the "OK" sign with his free hand. Christie rolled her eyes and shook her head. He didn't get it at all. He saw it as a piece of treasure, not a disgusting sign that someone was poaching in the park. Men were wired so differently she thought. The differences never ceased to amaze her. Having a minor in human behavior didn't prepare her at all for what life would be like with Jarred. She watched as Jarred put the trophy lure inside his pocket. He could buy hundreds of this type of lure with the money they made, but this like so many other past found objects would most likely become one of his favorites, and he didn't even like to fish. He'd better enjoy it while it lasted, because sometime in the next couple of years she would give it away to the Salvation Army, just like all the other things he managed to bring home.

The two of them continued around the Triumph and near the propeller they checked their air pressure gauges once again. They both had plenty of enriched air to make it back to shore underwater. They swam around the Cathedrals on their way back in and then they turned directions by forty-five degrees and kicked over to the Jackson. They crossed the bow and made their way over to the boat yard. They then headed east on Jetty Way back to shore. As they swam close to the Jetty, they turned south and curved around the rocks until they entered the little bay in front of the dressing rooms and the parking lot. They finally popped their heads out of the water and stood up when the water was only up to their chests. Christie was the first to spit her regulator out of her mouth.

"That was great!" she exclaimed. "Those nudibranchs were everywhere."

"Yeah," Jarred replied. "I've never seen'em laying eggs before."

"Shower first?" she asked. Jarred nodded in agreement. They took off their fins and walked through the water and up the beach to rinse off under the outdoor shower station. They both knew how fast you could ruin your gear if you didn't rinse off the salt as soon as possible. They stood under the outdoor showers while wearing all their gear and did a quick rinse. Pieces of brown kelp and lengths of sea grass slide down the sides of their drysuits and ran down the drain. Some of the Isopods and other small animals would tenaciously cling on to their gear until they got home. Jarred once even found a good-sized shrimp tucked inside a BC pocket as he was retrieving a small flashlight in the comfort of his garage.

After they turned off the showers they headed over to their brand new Chevy Tahoe. Standard procedure for Jarred was to rinse off both sets of dive gear at the dive site followed by letting the gear soak in warm water once they got home while Christie got the hot tub running and set out a tray of wine and snacks. First they'd drink a glass of Shiraz, then switch to a nice Chardonnay. Diving, followed by wine, and hot tubs had become a weekly ritual for the young couple.

Jarred was just helping Christie take off her tank when he saw Tom drive into the parking lot and park right next to them. Jarred and Christie knew all about Tom and his volunteers because of their instructor Phil who used to be an instructor in Bellingham for Adventures Down Under. Adventures Down Under is owned and operated by Ron Akeson. Ron had known Tom for a long time and had helped him in one capacity or another over the years. If you made a list of names in the Pacific Northwest dive community and drew lines between people who knew other instructors and dive shop owners, you would end up with a wall that looked something similar to a giant spider web. Ron Akeson for example is one of the top technical dive instructors in the northwest. He is crossed trained by more diving agencies than most divers even know exist. He's trained the owner of Diver's Inn in Hoodsport, who in turn has trained instructors in Edmonds and the greater Seattle area of which one of them was Phil who taught Jarred and Christie in their open water class. Betty Pratt the author of numerous books on northwest diving is close friends with Ron and still consults with Ron to this very day on upcoming books and possible new dive sites. There were literally thousands of well-known people that either knew Ron or Tom on a first name basis. If you go past Canada and up to the far end of Alaska, and you still couldn't break the chain of names. Divers up in Alaska may never have heard of Edmonds underwater park, but Ron Akeson flew up to Alaska a couple of times a year to teach tech dive instructors and every time he went up to Canada with his rebreather equipment, a crowd of divers quickly gathered around the van to see the ultimate in dive gear being used by someone who enjoyed sharing his knowledge and enthusiasm for diving to anyone willing to listen or show interest. Thus, you can see why, that after a short introduction period, everyone in the dive industry seems to know everyone else.

Tom got out of his truck and went back to open his tailgate.

"Hi Tom," Christie said.

"Hi," Tom answered. He vaguely remembered ever meeting them.

"What are you up to today?" she continued.

"Oh, just dropping off some more blocks." He answered.

"Did you have a good dive?"

"Oh, we had a blast." She answered. "And we found something you might be interested in." Tom set the wheel barrel down on the ground, stopped, and stepped over to the two divers.

"Oh, what did you find?" Tom asked.

"Go ahead and show him," Christie told Jarred. Jarred by now had taken off his BC and had to turn it over to find the correct pocket. He unzipped the pocket and pulled out the fishing lure.

"Christie found it on the Triumph. It was stuck in a piece of wood. I had to use my knife to pry it free," Jarred explained.

Tom looked at the lure. It was the same type his brother liked to use.

"You found a glow in the dark minnow." Tom stated.

"I think someone was fishing in the park," Christie spoke up.

"I think you're right." Tom responded. "And from the looks of it, they didn't do it too long ago."

"I think that's down right disgusting." Christie said.

"Whoever's doing it, they're taking a big risk." Tom interjected.

"Good, I hope they get caught soon." Jarred said. Tom was just about to turn back to his task at hand, when he stopped because of a sudden thought.

"Do you mind if I keep that for a few days?" Tom asked Jarred.

"Not at all." Jarred replied. He handed Tom the lure by the attached short strand of string.

"Thanks." Tom took hold of the string and carried the dangling lure back to his truck. He set it down in the corner next to the wheel well and began loading cement blocks on his wooden wheel barrel. He started wheeling four blocks at a time on the wheel barrel. As he reached the beach behind the restrooms on his second trip his wheel barrel dug into the sand and the rusted frame finally gave way and broke in two. The rusted wheel folded under the wheel barrel and he was stopped dead in his tracks. He figured it would happen someday, but he was hoping just to get a little more use out of the homemade contraption before it broke for good. He pushed the blocks into the sand and turned the wheel barrel over. He smiled when he saw that it was just a support rod that had given way. He could take that home and solder it back in place if he could find any metal left under all the rust.

He finished carrying the blocks down to the water line then dragged his wheel barrel back to his truck. As he got in his truck and looked down at the floor bed to his surprise he found the lure was no longer there. He looked around, but no one was near the truck. Jarred and Christie had left the park and were already on their way home for fine wine and hot jets of water. Few other people were in the parking lot and most of those people were parked down by the park's entrance. He got out of the truck and walked around to the passenger side. There on the ground almost under his front right tire was the lure. If he had backed up just a little, this one piece of evidence would have been destroyed. How it got there he hadn't a clue.

Back to Kevin's Boat

With the wheel barrel out of commission Tom packed it all up and left the parking lot. His first stop would be Everett. He only knew one person who had the gall to fish in a marine reserve. Kevin had told him last year about a man in California who poached over ninety lobsters in marine reserves. According to Kevin, the man got caught, paid a small fine, did a hundred hours of community service, and was then released on probation. During his probation, the man apparently couldn't help himself and got caught with another hundred illegal lobsters. He should have gotten five years in prison and over a hundred thousand dollars in fines, but because he was a good upstanding family man, he got six months in jail and fifteen thousand in fines.

Kevin told him himself that if he had been married and had kids, he would still have his boat and money in the bank. Kevin said there should be no difference between killing seals and poaching lobsters; both were against the law. Kevin told Tom the legal system wasn't fair and he hated the federal government. He hadn't brought up the subject lately, but Tom knew Kevin still carried a deep-seated grudge against all parties involved. It occurred to Tom that it could be his own brother who was fishing in the park. Even arriving at this conclusion made him feel empty inside as well as a little sad. He hoped he was wrong. He had to find out the truth about his brother as soon as possible if nothing more than to clear his brother's name in his own mind.

Tom pulled into the marina and slowly made his way down towards his brother's parked truck. He thought that if he took his time and was quiet enough, he just might be able to snoop around a little. He peered inside the back of his brother's truck and he could see dive gear strewn around the bed liner. A puddle of water lay directly below the back bumper. The puddle had a large dark ring around it suggesting that earlier the puddle had been larger, but it appeared to be drying up at a fairly good rate. Inside the truck he could see sandwich wrappers, discarded plastic orange juice containers, and a host of old candy wrappers. There was no sign of fishing gear in the truck and Tom thought that was a good sign. Maybe he was wrong about his brother.

Tom next went down to the boat. There were no signs of movement or life. He quietly boarded the back of Kevin's boat and looked around. The fishing pole was still where he first spotted it the other day. A glow in the dark minnow was attached to the end of the line. It looked identical to the minnow Tom just pulled out of his pocket. It could have been just a coincidence because the minnow lure was a popular fishing lure. He moved over to the back of the boat and looked down at the dingy. Some water had collected between the floorboards, and pieces of sunflower seeds were floating back and forth across the stagnant water's surface.

A small dingy could easily slip inside the park and go unnoticed he thought. Kevin had the means, but what would be his motive? Was he for some reason trying to get back at his brother? Was he trying to retaliate against the government and their fishing regulations? Or was he just trying to catch some fish and didn't care if the area was a designated marine reserve or not? Maybe Kevin thought that if that's where the big fish were, then that's where he was going to fish; no if's, and's, or but's about it. Kevin used a similar line of logic when he killed the seals for eating his salmon. Maybe the consequences of his actions weren't even a consideration. If this was the case, then over the last few years and especially after Kevin's brief stint in prison, Kevin hadn't changed a bit.

Tom solemnly moved over to the cabin door. He knocked a few short times, but no body answered. He waited for a moment and then knocked a little harder. He heard a muffled voice that sounded like his brother, but then the sound subsided and all was quiet again. This time Tom banged on the door and after a whirlwind of fowl language his brother threw open the door. He was standing in front of the door dressed only in his boxers, and looked as if he was ready to kill someone.

"What the . . ." Kevin started to roar, but he stopped when he noticed it was only Tom. "Oh, it's you." Kevin yawned and stretched his arms. Tom just stood there waiting for his brother to wake up. There was no sense saying a word till his brother cleared his thoughts. At first Kevin thought it was morning, but as he looked over and saw the sun setting he remembered what had happened last night. It took him close to two hours to swim across the canal and then another half hour to find a spot where he could haul up on shore and stash all his dive gear. His tennis shoes were soaked inside his wadded up duffel bag. He had kept his street clothes on as an additional layer to his fleece dry suit under garment, so after a long swim and wearing dry clothes and wet tennis shoes, he made his way up a rocky hillside to the main road, and started walking north with his thumb sticking out in hopes that he could get a ride. He walked till the sun started to rise and then a beat up white truck pulled over and gave him a ride. The man didn't say much, and the ride didn't take as long as he thought because between walking and swimming, Kevin had already gone quite a ways north from where he first dropped into the water. Once he got to the spot where he first left his truck, he had to go back south and find the spot where he stashed his dive gear. Then he had to go back north, catch a ferry, and try not to fall asleep as he made his way back to his boat in Everett.

"So what's up?" The dead tired diver asked his brother.

"This was found in the park today." Tom raised his hand and showed his brother the lure. Kevin glanced at it. It was a minnow and it had been tied to the line with a clinched half blood knot. It was a type of knot he liked to use.

"So?" Kevin said.

"I was wondering if it was one of yours." Tom flatly stated.

"I see." Kevin took a deep breath as he began to realize from years of experience that his brother was accusing him of something yet again that he didn't do. Immediately Kevin began to get mad. "You find a lure and you automatically suspect your brother. Is that it?"

"Well, it is the type you use." Tom replied.

"Along with thousands of other people who like to fish." Kevin responded. "Look, I already told you I'd never do anything that would land me back in jail. Why would I be risking my probation over a fish?" Tom was silent. He wanted to believe his brother, but couldn't. It was as if he was guilty until proven innocent in Tom's eye.

"Look," Tom began. "I didn't say it was you, I just had to make certain."

"Ok, so here's the deal. Every time someone commits a crime or does something wrong, you have to come out here first and ask me if I know anything about it." Kevin slammed the cabin door shut. Tom sighed and put the lure back in his pocket. Once again, he had tried to talk to his brother and it turned into another fight. He stepped off the boat and walked up to his car.

A second later the cabin door opened and Kevin stepped out holding a warm beer in his hand. He glared as he watched his brother get in the car. Kevin guzzled down the beer as his brother drove out of the parking lot. Kevin then took the empty can and smashed it flat against the gunwale. No matter what he did or didn't do, his brother already had him judged and sentenced. He looked over at his pole. He only had one minnow lure. He lost the rest when he was out fishing last week.

And that's the first time he noticed a piece of plastic shrink-wrap on the new lure attached to his fishing pole. It was the kind of plastic you see on new lures when you tried to remove them from their original packaging. The plastic was caught between two of the three hooks. But how could that be? He had cast that lure over a dozen times. He would have cleaned the plastic off the hook before he ever cast it in the water. That piece of plastic would have spooked the fish. He stepped over and examined the lure. He started to tear off the plastic film stuck between the hooks. How could he have ever missed it? This really made him mad. How many fish did he loose, because he didn't take the time to properly unwrap his lure? Was he just not thinking that day or what? He even had to tear sea grass off the hook last week, and still how could he have missed that piece of plastic wrapping?

Then it hit him. This hook was brand new. More importantly, he hadn't tied this hook. This hook was tied on using a Centauri knot. Whoever tied this brought the fishing line through the eye hole of the minnow's head one time, wrapped it around the line three times, then tied it off like a miniature hangman's noose. Kevin preferred using a clinched half blood knot on his lures. That way, instead of one strand of line going through the eye of a hook or lure, you had two wraps of line going through the eye of the hook and the wraps looked almost identical, but the clinched half blood knot had more strength and durability then the centauri knot currently tied on this lure. Someone had used his pole. Someone had had to replace his lure, and they messed up on the knot. Whoever used this pole didn't pay attention to detail, wasn't a true fisherman, or couldn't see the difference between knots in the first place. But when did they use his pole? Kevin trucked the dingy up to Everett Saturday morning so it had to be before then. Down in Edmonds he had the dingy in storage and sitting upside down against the fence. The pole was inside the dingy along with his two oars. Saturday when he came to pick up the dingy, it was wet and one of the oars had been broken. Whoever broke the oar, probably used his fishing pole too. That was nice of them. They took a joy ride in the dingy, lost his only lure, and replaced it, but didn't bother to replace the broken oar. Apparently they wanted to cover their tracks, but didn't care about covering all their tracks. He wondered why they even bothered replacing the lure?

Kevin moved to the back of his boat and stared down at the dingy. With one oar missing and no motor attached, it wasn't good for much. He put the dingy in the water just to get it off the beach and keep others from using it on a whim. The dingy was old and some of the paint was peeling off the wood, but the dingy could last another ten years before he donated it to his brother's park. Why did he even try to get along with his brother he wondered? No matter what he did, he never seemed to achieve equal status with his brother. He would have liked to tell his brother what he was up to lately, but he had been sworn to secrecy.

If it all worked out, he could get his confiscated boat back and possibly get his criminal record expunged. He was thinking about this when he happened to look down in the dingy and saw the pieces of sunflower seeds floating in a pool of water that had collected on the floor of the dingy. The seeds must have been in the boat for a long time. They were probably trapped in crevices and didn't expose themselves until they were floated out into the open by the accumulating water. Kevin didn't eat those nasty things. Sunflower seeds were too much work for too little pay off. However, he did know of one person that ate sunflower seeds and that was Ian.

Ian ate sunflower seeds and spit them out through the open space between his front teeth. Ian worked down at the marina and had access to the dingy anytime. But if Ian used the dingy, why did he replace the lure, and not the oar? And besides, Kevin would have given Ian permission to use the dingy anytime if he had just asked. Ian is the one that set him up with the geoduck poachers in the first place. He remembered how Ian had approached him down at the marina one day while Kevin was looking at a boat for sale. Ian heard from Tom what Kevin had done in Alaska and all about his conviction and jail time. To Ian, Kevin was the best recruit the geoduck operation could hire: someone already familiar with water and someone who didn't dare mention a thing about the operation for fear of landing back in prison. But little did Ian know that the minute Kevin agreed to work for them, he called the authorities and told them about the operation. Stopping a multimillion-dollar smuggling ring was Kevin's ticket to wiping his slate clean. It was his chance to get back on the right side of the law, and prove to his brother and mother that his life did have meaning. Any day now he could stop working on this boat the government loaned him, and start getting his original boat ready for fishing back up at Copper river. Forget Ian Kevin thought. Kevin would be out of this town soon enough. Come to think of it he owed Ian a thank you for getting him the geoduck job in the first place. Forget the oar, forget Ian, forget even his brother and his blasted underwater park, as soon as things wrapped up, he was out of here and back to Alaska.

Boat Call

Kevin went back into his cabin and grabbed another warm beer. He sat down on his sleeping bag and looked around to see if he still had an unopened packet of beef jerky lying around. He spotted an opened bag of jerky next to his night-light. He reached in and picked out the biggest piece left in the bag. He put it in his mouth and began to chew. It was hard as a rock and almost hurt his teeth too much to be worth the effort. He couldn't wait to get back to Alaska to the land of long legged king crab, king salmon, deer, moose, caribou, and elk. He would soon be smoking his own jerky and wouldn't have to eat this stringy garbage they sold down in the lower forty-eight states. Finally he couldn't stand it any more. He stood up and stepped out of the cabin. He went and leaned over the side of the boat and spit the jerky out into the water.

"You realize you're polluting the water," a deep voice resonated. Kevin flinched at the sound of the intruder. He turned to see the man he had nicknamed Blackbeard standing on the dock.

"Man, you scared me." Kevin exclaimed.

"Good," Blackbeard said. "Sometimes the only way you can tell if someone is truly alive is by whether they still fear the breath of death on the back of their neck."

"Nice poetry. I'm alive; if that's what you came to find out."

"That was part of it. Mind if I board?" Blackbeard asked. He didn't wait for a response. He climbed aboard and did a quick cursory examination of the boat. "So this is what you intend to take up to Alaska?"

"Who told you that?" Kevin asked.

"Ian told us. He told us all about you before we even considered bringing you on board and for all he told us, you still have been a big disappointment."

"As if I care," Kevin replied. "Was there something else or are you just wasting my time?"

"Time is something you may get a lot of." Blackbeard hinted.

"How so?" Kevin asked.

"There's a rumor that you were fishing in the park a few days ago when that diver died." said Blackbeard.

"What's your point?" Kevin asked as he put his hands on his hips. Blackbeard stepped up to Kevin and shook his right index finger in front of Kevin's face.

"Pulling little stunts like leaving the boat without permission will not be tolerated." Kevin took a step backward and held the palms of his hands up in a peaceful gesture.

"I can't afford to get caught," Kevin responded.

"None of us can," Blackbeard almost shouted. "Don't you get it? You dive over the side and someone sees you, they'll immediately look at us suspiciously. You freaked out and left us all holding our breath."

"Well that won't happen again, because I quit." Kevin snarled. He tried to move past Blackbeard, but Blackbeard blocked his past.

"You don't get it do you? Once you hire on, we tell you when you quit."

"Or what?" Kevin insisted.

"Or we frame you with some kind of accident." Blackbeard suggested.

"As the victim, or the perpetrator?" Kevin asked more out of amusement than anything else.

"Whatever it takes." Blackbeard answered.

"Not good enough. I just don't care." Kevin stated.

"Did you hear about your brother?" Blackbeard asked with a sinister grin. Kevin suddenly grabbed the taller man by the shirt.

"Leave my brother out of it. I hate that bastard."

"Ok, ok, I'm just the messenger. They just cut his net that's all. They just wanted to send you a message that's all." Kevin let go of Blackboard's shirt.

"Maybe I should send a message." Kevin replied.

"Don't do anything stupid. They don't tolerate stupidity."

"So what do they want from me?" Kevin finally asked.

"You take some time off to think things over, then you come back and follow our rules and work until we find a replacement. You do what you're told, no jumping off of boats, or any other weird stuff, we all make money, and those above me don't bother you or your family." Blackbeard finished the last sentence and braced himself for the hit he was ready to block and counter. Blackbeard was a black belt in karate, but he never liked to hint to that fact. He found it better to appear vulnerable. He liked the advantage of surprise when opponents underestimated his lethality. Kevin balled up his fist, but stopped short of hitting Blackbeard. He wanted to hit someone, but not the messenger. He knew others would retaliate for his actions. All he could do in the mean time was wait and see what happened next. His real covert mission was almost completed.

"You're right. Give me four days and I'll be fine." Kevin said.

"They'll give you two days, and you better be great." Blackbeard countered. Kevin felt the urge to deck him again. Blackbeard could sense the indecision in Kevin's eyes.

"You do your job and you'll be fine." Blackbeard added. Kevin resigned to his fate and his muscles relaxed. As soon as Blackbeard saw Kevin's shoulders slump and his head lowered. He turned and stepped off the boat. Kevin went back inside the cabin and peered from a window as Blackbeard walked up the ramp to his car. Kevin grinned and congratulated himself on his fine job of acting. The minute Blackbeard drove off Kevin grabbed the keys to his truck and decided to go pay a visit of his own.

Ian had used his rowboat; the remnants of sunflower seeds proved that. Ian must have tied the lure on his pole too. If Ian did both of these actions, then it was safe to assume Ian was poaching in the marine reserve, and they were going to frame Kevin for the incident. Well, if that was there plan, he wouldn't bother worrying about it, but what bothered him was what Blackbeard had said about his brother. If they were going to harass or hurt Tom, then he was definitely going to see what they were up to and stop them before they took further actions. It was time to pay Ian a visit.

Kevin Stepped out of his truck and looked around. It was dark down at the marina in Edmonds. It was quiet for a change. The birds had all gone to sleep and he heard the waves splashing against the shoreline. A cool breeze swept from the sound over the land and he could smell the salt in the air. Why would anyone want to spend all their life on land he wondered? Soon he would be out on the water and never look back at this insignificant spot of dried earth.

He looked out at all the boats stored in the marina. There

were few workboats in this Marina. This marina was filled predominately with weekend family fun boats, San Juan Island sleep over boats, and last but not least, the large and numerous executive blow your own horn and show off your exuberance for wasting money on white fiberglass coated floating alcohol laden and stereo music blasting "V" shaped barges. Small privately owned fishing boats were becoming a thing of the past.

Three quarters of the planet was covered by water, and it seemed to be turning into an exclusive recreational playground for those with extra cash and a little free time on their hands. Oh sure, there was still room for big commercial fishing vessels from countries such as Taiwan and Japan. Their governments bent over backwards to help their fishing industries just like our government at one time helped our oil and timber industries. Those countries have over fished and depleted the worlds major fish stocks. Of course no one said it to his or her face. That would not be diplomatic, but it's what everyone felt and said behind closed doors and in the back rooms of smoke filled bars down by the docks. This entire ocean, and barely any room or fish for small individual fishermen like himself.

Kevin went down a ramp and stopped next to a small sailboat. He knocked on the side of the cabin.

"Who's there?" Ian's raspy voice shouted out.

"Greenpeace! We have an award for you." Ian recognized the voice and turned on a light.

"I'll be right there," he called out. He put on a pair of pants, and stepped through the cabin hatchway. "What do you want?" he asked Kevin standing face to face. "It's got to be close to midnight."

"I want to know what you've been up to. You've been using my dingy and fishing in the park."

"Who told you that?" Ian asked.

"It doesn't matter. I just want to know what else you've been up to." Kevin said.

"That's it. I was told to go use your gear and go fish in the park."

"But why?" Kevin demanded.

"Insurance." Ian answered. They take insurance out on everybody. That way no one can say anything to anybody. That's how the operation's kept secret all these years."

194

"And what about you?" Kevin asked.

"Oh they've got me good. I can never leave." Ian solemnly answered. "It would be best for all if you came to realize that the same applies for you," Ian said with a sinister tone in his voice. "Now good night." Ian turned and went back down the hatchway.

Kevin stood there thinking about Blackbeard and Ian both had said. What did they plan to use to coerce him? Trumped up poaching charges? Threatening his family with bodily harm? The hatch to the sailboat slammed shut. If the lower echelon level authorities broke up this operation, maybe the geoduck organization would connect the dots back to him. The bad guys had the money, they had the power, and no one was going to let a multimillion-dollar operation go down the tubes without getting even with the people who brought it down. So how was he going to keep his name off Blackbeard and friend's list? He wasn't going to wait and find out.

Back at the House

Tom heard his brother's truck pull up in the driveway. He opened his eyes and looked at the clock sitting on the dresser. It was two o'clock in the morning. He rubbed his eyes, and thought about going back to sleep, but the sound of the garage door opening took care of that thought. He got out of bed and put his pants on.

Kevin backed his truck up to the garage after he made certain that there were no suspicious cars parked out on the street. He opened the garage door as quietly as he could and began to systematically collect his fishing and dive gear. He was in the middle of carrying two one hundred cubic foot tanks over to his truck when the door leading inside the house opened and out stepped his brother wearing nothing more than crumpled blue jeans.

"What's going on Kevin?" Kevin stopped and set the tanks down.

"I'm leaving." Kevin began. "I'm going back up to Alaska."

"Tonight?" Tom asked. He knew his brother wanted to get back up north, but he hadn't planned on him leaving this soon.

"That's the plan." Kevin said. He picked up the tanks and carried them to the back of his truck. He set them down again. He could only lift one at a time if he wanted to be quiet and not wake his mom.

"Are you going to say goodbye to mom?" Tom asked. Kevin stopped and shook his head.

"No, and I'd rather not say why." Kevin picked up one of the tanks and slid it inside the back of the truck.

"Look, I'm sorry about the lure," Tom began, but Kevin cut him off.

"That's it," Kevin said. "They said they heard rumors of me fishing the night that diver died." Kevin turned to face his brother. Tom just looked at him wondering what he was talking about. "Tom, do you know how that diver died?"

"They said he was hit on the head and drowned while unconscious," Tom said

"I see," Kevin replied.

"Why," Tom asked.

"He was hit on the head with my oar." Kevin blurted out.

He looked Tom right in the eyes. "Whoever used my row boat and fished illegally in the park, murdered that diver."

"But why?" Tom asked. Kevin wouldn't answer him.

"They also cut your net." Kevin stated. Kevin grabbed the tank he just put in his truck and pulled it back out.

"What are you talking about?" Tom asked.

"Don't you get it?" Kevin began to explain. "They framed me to keep me quiet. If I do anything they don't like or go anywhere they don't approve of, they'll turn me in to the authorities. I can't prove I didn't murder him and they could convince everyone I did."

"Who are they?" Tom asked.

"My geoduck buddies. One of them left his calling card on the floor of my dingy and if I'm not mistaken, he's the one that killed that diver."

"You mind giving me some names?" Tom asked.

"Sorry, I don't want you involved," Kevin said as he moved around the side of his truck. He got in and turned on the engine. Tom approached the drivers side to ask his brother a few more questions, but Kevin floored it and the truck took off racing down the street with the back tail gate still down and the canopy top up. A shirt fell out the back end of the truck as he turned around the corner.

Tom was worried about his brother. He grabbed a pair of shoes and shirt and got in his truck. It was now nearly three in the morning. The only clue Tom had about his brother's whereabouts was the mention of the dingy. He drove as fast as he could up to Kevin's boat. He hoped to find Kevin there, but he doubted it.

Tom pulled the truck into the marina and immediately noticed that Kevin's truck was nowhere in sight. The area was pitch black except for one nearby streetlight. Tom grabbed a flashlight under his seat and headed down to Kevin's boat. His boat was still moored in its berth. Tom stepped on board the boat and went to the stern and looked over the side at the dingy. The dingy was tied to the side of the boat by a nylon-braided line. Tom pulled on the line and the dingy moved towards the boat. Tom turned on the flashlight and peered down into the dingy. The dingy was empty, save for one oar and some water floating across the floorboards. Then he saw it. Pieces of sunflower seeds were floating in the water and lying on the floorboards. The only one he knew who ate sunflower seeds was Ian. He sighed with frustration. He had come all the way up to Everett just to find out that his brother was back down in Edmonds. As he turned around to face the cabin door, he noticed that the door was open. He pointed the flashlight inside the cabin and saw that the cabin looked ran sacked and most of the personal possessions were missing. It looked like his brother was leaving for good. He turned off his light and got out of the boat.

A Sinking Feeling

It was dark when Kevin arrived at the marina, but the street lights more than adequately lit up the night. A train roared by as he stepped out of his truck. It was a short train consisting on twenty some cars. After the train went by the area was quiet except for the sound of the waves splashing against pilings. Kevin didn't know what to expect or what was going on, but if he had learned anything from knowing Ian the past few years, anything was possible, especially if it dealt with cash under the table.

Kevin marched down the ramp to Ian's boat. He could see Ian's silhouette outlined by the moonlight. Ian was sitting in the back of the boat smoking a cigar.

"Are you expecting someone?" Kevin asked. Ian looked up at him but he had a dazed expression on his face. As Kevin waited for a response, Ian revealed a paper bag he had placed between his knees and took a sip from a partially exposed bottle. Kevin could smell the whisky from where he was standing.

"Police, FBI, Fish and Wildlife . . . any one of them." Ian slurred.

"Why? What happened?" Kevin asked. He climbed on board and took a seat across from Ian.

"They busted the geoducks," Ian began. "I'm not saying it was anybody's fault, but they closed the operation down and confiscated the boats."

"How long ago?" Kevin asked.

"Less than an hour ago." Ian said as he brought the bottle back up to his lips.

"There goes my new job," Kevin said with a hint of sarcasm. Ian looked at him and shook his head.

"What are you complaining about? You jumped ship just the other night."

"I had to Ian. A boat came too close and I couldn't afford to get caught."

"You're lucky the operation didn't get caught that night or they would have blamed you." Ian said. "But I guess that's beside the point now that the operations been shut down."

"Well, I can't say I enjoyed it." Kevin began. "Working underwater in the cover of darkness was never anything I wanted to do in the first place."

"There'll be another operation soon enough. There's too much money to be made and too many people need geoduck for sushi," Ian said.

"No way. Not me." Kevin stated. "I don't care how much they get per pound." Ian waved his hand as if ignoring Kevin. He then took another sip.

"That's where you are wrong Kevin. You don't have a choice."

"How so?" Kevin asked. Ian took another sip before elaborating.

"There was a murder in the park." Ian began.

"So?" Kevin tersely replied.

"All the evidence points to you," Ian smugly confessed.

"You mean like my row boat?"

"That would be one clue," Ian answered.

"And your sunflower seeds?" Kevin asked. Ian looked him in the eye.

"So you know." Ian said.

"I know that you tried to frame me, but why?" Kevin asked.

"Why? . . .That's obvious." Ian blurted out. "They told me we needed something to hold over your head. I thought that evidence pointing to someone with your past that had poached in the park was perfect. After that, you would have to do as we say or risk going back to prison."

"And the murder?" Kevin asked.

"Well that was just pure luck." Ian confessed with a devilish smile. "My goal at the time was to snag a few lures on the side of the Triumph and then leave the empty wrappers hidden in the dingy. I thought it was a good plan, but then that jerk of a diver surfaced and started yelling at me for fishing in the park. I hit him with the oar and he sank back underwater. I spent two days searching the shore to find the end of that paddle."

"So you killed him." Kevin said. "How was that pure luck?" Ian looked at him in dismay.

"Don't you get it?" Ian asked incredulously. "Setting you up as a poacher was thinking small compared to setting you up as a murderer." Kevin shook his head in disgust.

"What now Ian? You killed a man, and the operation is shut down." Ian shrugged his shoulders.

———

"Oh the operation's shut down, but only for a little while. The price we get for seafood in Asia is too high to give up for very long. Another crew, another boat, and business will be booming all over again."

Kevin glared at Ian for a brief moment.

"I'm through with all of you Ian." Kevin turned to leave the boat.

"And we're through with you." Ian replied. As Kevin stepped back and turned towards the dock Ian brought a well weathered two by four pine board down on the back of Kevin's head. Kevin's legs buckled immediately and he fell to the floor of the boat. Ian looked down at the unconscious figure and then he looked around to see if anyone had witnessed the event. The coast seemed to be clear.

Tom finally arrived at the marina, but there was no one was insight. He grabbed his long metal security guard type flashlight he kept under his front seat and got out of the truck. He scanned the marina, but didn't see any signs of life. He shut the door to his truck and the sound seemed to echo in the mostly empty parking lot. His brother had to be here somewhere he thought. Where else could he go? Because of the time of night, it had taken him less than a half hour to drive back down to Edmonds. It used to be Tom had the only car on the road at night in Seattle. Now traffic was busy around the clock, but he still managed to make good time driving down to the Edmonds marina. If it had been daylight, the trip would have taken him over an hour and a half. The Seattle area was twenty years behind other major west coast cities like Portland and San Francisco when it came to mass transportation. Los Angeles may have barely beat out Seattle when it comes to gridlock traffic, but even Los Angeles grid lock traffic couldn't always move as slow as the traffic in Seattle. He had lost a lot of time held up by traffic and wondered where Ian and Kevin could have gone by now?

Tom turned on his flashlight and went down to Ian's boat. From the dim light he could see that the cabin door was slightly ajar. Ian must have left in a hurry to forget something as simple as shutting a door Tom thought. He climbed aboard and opened the door as wide as it would go. It was dark inside and smelled of stale beer and soiled clothes. Tom shinned the light inside. The inside of the cabin looked like the city dump. He stood there for a moment wondering weather to venture inside the cabin or not. A noise of a metal barrel being bumped against another barrel made him turn his gaze to the far side of the marina. It was too dark to see anything that far away. He listened for a moment, but heard no further noises. He stepped back from the cabin and almost tripped over a piece of wood. He pushed the piece of lumber to the side with a sweeping motion of his foot. He noticed a streak of wet liquid smear on the deck next to one end of the two by four. Tom bent over to get a better view. The substance in question appeared to be fresh blood. It looked like either some unlucky fish or some poor human recently took a terrible blow from this piece of wood. He directed his flashlight around the deck floor and spotted two drops of blood adjacent to where he boarded the boat. A third drop of blood was smudged with the outline of what appeared to be Tom's own shoes. The droplets of blood seemed to be trailing away from the boat. With no further clues available Tom decided to head in the direction of where he thought he had just heard the noise.

As he walked across the deserted marina he heard what he thought was someone pounding inside a boat's hull. He quickened his steps in the direction of the noise. He heard an engine sputter to life. He could see someone down on a nearby dock releasing the mooring lines from a thirty-foot long motorboat. The gray outline of a man that looked like Ian threw the last line on the boat and climbed aboard the vessel.

The vessel slowly pulled away from its berth. There was no way Tom could ever make it down in time to hail the boat. A few more minutes and the boat would pick up speed and be out of the man made harbor and disappear for good. Tom's shoulders slumped and he was about to turn around in disappointment, but out of the corner of his eye he saw something move away from the pier directly behind the boat. It was low, flat, and longer than the boat. It was a barge! That was why the boat was still traveling so slow. The boat was towing a barge.

Tom quickly thought about how he could catch up to the boat. Just about anything would work at the speed the barge was moving. He spied a small zodiac tied to the back of a big cabin cruiser. He ran down the ramp and climbed aboard. He turned the motor on and gave it a couple of cranks. The motor started with a roar. He cut back the throttle and untied the line connecting the small craft from it's mother ship. He shifted out of neutral and cranked the engine. It was too dark to read the writing on the handle. He cranked the handle and the zodiac went into reverse and rammed into the back of the big cabin cruiser. Tom was almost thrown out of the boat, but his chest hit the engine and broke his flight. Hitting the engine knocked the wind out of him, but he managed to cut the power as he gasped for air. He shifted the other direction and slowly eased the boat forward. He could no longer see the barge or the towing boat. They were around the corner of the bolder formed breakwater and out of the marina.

As soon as Tom got his breath back, he gunned the engine and headed out of the marina. Once he cornered the breakwater wall he slowed down and looked for any signs of the boat and the barge in tow. With the lights of the marina now behind him, the rest of the Puget Sound appeared darker than he expected. A few boats slowly swept through the waters, but only three vessels seemed likely candidates to chase after. He couldn't see the barge at all, but he figured that was because of its low profile in the water. Tom chose one heading straight out away from him thinking the barge must be directly behind the boat. It was a good theory, but a few minutes later as he found that the boat was moving away too fast to be pulling a barge.

He had picked the wrong boat, and he didn't have time to hunt down the right boat. Tom shifted into neutral and the zodiac began to slow to a stop. Cold saltwater splashed against the sides of the rubber craft. Tom looked in all directions. Any other time it would a beautiful view of the distant shorelines with the city lights refracting off the water, but tonight Tom was desperately searching the surrounding waters. He didn't want to think about it until now, but deep down Tom knew that it was his brother's blood he saw on Ian's boat.

Kevin had gotten himself into something worse than Tom had ever expected. Tom's options were limited. He could go back to shore and call the police and tell them what? That he had found some drops of blood on a boat and that his brother was missing? They would tell him there was nothing they could do about it. It was probably fish blood. Fishermen used 2x4 boards all the time to kill fish. It was a lot easier removing a hook from a fish that wasn't flopping around, safer too. And even if the police did send out a patrol boat, where would they look? Tom desperately searched for any signs of the trailing barge. North of him he saw a large ferry departing from Edmonds and bound for Kingston. The bright lights from the ferry reflected off the surrounding water. Right behind the ferry was the underwater park, but the ferry blocked Tom's view of the park. Tom turned and looked southward.

A large boat was coming his way. Most likely it was headed for the entrance of the harbor from which he just departed, but at the speed it was traveling, it couldn't be towing a barge. Tom was ready to give up his search. He was wasting precious time bobbing around in the middle of the Puget Sound. It had only taken him a few minutes to depart the harbor, and already the boat along with the barge was nowhere in sight. It seemed impossible that it could have disappeared so quickly. Tom looked one last time as far as he could see from south towards points west and then northward. He suddenly saw something that looked out of place.

As the ferry moved further away from the dock in Edmonds, a boat in the distance behind the ferry came in to view. The boat was moving in the direction of the marine reserve, and the shadow of the barge was directly behind the boat. What was Ian up to Tom wondered. He crouched down and shifted the motor back to forward. The motor instantly shut off. Tom reached for the starter cord and pulled it back. Nothing happened. He pulled the cord again and the motor froze in the middle of his pull. He felt his shoulder jerk to a stop followed by the handle of the cord ripping away from his hand's tight grip. His hand began to burn with pain. He ignored the pain and tried to pull the cord again. The motor was frozen. He couldn't get the cord to budge one inch.

He stopped and looked over at the marine reserve. The boat and the barge had come to a stop in what appeared to be inside the marine reserve boundaries. He couldn't tell what they were up to. The boat was too far away, but more importantly he wondered whether his brother was part of the crew, or being held against his will by the crew. The fact that the boat and barge had come to a stop in the park added to his uncertainty of the situation. What were they be doing in the park? Was this his brother's idea? Tom sat in the zodiac looking out at the park. He needed to get the engine working again. He turned on his flashlight and looked the engine over. A huge wave hit against the side of the zodiac and splashed over the side and drenched him with cold salt water. He realized he was in serious danger. He knew of two dive boats that capsized after their engines flooded. Without engine power to turn you into the on coming waves, water could splash over the side and fill a craft quickly. He spit out the water that hit him in the face and mouth. The wind hit his wet clothing and he felt his upper torso begin to get chilled. Tom was getting cold, the motor still wouldn't start, he was loosing precious time, and coming out in the in the Puget Sound in nothing more than a small raft had turned into an extremely risky, if not stupid idea. If he died from drowning or hypothermia, he was a sure bet for the annual Darwinian award.

The Nordic tug entered the northern end of the park. The boat was far enough away so that only a trained eye could tell the boat had crossed the park boundary. Ian set the engines in neutral. He took a sip from his bottle of whiskey, grabbed a wrench as long as his forearm, and went back to the stern of the boat. The barge still moved forward on it's own momentum and bumped into the back of the boat. Ian jumped down on to the deck of the barge. He quickly moved to the back end of the barge. He looked down by his shoes. There was a closed hatch located at a slight angle off the deck, which lead inside the hull of the barge. A lock was clasped shut through a raised eyelet. Ian took the wrench in hand and pounded twice on the hatch cover.

"Hey, you awake down there yet?" Ian said with a slight slur.

"Let me out of here you drunken psycho." Kevin's muffled voice sounded out. Kevin banged his fists against the underside of the hatch cover. There was enough light filtering through for Kevin to vaguely make out his surroundings. He was stuck in a small compartment where at one time sleeping bunks rested against the walls with enough room for four people to sleep overnight. A small tabletop was welded into the wall with enough room to hold a coffee pot and not much else. A shelf that was recessed into the wall was barren except for an old rusted out metal first aid box and of course the metal narrow stairs that led out of the room to the main deck.

"Hey, is that anyway to talk to the only guy with a key?"

Ian yelled down and broke Kevin's train of thought.

"Let me out of here!" Kevin pounded again on the hatch with a closed fist as he stood perched on the stairs and peered out through the grated metal door.

"I don't think so," Ian replied. "I wouldn't want you to miss all the fun. You see I plan on sinking this barge right here. I've got enough toxic waste on this boat to kill every fish in the park and maybe you too. That is, if you don't drown first." Ian started to laugh then abruptly stopped. "In a way, this might be the first boat you've sunk in the park, but it will be the last one sunk on purpose for quite awhile." Ian started laughing again but stopped when he heard the sound of a small engine approaching. He was going to open the lid on every drum, but what good would that do if whoever was coming nearer stopped him from sinking the barge? Damn, he thought to himself.

He decided a change of plans was in order. He decided to open up the hull cocks so water would start to pour in the barge. Then he would open up as many barrels of the contaminated sludge as time permitted. It may not create the level of pollution he originally desired, but it would insure Kevin drowned before anyone could try and save him. Ian went to the stern of the barge. He groped around in the darkness until he found a metal cover the size of a small paperback novel. He lifted the lid and reached down inside with his right arm. It was wet inside. He reached down into the cold stagnant water until his hand came into contact with a lever. He turned the lever counter clockwise. The sound of water flowing into the hull could be faintly heard. He moved over to the other end of the stern. The sound of Kevin's fists began to hit against the hatch cover more frenzied than before.

Kevin stopped pounding on the hatch when he realized the act was useless. Instead, he reached for the first aid kit. Maybe there was something inside he could use to free himself he thought. He opened the first aid kit on the metal counter and looked at the contents. Inside he found old gauze, bandages, and a pair of rusted scissors. He felt totally frustrated. He couldn't use anything to make his escape possible. Then he noticed another small tin box located right behind where the first aid kit had stood. He reached up and pulled that down too. Inside he found a plastic pistol and two large cartridges. It was a flare gun.

He could use it to fire signals in the sky and just about nothing else. If he fired it off in his confined chamber, he could loose most of the hair on his head, but it wouldn't do a bit of good to get anyone else's attention. He put it back on the shelf and hid it back behind the first aid kit just in case.

Ian smiled as he opened the other small cover. He turned the lever and began letting more water seep inside the barge. Ian looked up and saw the approaching zodiac. He wouldn't have time to open any toxic barrels at the rate things were progressing.

Tom finally got the motor to work again and the zodiac was closing in on the barge. Ian still had to get to the main boat and cut the towlines. Ian dropped the big wrench on the deck of the barge and started running towards the Nordic tug. He had a handgun conveniently located right beside the steering wheel to take care of situations like this. He didn't know who was in the zodiac, but they weren't invited and definitely unexpected. He got to the front of the barge just as the zodiac reached the back of the barge. Ian was ready to jump back aboard the Nordic tug when he realized that the currents must have changed directions and instead of the barge being mere inches away from the boat, there was now a gulf of some ten feet between the barge and the boat. He didn't know what to do. All his plans were failing fast. He turned to look back behind him as a single stream of light blinded his eyesight.

Tom shut down the zodiac's engine a split second before the rubberized boat touched the back of the barge. He didn't bother tying the zodiac off to the barge; he just grabbed his flashlight and climbed aboard the barge as fast as he could move. He shined his light forward and saw Ian at the other end of the barge turning to face him.

"Where's my brother?" Tom yelled as loud as he could. Ian ignored the question and turned back to face the boat.

"Here, grab hold of this," Blackbeard said to Ian. Ian at first was stunned to see him. The man moved at will around like a Ninja ghost. He was holding out a long wooden pole with a smooth hook at the end used to catch hold of ropes and lines. Ian hesitated at first, but found he didn't have much choice. He grabbed hold of the pole with both hands. He expected Blackbeard to slowly pull on the other end causing the boat to move closer to the barge. Ian felt the slow pull on his arms and braced himself. Suddenly Blackbeard jerked the pole back towards the boat and Ian lost his balance and went face first over the side of the barge. Ian almost hit his head on the side of the boat, but the pole slipped out of his fingers. Ian looked bewildered as he hit the water and immediately began to sink beneath the surface. The water was freezing cold and he was too stunned to move. Blackbeard watched Ian go under the surface. He had found the gun next to the steering wheel and was going to shoot Ian, but if Ian drowned, then things would be a lot simpler and less messy. Ian came to the surface and reached out towards the boat. Blackbeard swung the pole and hit Ian on the right wrist. A bone snapped and Ian yelled out in pain. Ian turned to retreat towards the barge, but he started to go under the surface again and this time he didn't come back up. The alcohol, the cold water, and his poor physical health had finally taken their toll.

"I told you alcohol would be the death of you," Blackbeard said with a sick smile on his face. He watched until he could no longer see the outline of Ian's face with his wide-open eyes looking up at the surface. Blackbeard heard a loud noise and looked over immediately towards the barge.

Tom heard the pounding noises coming from the locked metal hatch. "Kevin? Is that you?" Tom yelled

"I'm in here," a hysterical voice screamed back. "The barge is sinking."

Tom had to get the lock off and get his brother out fast. Tom quickly turned the beam of the flashlight loose on the surrounding deck and spotted the long silver wrench. He pickup up the big piece of metal and brought it over to the hatch. The lock appeared new, but the metal hatch was old and rusted. He took the wrench and delivered a strong blow down on the lock with all his might. With a loud thud the wrench hit the lock and the metal around the lock began to give way.

Blackbeard saw the figure hunched over the hatch trying to hammer it open. Without hesitating he jumped over onto the barge and ran towards the hunched over figure to properly greet Tom.

Tom brought the wrench down once more on the lock. The lock showed little wear and tear, but the rusted metal behind it was almost completely torn apart. One more strike and the metal backing would give way and the lock would fall off. For some strange reason Tom suddenly felt a cold hard rubber sole press against the side of his face and his entire head lifted up along with his shoulders and the rest of his body. The wrench fell out of his hands as his body arched in the air and came down to rest a few feet from where he was originally assaulted. His body fell limp and his eyes closed.

Blackbeard had taken Tom out with one swift kick. He reached down and picked up the flashlight and the wrench.

"Sorry Kevin. It looks like the rescue attempt failed." Blackbeard said as he banged the wrench against the hatch. He took one last look at Tom's crumpled body and then walked back towards the Nordic tug.

Kevin listened as Blackbeard walked away. It was strangely quiet once again except for the sound of water seeping in side the compartment. He knew he only had a few minutes more before the water would start to fill the room at an accelerating pace. He had little options left. His fists were sore and bleeding. He turned his shoulder at the grated metal door, ran up the stairs, and rammed it with all his might. To his surprise, the door budged just a little bit. He did it again and the door opened a quarter of and inch. His shoulder quickly became inflamed with pain, so he turned and used his left shoulder as a battering ram. One hard hit and the lock finally fell off the surrounding metal and the door opened wide.

It was dark outside, but from where Kevin was sitting he could clearly make out his brother's limp body lying on the deck. He started to exit the hold's doorway, when a bullet whizzed by his head and caused him to stop and rethink his movements. He pulled himself back down the stairs inside the cramped room and grabbed the flare gun. He put one round in the chamber and snapped it shut. The water was now up past his knees. He wouldn't have long for a stand off. The suction of the barge pulling him down under the water's surface would soon be a greater threat than any gunfire directed his way.

He peered out the hatch and a bullet hit him in the top of his left shoulder. Blackbeard cursed at the role of the waves for saving Kevin from the last shot. Kevin aimed the flare gun at the boat and fired. Blackbeard was momentarily blinded as the bright flare came straight at him. He ducked and the flare passed over him and imbedded somewhere deep within the boat. The hot fire burned right through several layers of fiberglass, igniting everything in its path. Fire started to erupt on the boat, but there was no time to put it out. Blackbeard realized that he couldn't afford another salvo from the flare gun or he would be standing on a floating bonfire. He also had to stop Kevin from firing another round before he could begin to contain the existing fire. He should have killed Kevin long ago he thought in hindsight. He quickly rose up and jumped onto the barge.

Kevin had just finished reloading the flare gun when Blackbeard approached him with an insane look frozen on his face. Kevin fired right at Blackbeard's face. The blast wouldn't be enough to knock Blackbeard over, but it could blind him and that was Kevin's primary goal. If he missed, then Blackbeard would take him out just like he did his brother Tom. The gun fired and the flare shot out at Blackbeard's face. Blackbeard jerked his head to the side and only part of the flare connected with his skin. He immediately screamed as he fell to the ground and rolled in pain. The smell of burned skin and hair was nauseating, but after a quick glance to see that Blackbeard was still on the ground, Kevin didn't give him another thought.

Kevin went over to his brother and tried to shake him awake. His brother was out cold.   With the barge starting to list and the boat fire spreading out of control, there was only one thing left to do. He took off his shoes, then he dragged his brother over to the side of the barge. He pulled them both into the bitter cold water. Kevin knew he would have to swim for the two of them. With one eye fixed on his brother to make sure his head stayed above the water, Kevin started towing his brother towards shore.

Final Farewell

Kevin stood on the beach wearing blue jeans and a red and black-checkered logger shirt. The sun was already beginning to shine and soon it would be that time of year to find where he put his sunglasses. Hard to believe he was in Edmonds, but the weather was something the residents of this local area of Seattle liked to keep to themselves. Prices of property more than doubled even under the auspices that it always rained in the northwest. Gray overcast days were the last defense against vast migrations of new residents from California and points beyond. More people, meant more divers, and more fishing, and less of everything left over for commercial fishermen like himself. Kevin was leaving the northwest for good. He watched as his brother came out of the water along with his dive buddy Paul. They left their homemade floating basket with an attached dive flag floating in shallow water. Tom and Paul took off their fins and masks then marched over to where Kevin was standing.

"So are you leaving now?" Tom asked.

"Yeah, thought I better get going north where it's a little less crowded and a heck of a lot safer." Kevin replied.

Tom took off his cut up neoprene glove and extended his wet hand. Kevin reached out and shook his brother's hand.

"Well bro, you did a good job sinking those two boats. The barge came to rest upright on the bottom. It'll make a good flat platform to teach dive skills on. What didn't burn on the Nordic tug before the barge pulled it down, is on its starboard side and resting five feet from the barge."

"What about the barrels?" Kevin asked.

"We hauled those up last weekend while your brother was beauty resting in the hospital with his so called concussion," Paul replied. Tom shook his head in disbelief. Tom and Paul unbuckled their tanks, slid them off their shoulders, and dropped the equipment on the sand.

"So did they ever recover the other body?" Kevin asked. Tom wiped the saltwater out of his hair.

"Nope, just Ian's." I can't imagine he made it to shore in his condition," Tom said.

"Neither can I," said Kevin. "But a white Bayliner was seen near the park right after the fire broke out.

211

"Who was he?" Paul asked.

"You know, we never did get his real name," Kevin said. "We just called him Blackbeard."

"Whose we?" Tom asked. That, my brother, I can never tell you."

"Well, thanks for saving my life again Kevin."

"And thanks for saving my life Tom." Kevin turned and started walking up the beach towards the parking lot. Tom and Paul watched him leave then turned their attention back to the water. They looked out at the park as if to find something that wasn't there, and simultaneously began to talk about what they wanted to see done next to the park. Just then Gina, Vic, and John surfaced and spit out their regulators.

"Are you two still standing there?" Gina asked incredulously. "Get your tanks up to the truck or we're going to be late for dinner. You know … at your mothers." She rolled her eyes in disbelief."

"We better do what she says, Paul quickly stated. Tom stopped and gawked at his dive buddy.

"Did she take over while I was gone?"

"No buddy," Paul replied. "She did that long before you got kicked in the head. You were just the last to figure it out." Paul and Tom broke out laughing. They waited for the other three divers to join them and they all marched up the beach together.

The End